THE GRAPPLING HOOK

and Other Stories from The War in Iraq

William F. X. Maughan

UNIVERSITY OF SCRANTON PRESS
Scranton and London

Library of Congress Cataloging-in-Publication Data

Library of Congress Cataloging-in-Publication Data

William F.X. Maughan, 1957-
 The grappling hook : and other stories from the war in
Iraq / William F.X. Maughan.
   p. cm.
 Includes bibliographical references and index.
 ISBN 978-1-58966-179-0 (pbk. : alk. paper)
 1. Iraq War, 2003---Personal narratives, American. 2. Maughan,
F. X. William, 1957- 3. Soldiers--United States--Biography. I.
Title.
 DS79.76.M673 2008
 956.7044'3373092--dc22
 [B]

                                                 2008031031

Distribution:

UNIVERSITY OF SCRANTON PRESS
Chicago Distribution Center
11030 S. Langley
Chicago, IL 60628

Dedication

This book is dedicated to my forefathers, exiled sons of Ireland, pious Catholics, dedicated family men, loving husbands, and devoted fathers—loyal Americans all. Each of them took his turn in answering the call of his country. Everything good in my life was passed on to me by these men and their wives.

William F. Maughan

U.S. Marine Corps and NYC Police Department

1928–2003

William Moughan

U.S. Army

1890–1966

Hugh A. Halligan

U.S. Army and NYC Fire Department

1896–1987

Acknowledgments

I owe many thanks to many people and, hard as I try not to, I am bound to leave somebody out. For this I apologize but the alternative of naming nobody would be even worse. So here goes.

I owe Dr. Maria Poggi Johnson and her husband Glen Johnson more than words can express. Maria was my first Theology Professor at the University of Scranton and her passion and intellect kept me coming back for more. I spent many an evening in the Johnson home, first as a student soaking up their knowledge and later as a friend. They kept the faith with me while I was in Iraq, a time when true friends were as scarce as a cool breeze in the Iraqi desert in August. It was Maria who first told me I could be a writer and insisted I try. I sent my journals written in Iraq to Maria and she coached me to become a better writer. I hope I did.

I owe my roommate, Sergeant Johnny "T" Evans, for his friendship and humor. He also encouraged me to write and gave me privacy to do so, encouragement when I lapsed, and good will at all times. Many thanks are due SFC Joe Sturges, another old Marine turned Guardsman who shared his experience, strength, hope, and way-loud music with me. I will always remember two First Class

Sergeants, Russ Cramer and Brian Milore, for their pro-
foundly inspiring character, selfless leadership, and honorable fellowship. They have returned to their "civilian"
jobs with the Pennsylvania State Police. Stay safe, men.

First Sergeant Mike Horn pulled a dozen strings to
get this old sergeant back in the battle and for this, and
for many more favors, I hope to have an opportunity to
do him a good turn someday. Father Lou Kaminski was
my Chaplain and friend in Iraq. He is a devoted priest
and a fine officer.

I couldn't have done much without the support of my
sister, Eileen Vatter. She and her family sent unending
good wishes and care packages to my soldiers and me,
along with their prayers. I will always have a soft spot for
Joan Ryan and Sean Halligan, an aunt and a cousin, who
were so supportive and giving. I owe John Prevoznik for
his friendship as well. He and his wife Michelle put my
personal, legal, and business affairs in order for me and
kept them in order for me while I was away.

I am grateful for my sons, Billy and Matthew, who not
only supported me while I was in Iraq but did the hard
work of editing a story draft or two for me. I am blessed
by a daughter Mary and by my stepdaughter Carla and
am grateful for their cheering me on as this book came
together.

My oldest daughter Kelly was my greatest support
while I was overseas. She helped me in tasks too personal
to mention but too important to have gone undone. She
and her fiancé, Matthew Ferguson, also took their turns
at editing story drafts. Matthew is a wonderful addition
to our family and this is as it should be. Kelly deserves

the very best and I couldn't have parted with her so happily had she not chosen such a fine man. Much love and blessings to you both on your coming marriage.

I am grateful to Jeff Gainey at the University of Scranton Press who provided this opportunity to me and special thanks go to my editor, John Hunckler. My rough work didn't seem to exhaust his considerable skills or his patience. The outstanding drawing of the Halligan Tool on page 3 is the contribution of Matt Hunckler.

Lastly, I will spend the rest of my life trying to match my wife Jane's gifts of devotion, loyalty, encouragement, and love. She has made my world new and joyous and she made the writing of this book possible, selflessly giving up many hours of our time together so I could write, and cheerfully helping in the logistics of its production, but mostly in her unyielding belief in me.

These stories, while gleaned from this author's experience in the Iraq war are fictional. Any resemblance to actual people or events is coincidental. The soldiers are composites of a thousand warriors I have met. If you have been deployed to Iraq recently, or for that matter, any war-zone at any time, you might think you recognize the soldiers and Marines in these stories though. I tried to recreate the timeless traits and common characteristics of these incredible men and women. The incidents are all based on actual events, but always altered to keep them fictional.

Contents

A Brief Introduction

Wikipedia says, "Grappling hooks were originally used in naval warfare to catch the rigging of an enemy ship so that it could be drawn in and boarded. Later, grappling hooks were also used in rescue work or to assist in scaling walls." In the title story, "The Grappling Hook," you'll learn about a more dubious combat application of this device. But my first story—while, strictly speaking, not a war story—connects through a more common (although still low-tech) implement designed to protect heroes and rescue lives, the Halligan tool.

A Halligan tool is a device commonly used by firefighters. It's also carried by some U.S. troops in Iraq. It was designed by and named after Hugh Halligan—a First Deputy Fire Chief in the New York City Fire Department—in 1948. A multipurpose tool for prying, twisting, punching, or striking, it consists of a tapered pick and a blade (wedge or adz) on one end of a metal bar with a claw or fork on the other end. It is a dependable rescue device, especially useful in quickly forcing open many types of locked doors.

The true Halligan is a forged tool, of one-piece construction, available in a number of lengths. A tool of similar design, made of two or more metal components fastened or welded together, is not considered to be an authentic *Halligan tool* by those who use it. Such a counterfeit is often disparagingly referred to by some as a *Hooligan tool.*

Hugh Halligan was my grandfather. I called him Pop. To introduce him, me, and this collection of short stories about U.S. troops in the War in Iraq, I'll begin by sharing the most memorable day I ever spent with Pop. This day, the one you will read about shortly, was brought to my mind on another day, years later, while I served in Iraq. I was standing in the turret of an up-armored Humvee, manning a U.S. 240B machine gun. My mission was to provide security for the Army Engineers who were replacing a broken water main (sabotaged by terrorists *again*). With one eye on the horizon, and the other on the soldiers, I watched as one particular soldier returned to his truck and pulled out a Halligan tool. I watched him return to his work site, and put the tool to use; in this case he was tearing apart the cemented joints of the destroyed water main.

Comforted by this little touch of home in a desert eight thousand miles from all that was familiar to me, I thought then that Pop would have been awfully happy to see U.S. soldiers making use of his invention almost a century after he had served in his own war, in the same Army. I thought then that I'd include a story about Pop and his Halligan tool when I got home and wrote that book I dreamed of, this book you are holding in your hands now. This collection is, in part, a tribute to my grandfather, the late Chief Hugh A. Halligan, or as I remember him, *Pop.*

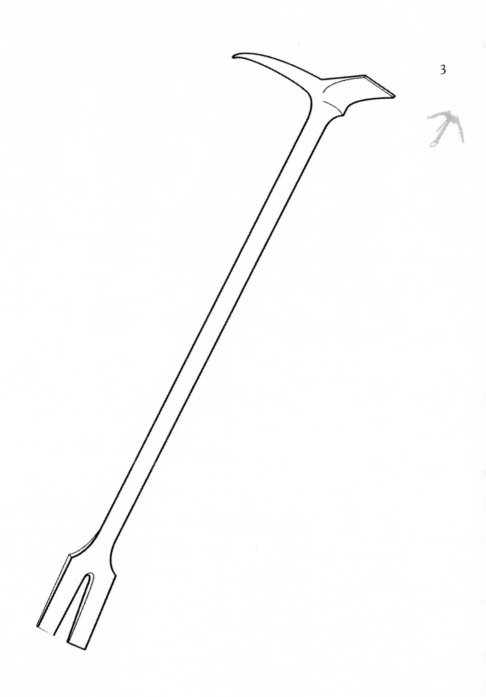

3

Hughie and Me

My grandfather was bent over the bathroom sink, washing his face. I watched; I knew this routine by heart. A frequent visitor to our house, he'd use the bathroom next to the bedroom I shared with my brother. His daily grooming consisted of brushing his teeth, shaving, washing his face and hands, and combing his hair, all done in less than five minutes. To this day, I have never met a more unassuming man. He was completely unpretentious, so that grooming was a purely functional exercise—certainly not a beauty routine. There was not a shred of vanity or ego in the man. There was no room for it, his heart and soul commandeering every corner.

He finished, as always, by putting his electric razor back in its case and putting the case in the plastic bag that functioned as his toilet kit. That razor, like everything else he owned that had a market value greater than a dollar, was given to him by one of his five children. Buying a gift for him was always tough on them. Hughie simply had no desire for material goods, so anything bought for him that wouldn't be a complete waste of money had to have some practical value. I still have the razor; it is the only physical object of his I have kept. I never use it, of course, but it is mine.

I expected him to turn around, see me watching him, smile benignly, and take his leave. But not this time.

When he turned and looked at me, he was serious and direct, "We're going for a ride, leaving in a few minutes."

This was not simply unusual; it was unique. I remember this day as the one and only time Hughie and I went somewhere and spent the day together, alone. I am grateful that I knew enough, even then, to cherish it. I checked with my mother who confirmed that I was indeed to spend the day with my grandfather. He was heading to Newark, New Jersey to pick up some "heavy things" and he needed my help. At ten years old and ninety pounds, I thought it made perfect sense that Hughie would need me along in case there was some heavy lifting to do. He appeared in the driveway a few minutes later, wearing his work clothes and heading for the blue Rambler that functioned as the family car for my grandmother and him. It was also occasionally a utility vehicle and sometimes storage shed. This day, it would be the company truck.

There are many powerful memories from that day, but one of the most lasting is that of my grandfather's attire. Already the least vain man in the universe, he simply outdid himself when he put on his "work clothes." He was wearing heavy twill trousers, a flannel shirt, a jacket, and a fedora—all the same color. I don't mean to say that all these clothes had started their long, long lives the same color. They simply had *become* the same color, a sort of dirty-brown, dusty-gray, certainly black, but maybe a touch of what was once a maybe-green or a kind-of-red color. There was evidence of a dozen paint jobs remembered in them. There were tar stains and grass stains and good old dirt. He had a half-dozen knots in one shoelace and, I swear to God, package twine functioning as a shoelace on the other shoe. The belt (I'm still under oath here) had electrical tape holding it together. Hughie *loved* his electrical tape. He taped his prayer books together. He repaired his radio and coffee cup with it, and he used it to get another decade or so out of his shoes or furniture. As I got in the Rambler, I noticed that electrical tape also functioned fairly well for repairing the tears in a car seat, holding the antenna on, and keeping the armrest in place.

"Let's say a quick rosary so we can bring the Blessed Mother along for the ride," he said.

"I believe in God …," he began, not bothering to wait for my agreement.

I prayed along with him as best I could. I knew praying was a worthwhile enterprise and I also knew it was boring. Sometimes, Pop would forget that he had a partner in this particular rosary and would pray in whispered intensity. Then he'd remember I was there and he'd speak louder and more slowly, his face animating at the remembrance of our collaboration. When it was over, we had made it to the parkway and were on our way to some place called Newark. I did not learn of our mission till I asked him directly. All my grandmother had said was that we were going to see "The German."

Well, that at least explained Pop's wardrobe. He was dressed to fight the Germans and he wanted *me* with him! After all, this was barely twenty years after World War II and my conception of the Germans was that they were perpetual global belligerents who needed to have their Teutonic asses kicked at least once a generation. It had fallen on the shoulders of America's boys to do that ass-kicking. It was part of the job description of "American Boy." Pop had been in the Army during World War I. On military leave from the New York City Fire Department, he enlisted in one of the New York regiments. The war ended before he got to the fighting, but he had at least one brother who was in the heart of the heat.

Father James Halligan served as Chaplain in what became known as, "The Lost Battalion." In the lexicon of the U.S. Army, *lost* means "men who were sent, based on ridiculously poor intelligence, into enemy territory with inadequate arms, food, manpower, and support, only to be cut off and decimated." I hated to think what the Army lexicon has for the word *screwed*.

Pop did his part though. He was a legendary piano player and he had written a song encouraging his fellows to "wave the flag, crush the Hun, and hurry home to Mom's apple pie." Or something like that. It had limited marketing success and I only heard it sung once (by Pop, while at the piano), but I am certain of its existence. It has been mentioned by more than one younger fireman who remembered Hughie Halligan as the Piano Man of countless celebrations.

Most of the ride was in silence, and with Pop's bad hearing, I got to pick my radio station. Of course, I knew that we weren't going to actually fight some Germans, but the idea of any contact at all with a member of this infamous horde was exciting in itself. Our arrival at the German's was not a letdown. The place where the Rambler finally stopped was not a battlefield, but it was just as new and exciting to a boy from the suburbs of Whitelandia.

In Newark, there is a section where the buildings and streets have taken on that same dingy brown and gray. All that was there was there for a purpose rather than for any aesthetic value. The stones and steel were imposing, the countless scars and marks and chips unable to lessen the impression of permanent strength and utility. We were in a land of factories and warehouses. Looking up at the cranes and hoists and lifts that formed this industrial forest, I had stepped in a puddle of goop. Everywhere, the ground was covered with a tar-like substance formed from a century of oil spills, hydraulic leaks, and human litter. The "cleanups" involved throwing dirt, sand, or gravel on the spill till it formed a solid toxic nightmare. As for the mess I had made of my sneakers, Mom would certainly have to be made to understand that you must accept certain costs when you spend a day in Mantown. After all, what do dirty Keds amount to when one is involved in all this power and building?

While I was escaping the tar pit, Pop had moved toward the open truck bay where appeared the man who was undoubtedly "The German." He wasn't wearing a sign or anything else that identified him by ethnicity, but he couldn't hide from me the "I'd rather be attacking a small border country" look on his face.

This was the German. He was as old as Pop and was clothed in the same gray-brown standard as Pop, only the German's outfit was covered by a huge leather apron. He had forearms that were considerably larger than his upper arms and his hands were absolutely huge, with the lines between wrists, palms, and fingers not all that clear. He, like the city in which we stood, had been built for utility.

I was only partly surprised when he and Pop greeted each other warmly. The union of their shaking hands looked like a huge mound of muscle and gristle.

My grandfather and the German were somehow cut of the same cloth after all. Hughie Halligan, a gentleman of kindness, piety, and prayer, a scholar whose career brought him within striking distance of the highest executive office in the largest fire department in the world was also a working man, a man's man. He was at home in the steel and the sweat. He spoke the language of the everyman.

The German nodded to me and I scurried to catch up as he led Pop inside. We (we!) walked over (they walked, I ran to keep up) to a pallet where there lay two dozen Halligan tools. Pop picked one up and inspected it very carefully, paying particular attention to the end where the pick and wedge portions are situated at right angles to each other. He and the German discussed this particular point with mutual pride and satisfaction. The German, this muscle with a face, waited for my grandfather's approval.

As Pop offered his approval to the German, I learned something that day that I have held onto ever since. Looking him directly in the eye and reaching for his hand again, Hughie told him the tools were wonderful! The job was perfect! Hughie said the words, "Thank you!" more than once after him as the German hurried to his office to get the paperwork. Turning to me in the middle of the noise and confusion of Mantown, Pop said, "You get more out of a man by patting him on the back than by kicking him in the pants."

He checked to see that each tool had the acronym, AMDG, stamped on the flat part of the forked end. They all did. AMDG, he instructed, was for the Latin expression *Ad Majorem Dei Gloriam*—for the greater glory of God. These letters appear, in tribute to God, as the final punctuation of many theological works, especially among the Jesuit scholars. A voracious reader, Pop had seen it enough times to know it belonged on his magnum opus, the Halligan Tool.

Pop and I loaded these tools into the back of the Rambler. He grabbed two at a time and I was able to muscle only one each trip. The German pitched in. Neither man made anything at all of my inability to carry much weight. In fact, I thrived on their camaraderie and soaked up their nods of approval. They didn't pay much attention to each other's contribution either. Each man did what he could, at his own pace till the job was done. Citizenship in Mantown requires each man to carry his weight, without prodding. Tools loaded, the men bid farewell once more and Hughie and I were on our way home. Now Pop would have to suffer the death of a thousand questions. Such is the fate of a man alone with a ten-year-old boy.

I asked him what the German and he had been discussing regarding the tool head and he explained the point at length with a level of enthusiasm more often found in a mother discussing her first newborn. It seems the German was the last guy he could find who would forge the Halligan tool in *one* piece.

There had been attempts by others to manufacture the tool, and they always resorted to a two-piece process—where the long end with the fork was forged and then welded onto the separately forged pick-wedge end. The welded model would be cheaper and easier to produce but Hughie would have none of it. He was convinced the weld point would be a weak spot when submitted to the heat and pressure of a fire and he would not put anything but the best equipment in the hands of a fireman—"his kids," as he called the men.

Hughie loved his firemen, and he called them his kids more than anything else. In the advance of old age, when the story of a man's life begins to distill to a handful of the same old stories, there were two things Pop mentioned repeatedly.

"I never had a man knocked down by smoke, Kid"— attributing this remarkable record to his saying a "Hail Mary" each time he put on his hat to go to a fire. And, "When you're going through a window or door, reach in with the tool first and make sure you have a floor. The floors go before the walls."

He'd let a billion-dollar building burn to the ground before he'd knowingly risk the life of one of his kids and he never, ever took an ounce of credit for his accomplishments. Everything he ever did, including the invention of the Halligan tool, was through the intercession of the Blessed Mother and the Grace of her Son.

We arrived at my house in about forty minutes, the Rambler scraping the driveway apron. The noise was alarmingly loud. We had been driving on a major turnpike with the rear of the automobile barely six inches from the pavement. Yikes!

Pop silently began working. He gave me no direction, allowing me to fit myself into his plans as I discovered them. He set up some sawhorses and moved the tools from the car trunk to the platform he had created for them. He donned a welder's mask and this took some doing as the straps had long since been destroyed and replaced by a rope-and-twine rig. He took a single tool and began to grind it on the steel wheel of the grinder he had positioned on my father's workbench.

I watched him work, through a shower of sparks, as he ground off the seam that outlined each tool. It didn't seem to be hard work, but it was tedious. He was intent on his task and focused on each tool till the seam was gone, running his open hand along the shaft to ensure that no edge or burr would hinder his kids. When he was satisfied, he ran the whole tool along the spinning brush on the opposite end of the machine that held the grinder. The finished product was shinier and smoother, though still rough looking. He placed the ground and sanded tools back on the sawhorses as he completed this operation.

He invited me to paint them, pointing to a can with an old brush lying across the open rim. The paint inside was a beautiful silver, but it had a terrible odor. I was to learn that this paint contained an aluminum alloy along with some rust retardant and that it was, of course, fireproof. It was difficult to mix. No matter how long I stirred the paint, there continued to be different colored swirls, all different shades of gray, refusing to merge and blend. Though I was normally enthusiastic about any chance to wield a paintbrush, the stench from that paint, along with the difficulty of painting something with so many irregular surfaces, made this job long and hard.

We worked in silence for a few hours, with Pop regularly glancing over to see how I was doing. It was a whole different experience working with a grandfather instead of a mother or a teacher. He never mentioned the paint I got on my clothes, in my hair, or on my sister's bicycle. I don't know what he was thinking, but he never said a word to criticize the incredible mess I was making while I learned how to paint the tools. Apparently, in this kind of work, you learn as you go along and everyone understands this process.

We worked like this for a few hours and I can't say I enjoyed the actual job much. This says something about the value of time spent. I am sure there were many hours spent doing things I enjoyed in the days immediately preceding the day with Hughie and the Halligan tools, and I am sure there were many days just afterwards that included a lot more fun. But I can't remember a minute of those days, but that day spent with Pop has left me with a hundred clear details almost four decades later.

Pop knew how to lead by example and he knew enough to let me observe and figure things out for myself. So, on that day, I tried and failed and tried and failed till I tried and got it somewhat right, with no more than a dozen words from him. And if I got a little paint on my clothing along the way, there's a lesson in there too. I wouldn't take anything in trade for the time I spent with Hughie that day.

The tools were left to dry, Pop and I watched the Yankees win on the Yankee channel (New York City's Channel 11—in the days when there were three national networks and major markets like ours had an additional channel or two), and then we had dinner with the rest of the family. During dinner, my grandmother asked Pop where these tools were going and he named the towns.

She was as intimately involved in his tool business as she was in the rest of his life. And she adopted a different manner, as husband and wife assumed their business-partner roles.

"Should I make up an invoice?" she asked.

"Sure," he said, after smiling at her with his eyes as well as his lips.

"I'll bet," she answered, with only a hint of resigned sarcasm, as her intended frown died to her own smiling eyes and lips.

It seemed to me she was constantly trying to keep some sense of the practical in his life of charity. They loved each other dearly, all the more so because each one had a way of loving the best qualities of the other. Pop gave stuff away and Nana kept the books, in the business as well as in the home.

For Pop, everything was given to him by God and was for God's use. Pop told me directly, more than once, that the Halligan tool was given to him by the Blessed Virgin in response to his desperate prayer. He consecrated it to her and made it available to her kids, the men on the big red trucks. There was no one who would be turned away from his open home and ready wallet. Every mission, every religious order, and every orphanage had his name, and if a firehouse told him they needed a tool and they had no money, he gave them a tool. Nana, though primarily a homemaker, was a bit more worldly than Pop. She knew people could take advantage of him, and keeping Pop from getting hurt was part of her gift to him.

After dinner, it was back to the garage where Pop packaged the tools for shipping. He put two or three tools together and encased them in a fashion that was pure Hughie Halligan. He had scraps of cardboard he had made from boxes he'd bummed from the local grocery store. He wrapped the scraps around the tool heads, taped them (duct tape this time, probably because it matched the tools better than electrical tape) and secured the whole magilla with package twine. I'm guessing that, if there were any firemen like Hughie at the firehouses where those tools arrived, that twine ended up in the laces of some brave man's shoes.

The key was to leave enough cardboard visible so that a shipping label and postage could be affixed, so this particular job required an expertise best left to the master. He did allow me to hold the cutting knife and he offered me the tape or twine between his hands to allow me to do the cutting. This was big stuff. When a grown man gives a boy a knife for the cutting job, he's saying a lot about that boy's ability, his maturity, and his manliness. Without actually speaking, Pop was saying, "You're ready now. You can handle the knife and I don't have to remind you to be careful."

The next day, we put the tools back in the Rambler and drove to the post office to ship them. I was getting pretty sharp by now and was able to figure out for myself why we had to go to the post office instead of just putting them in the mailbox. The man at the post office started to give Pop a hard time and Pop assumed an extremely deferential and humble manner. I didn't hear the details, but Pop apparently had to plead with the man to accept and ship the nontraditional parcel, wrapped in such an unorthodox manner. The man who stood with the German as his equal was simply a humble pleader of causes before the tyrannical civil servant. I don't remember all the details, but I do remember we left without the tools and everyone was happy.

Especially me.

Sniper School Tryout Day

The day began with the usual monotony. Specialist Moran fell out with the rest of the company for the First Sergeant's morning formation. Automatically, he made his way to his spot. He stood in the third position down from his squad leader, who was the first man in the third row of the scout platoon which fell in line as the fourth platoon down in the company of five platoons. The platoon sergeants stood in their places at the front of each platoon, and the platoon leaders, the officers, milled around behind their respective platoons. At the front of the whole thing was the company staff, officers off to the side and the First Sergeant at the head.

After taking care of the usual business, announcing new rules and new plans and yelling at everyone about one thing or another for a few minutes, the First Sergeant called about a dozen names of soldiers who were to report to his office after formation for "something special." Moran was one of these. On arriving at Top's office (*Top* is the familiar term for first sergeants, shortened from *Top Soldier*), the men were told that they were on the list of 201 men—from a brigade of 3,600—who met the minimum requirements to attend sniper school. The criteria established were that each soldier must have fired "expert" with his rifle, must have passed his latest annual Army Physical Test and must have 20/20 vision. Of course, these criteria were not alone enough to earn a spot in the Army's Sniper School at Little Rock, Arkansas, but were sufficient for each of the men to compete for the forty slots that had been made available to the brigade.

It is highly unusual to have so many snipers in a unit of this size and type. Also, the role of sniper usually is a primary and sole profession. A sniper is normally not also a cavalry scout, or rifleman, or mortar man and each member of Moran's unit was already one of these. The men met this news of their "selection" with suspicion. Many a soldier's worst days have begun with his being selected. Being selected is often what happens to soldiers who do not volunteer.

The First Sergeant explained that the situation in Iraq was such that almost all the casualties suffered by American troops were from Improvised Explosive Devices, always referred to as IEDs. (Everything in the Army must be capable of reduction to an acronym or it is not allowed to exist.) The Coalition forces in Iraq were uncovering and intentionally detonating about sixty of these killers on an average day. Almost all were discovered before they performed their evil missions, but whenever one managed to detonate before it was detected, soldiers died. They died in ugly and bloody surprise explosions, explosions they never heard.

At this point in the war, the spring of 2005, Specialist Moran was training to go to war in a country that had been declared liberated more than a year before. The present combat operations were about defeating a growing insurgency. It was an international war, with radical Islamic elements from all over the Arab street providing men and material to the insurgents in Iraq. They couldn't fight the powerful coalition head on, so they attacked the American lead forces with time-tested guerilla tactics. They used quick ambushes, booby traps, and IEDs. They terrorized those who helped the troops and this was effective in limiting the trustworthy intelligence and civilian logistical support the Coalition needed.

The Commanding General of Moran's brigade combat team decided that rather than try to react to these killers at the point of explosion, it was preferable to detect the IED before it was set in place, preferably while it was still in the hands of the insurgent. For this, he planned to use troops who were trained to move through the battlefield undetected, to take cover in strategic locations and to kill specific isolated individuals—as they placed the bombs. Snipers could take concealed positions in areas in which IEDs were likely to be placed, or had been placed in the past. (Yes, these particular terrorists had noticed the American belief that lightning doesn't strike twice in the same place, had seen the resulting complacency immediately *after* an IED incident, and then exploited that by placing a bomb in exactly the same spot.) Rotten sports, these terrorists.

The sniper, when placed, would remain concealed and observe the terrain with naked eyes, night-vision goggles, motion-detection equipment, and infrared spotting scopes. When he saw anyone attempting to place an IED, he'd kill him with one shot, and *only* one shot, fired from a .50-caliber rifle, specifically designed for his craft.

This $9,000 rifle had its sound as well as its muzzle flash suppressed so that the sniper could remain in position after his kill. If he was lucky, he could kill one or two additional enemies when they'd come to find out what happened to the original bomber. This was a great idea. Indeed, it was a cool job.

So Moran found himself in the company of 201 men who were being considered for this role. He was excited about the possibility of securing a job like this. After all, the age waiver he had to secure in order to get into the Guard (Moran was forty-seven years old) had only approved him for noncombat positions. Additionally, failing the hearing test (miserably it seems, he was down 50% in his left ear and about 35% in his right) also prohibited his active participation at the front. With the help of a savvy first sergeant who knew how to get away with just about anything, he had managed to enlist in, and to secure a place in the ranks of a cavalry scout platoon, and scouts are absolutely combat soldiers. In fact, scouts are considered a cut about the average infantryman. They face greater dangers, need more specialized skills (not to mention nerves of steel), and of course, they must be in a high state of physical fitness.

As far as that went, Moran had managed to meet or exceed all the requirements of this position, despite his age and hearing problems. A former Marine, Moran had never stopped thinking of himself as a Marine. He'd stayed physically fit his whole life. Throughout the Army train-up, he'd never missed an opportunity to show up the younger guys. Of course he wasn't as strong or as fast as he had been twenty years before, but he still managed to come out stronger and faster than many of the younger guys often enough. When he did, he'd tell anyone who'd listen, "Not bad for an old guy, right kid?" He thought his body was ready for the challenge that the tryout for sniper school would be. His ego certainly was.

The soldiers met at the athletic field at 7:30 AM that next Saturday. They were told to bring their packs fully loaded for a three-day field exercise, even though they'd only be there for the day. The purpose of the three-day load was to get the pack up to sixty pounds. Extra uniform, socks, six meals, raingear, first-aid kit, a gallon of water, and a few other items make a pretty big load. When Moran checked in with all his gear, packed as prescribed, he was relieved to find that the 201 candidates had been reduced to 142. The others chose not to compete, the reasons given usually referred to the distaste for personal killing.

Moran thought those who didn't report due to some personal moral repugnance were weak and silly. His thinking was that if he managed to kill one person in the act of placing an IED, he was saving many lives, and American lives at that. War is war and dead is dead and attempts to distinguish between one type of killing and another is so much mental exercising and moral relativizing. Those discussions and distinctions belonged in the seminar rooms of the academy or in liberal think tanks.

The assembled men were introduced to the existing sniper team from the brigade. There were six men, and every one of them was a former Marine. It seems that the Corps wasn't treating them right, or something like that. They announced that they had a program planned for the day that would surely see the field reduced to only the forty soldiers for which they had seats. It was the usual, "We won't have to tell you to leave; 102 of you will quit before the day ends. Very few people have what it takes to become one of us and that is nothing to be ashamed of, but make no mistake about it, *you* will eliminate yourselves. We will not have to tell you to go." Moran thought, "Okay, fair enough. Let's do this."

First, the men were required to qualify in the regular Army Fitness Test. In this, each soldier has to run two miles, do as many push-ups as he can in two minutes and then as many sit-ups as he can for another two minutes. Each event is awarded points and there is a minimum and a maximum. Moran always did very well here, the primary reason being that it was age-adjusted. Moran hated the age adjustment. He didn't like *any* form of affirmative action, and his opinion was no different when he was the beneficiary. Besides, he could hold his own in this test with the soldiers half his age and the age adjustment took the fun out of it. So, he gave this particular test everything he had and scored a respectable (though age-weighted, damn it) 263 points out of 300, well ahead of the 180-point minimum. (Score: old guy, 1; phony tough Marines, 0.)

Next, they "rucked up," which is to say they loaded their packs on their backs. They were marched, single file, past ten objects placed in a line on the ground. This eclectic collection of items made as much sense as anything else in the Army; they were completely unrelated, and in some instances, unrecognizable. They marched around these objects three times and then they were marched away from them. They were then told to remember these objects; they'd have to recall and record them all some time later in the day. Moran developed a pretty fair system for remembering them. There were the B's—a Bic lighter (red, disposable), a ballpoint pen (silver, pocket-clip, click-top) and a box of band-aids (J&J, large size, 60-count, plastic). Then there was the Bell and Howell rifle scope, the sniper veil, and pants to a "ghillie suit" (pants with artificial camouflage secured in abundance). There was an eight-ounce bottle of Coppertone sunscreen # 8, a blue stuffed rabbit, an Eveready nine-volt battery, and finally, a Black and Decker steam iron. There were, of course, some details to these latter items that some could recall and others couldn't, but that's all Moran could remember, and later on, that's what he'd tell them when they asked.

Then they hit the road, and it purely sucked. They single-filed along the shoulder of the road with the instructors driving along the road or stationed along the route, encouraging them with the charmingly innovative motivational method of insulting and taunting the men. Moran handled that well enough; it was so expected that it didn't seem real. He just tuned them out and put one foot in front of the other, recalling the tools he'd learned at Parris Island two decades before. He retreated inside his own head and made a pleasant place for himself.

He'd built a nice world in his head and Moran had been a constant traveler there. From the drill field at Parris Island, through the combat of his first hitch in the Marines, and into the hostile marriage that had marked his life since, Moran knew how to retreat to the comfort of his own mind. He'd learned how to make a pleasant place there. Nobody argued with him. Everyone agreed with him. The whole world made sense, in his head.

As they forcemarched along, he recalled beaches. He recalled women. He recalled women on beaches. He did math problems, composed lectures, wrote letters, said prayers, thought about old jokes and bad beer, and just put one foot in front of the other. The pace was brutal though, and at some point in the morning, he found himself at the rear of the pack. Guess who else was at the rear of the pack? The meanest of the instructors, that's who.

At one point, he was dead last and he had one of those bastards on either side. Their mission was to pick off the weakest of the herd and, that's who he'd become, the weakest of the herd.

"You don't want to be *last*, do you, gramps?"

"Look at you *now*! How do you figure you're going to make it through this *day?*"

"Hey, Old Man, we haven't started the hard stuff yet. Nobody expects you to make this."

"No one is going to fault you for dropping out. Why kill yourself for nothing?"

"You are sweating like a pig! Drink water!"

The key for the old soldier was to not let them into the pleasant places in his head. After all, this kind of talk does not sit well on the white sands of a Caribbean beach. Keep it out. Avoid the temptation to tell them off in your head. These guys were not allowed on his beach and they certainly weren't going to meet the women there either. If he didn't hear it, it wasn't said.

But it did get him moving. In order to remain undisturbed in the pleasant places of his head, he'd have to get away from these guys and that required that he get out of the last spot. These guys were thinning the herd by isolating and destroying the weakest members. The most competitive place in the world can sometimes be the fight to be second to last.

He focused on the back of the second to last soldier five meters ahead of him, and he walked faster. It didn't seem like he was getting any closer, but he knew he was trying harder and it hurt more, so it must have been faster. For a while, he could have sworn that this kid was speeding up as well but the space between them got shorter eventually and he was huffing and puffing like a locomotive. His mouth was dry and his lungs burned. It took a long time for Moran to pass the younger soldier, but pass him he did. Once there, he focused on the next wet, green back. It went on like this for a full hour until they arrived at a new field, about three miles from their starting point. And by then there were about a dozen men behind him. "Gramps, my ass," he muttered to himself.

The instructors had anticipated that the soldiers would make the mistake of thinking that the field was their destination. When they arrived there, and everyone slowed to a crawling gaggle, they backed off a bit. They most enjoyed ignoring those soldiers who removed their rucks to sit down. Taking just enough time to relish the moment and savor the pain they were about to cause, they started screaming.

"*Who* told you to stop?"

"Put that goddamned ruck back on. On your feet!"

"Turn around and head down the other side of the road. Move it! Now!"

"You think this is *over*? We haven't even *started* yet."

The general response was grief—not anger, but grief. Real sadness. Beaten and tired, they headed down the same road they had just come in on. About a quarter of a mile down the road, one of the instructors was stationed; he told them to turn around again and go back to the field where they had just been turned around. This they did. This last cruelty met with success for the instructors.

When Moran returned to the field, he saw seven men standing in a group, apart from the returnees. The frustration and stress had taken a toll and these seven had quit at the turnaround. They were still useful to the instructors however, as they were being treated to ice cold sodas, sports bars, and fresh fruit. They were served their refreshments within sight of the remaining soldiers. This was very unsettling and it caused two more to drop out. After all, there were no negative consequences, the pain would stop and the soda looked too damned cold.

This struck Moran as being way too obvious to have been so successful, but he was wrong. More men dropped out and, as they did, they were told, "Good effort. Tough day. You gave it your best." Moran was exhilarated by the men dropping out. This meant that the herd was being culled, that he had survived, that the day would end, that his chances for success had just increased. "Bring it on!" he thought.

At the next field, they were given a land-navigation test. Equipped with a map given to them, and the pencil and protractor they had been instructed to bring, they had half an hour to answer twenty-five questions on a written test. Most were of the situational type: "You see a water tower at 270 degrees and a hilltop at 21 degrees. Give the grid coordinate for *your* position." Some were meant to test the fine points of map reading, "How high is the hill located 1,000 meters to the left of the cemetery in the town?"

The test completed, they rucked up again and marched back to the original field. It was the same brisk—almost running—walk and it was on this leg that Moran got two blisters about the size of a half dollar—one on the ball of each foot. Identical twin blisters. He knew blisters are a product of a lot of heat and rubbing but these particular blisters seemed to appear instantly and from out of no-where.

Blisters or not, on this leg of the march he managed to completely avoid the dreaded last place, but he was still close enough to hear the abuse the poor guy who happened to occupy that spot was getting. He had never known there were so many synonyms for *fat*, but apparently there are plenty and this guy was treated to every one of them—loudly and maliciously.

He knew he was to struggle all day. He was dog-tired and the sun was barely high in the sky. After all, he really *was* an old man and it really *was* ridiculous that he would try this. The reality was that this was going to be tough, really tough, not phony tough. He knew that to think this way was to let the enemy in and would do the tormenters' job for them. He took an immediate flight back to the pleasant place on the beach.

The test for the second leg was in two parts. First they were given ten minutes to describe the ten items

they were shown earlier in the day. ("Was that *today*?")
The next fifty minutes were filled by another twenty-
five-question written test. This test was on the format of,
and requirements for, the Operations Order. This is the
document that orders a mission. It has five sections. Not
four sections, not six sections—*five* sections. They are
Situation, Mission, Execution, Supply and Support, and
Command and Communication. Within these five sections are found countless excruciating details described
in extremely specific terms and orders, using very particular nomenclature. Moran had first learned this order
format twenty-five years earlier in the Marine Corps and
it hadn't changed a bit, though the Army had taken fas-
tidiousness to a new level in its particular religion of ad-
herence to this sacred form. Ergo, a soldier has to know
it completely.

He passed this test with results that were about average, however, and he had a very difficult time getting
off the ground for the third leg. In fact, he couldn't get
off the ground at all. He had heat cramps in his long
muscles and abdomen already. Heat cramps—in fact, all
heat maladies—are largely caused by dehydration rather than temperature. It was only about seventy degrees
but the flowing perspiration made days like this a battle
against dehydration. The athlete has to drink more than
he sweats—it's as simple as that. And he sweats a lot.

Moran forced a quart of water down and tried for
a second quart until his belly started to swell. He was
behind on fluids, and having been in this condition
before, he was scared. It was noon, the sun was high, he'd

been fighting to stay out of last place all day, and he had heat cramps already. He wasn't scared that he would go down as a heat casualty. After all, the Army successfully handled heat casualties every day. If he dropped, he'd be whisked away in an olive-drab ambulance to a special room in the dispensary which contained a tub with icy cold water. He'd get dunked in the tank, but only for thirty seconds (the cold can kill in five minutes).

Moran had never been in the tank but he'd known plenty of men who had been there. It's shocking and painful and everyone who gets dunked screams. After the dunking, the soldier gets to take a long nap with an IV in each arm and spends two days watching TV and drinking iced tea. Nope, dehydration was starting to look pretty good to Specialist Moran.

He wouldn't quit. He knew that now. But he damn sure could pass out. That might happen.

This next leg of the march was just as long but it was in another direction. The men got to see different pavement and walk on entirely new gravel. The scenery didn't matter to Moran. He was back in his head in no time. He was not competing to stay out of last place this time; he had moved up considerably in the pack, almost to the middle. Soldiers were fading and dropping out. Sometimes Moran felt bad for them. All this work and suffering for nothing. At least this was over for the dropouts. They would eat and sleep. Moran was starving and exhausted.

An hour later, they were down to about ninety soldiers and these men took the next test. It was a first-aid test. There were twenty-five written questions, including some on heat casualties. Some of the men's brains had already become too cooked to answer coherently and the instructors intently corrected the exams, looking for those for whom the effects of the dehydration would be first manifested in the brain. They pulled a few men based on bizarre answers to the exam, scribbled handwriting, or gibberish. The rest rucked up and took off again.

Moran drank two more quarts of water and joined the pack. About halfway through the next leg, and for only the second time in his entire life, he hit the wall. The first time was right around mile twenty-two of the New York City Marathon he'd run in 1989. When you hit the wall, there's no mistaking what it is and there's no accurate way to describe it. He'd read many accounts of this phenomenon while training for the marathon. He'd wanted to be prepared for it. When he had hit it then, as when he hit it this time, there was absolutely no mistaking what had happened.

He had hit the wall. After moving mile after mile on pure will and muscle memory, a message came from the last little sane part of his brain that was still uncooked. It was delivered to every cell in his body at the exact same moment. It simply said, "Stop. You can go no further. You are out of fluid. You have depleted your stores of sodium and electrolytes. Your muscles have no food left in them. Your brain is heating up and very soon, you will likely be an idiot. You will stop. Now."

The best description Moran had ever read about hitting the wall was that it was as though a wall of gelatin suddenly appears in front of you and you slam into it. Momentum keeps taking you forward a bit, but the same effort you were expending just a moment before will not move you a bit. It is here that you have to exert more effort, while your body is demanding that you cease all effort and lie down. Oh yeah, and you get a big headache too, a huge, brain-pounding headache.

He had run through the wall in the marathon. He'd been trained that a runner could override the wall's screaming at him to stop. He had used pure will to wrest himself from the arms of the cruel wall. He had been permanently changed by the experience. Running was never as fun as it had once been after he'd hit the wall. Physical exhaustion was never a "good kind of tired" again. Running and pain always brought back the memory of the day he hit the wall. When he'd finished the marathon, his training partner was waiting at the finish line to congratulate him.

"Great time, especially for a first marathon! How do you feel?"

"Terrible, and my first marathon is also my last marathon, Mitch."

"Oh, everyone says that. You'll see. In a few weeks, you'll be eager to do another one."

Mitch was wrong. Moran was never again tempted to run anything more than a few miles. The wall had humbled him. But it had schooled him too. Moran was up against the wall again. He endured the bone-rattling pain and staggered forward, putting one foot in front of the other for the next minute or two—and then it passed.

He wasn't restored of course, just running on fumes. Two instructors were at his side by now. They had seen him hit the wall. Oh yeah, you can *see* someone hit the wall. The body jerks, staggers, and quivers all over. It looks exactly the way it feels. The man looks as though he ran into a wall of gelatin. It is something to see.

Moran wouldn't recommend seeking out the experience, though.

"Drop out."

"No."

"No. Really. No bullshit, now. You are done."

"We made a deal, Sergeant. I am done when I say I'm done."

"You've given it everything. 110%. That's all you can do."

"I was in the *Old* Corps, Sergeant. What are you talking about? We did this every day. See you at the finish."

Their "Marine aura" was their calling card around here, and they didn't like the "Old Corps" crack. Marines have always been told that things were harder in the Old Corps and that the present-day Marine has it comparatively easy. Every Marine has been told this, and has been told it often—sometimes by the guy who signed up a week before *he* did. Not being tough enough is very scary for a Marine. They allowed Moran to keep on truckin', but they were by his side the whole way home. He didn't enjoy their company, but he welcomedthe security brought by their presence. He wanted some help handy if he dropped, and he enjoyed their anxiety. They stopped taunting him and even encouraged him. The occasional stage whisper from one to the other—"What if we kill the old guy?"—showed more respect and real concern than cruelty.

When they finally arrived back at the field, they were immediately forced to drink water. This is worse than it sounds. Each soldier must down two quarts of water under supervision. This makes sense of course, but this medicine can be worse than the dehydration for some. Some get intense abdominal cramps from the cold water hitting their hot stomachs. Some vomit. Moran did okay though. He'd been drinking all day and he was conscious to keep his stomach as stretched as he could, turning it into a holding tank of sorts, constantly filling it.

The final test was a sneaky killer. They required them to dump their rucksacks on the ground in front of them, where they were inventoried. The instructors checked the contents to see if each soldier was still in possession of all the items he had been required to bring. They did this at the end of the day because, apparently, it is common for soldiers to dump the weight of their rucks while on road marches. Well hell, Moran would have done it himself, if he had thought of it. Sure as shit, they caught about a half dozen guys—and then there were seventy-two.

Hmmm . . . the instructors had guaranteed they'd be down to forty before the day was done and here they were—all seventy-two of them. It's fun to watch a lifer, Army or Marine, get stumped and start to think. These guys looked like they were confused, trying to figure out how to deal with the seventy-two guys that were supposed to be forty guys. They huddled at the other end of the field, out of the soldiers' hearing, for a full quarter of an hour. The seventy-two had fun imagining all the crazy solutions the instructors might be suggesting. The soldiers were proud and pumped up and getting cocky.

"Hey, I got it! They'll split us up and have us hunt each other till we're down to forty!"

"Nah, you'd have to split us in half. Then, they'd end up with thirty-six."

"Yeah, right. Maybe they'll do a final road march till thirty-two more drop."

"Nope, if they break their own rules, their heads will really explode."

"Hey, isn't that Sergeant Groff opening a manual?"

"Sure is. God, I can't believe it. Duhhhh . . . it's gotta be here somewheres."

"What a lifer! Every problem has a solution in a freakin' manual!"

"Bet one of their heads explodes."

"Maybe they void the whole day. Reschedule and start all over."

"Holy Shit!"

"God! Nooooo, not again!"

That kind of solution is exactly like something a book-driven lifer would come up with.

It was a long forty-five minutes waiting for these guys to figure out what to do with seventy-two men when their brains were programmed for forty. Of course, the instructors were tired and hot, too.

Some soldiers dropped everything and lay on the ground, fast asleep in minutes. Others sat around, smoking and joking. Moran did neither. He anticipated the pain of getting back up and rucking up again, so he stood while waiting this crew out. He leaned against the cyclone fence, with the bottom of his ruck resting on the top of the fence. The fence took the whole weight of the ruck, and he found that if he bent his knees a bit, it took some of his weight as well. He drank some more water, smoked four cigarettes and listened to the chatter while the board of directors deliberated.

The chatter hasn't changed in twenty-five years, so listening to these guys wasn't likely to give him anything new to chuckle about. More often, it brought memories. Memories of marines from their fathers' generation shucking the same jive, practicing the same acts, the same sex-obsessed, booze-lovin', macho banter. God, he loved it. Twenty years, a college education, mortgages, a wife and kids—all did nothing to lessen his love for the world of the warrior. He loved it, even the stupid, painful, boring parts. He loved this shit.

He had stopped caring about whether he made it to sniper school by this point. Eons and eons ago, about 9:00 that morning, the challenge had become something else entirely. It had become an opportunity to win a big victory over *self*, so he'd just keep it in the day. Screw these guys anyway. If being a sniper is this damned demanding physically, he really *didn't* want it. He didn't know what he had thought. Maybe he had thought they would drive him out to his sniper's perch and helicopter afternoon tea out to him as well. Apparently, not. There was a lot more to this job than the skillful pulling of a trigger for a man of steel nerves. He'd placed himself in the day for the challenge of the test itself. He'd done his best and he'd done well enough to please himself. He hadn't quit. That was enough.

The pack of lifers arrived and announced, with some solemnity, that they had found a solution. They would interview each of the seventy-two and pick their favorite forty. They scheduled them from 9:00 AM to 5:00 PM the next day, Sunday.

A corporate solution that sort of made sense? That was a first.

At the end of the announcement, they asked if there were any questions and Moran asked if he could reschedule to another time slot. The only Mass on base was at 2:00 PM, the same time he was scheduled to interview, and he offered to be there at any other time but that. They were incredulous—and stony silent. The Lieutenant in charge of the group, who until then had been an enigmatic mute, hanging in the shadows, just watching and listening, confronted Moran. In front of almost eighty soldiers, he said, "Maybe you don't want this enough, Specialist. Maybe you need to examine your priorities."

"I absolutely want this, Sir, and I am most sure of my priorities. I *will* attend Mass tomorrow. It is not a choice between one duty and the other. My duties as an American soldier and my duties as a Catholic are not in conflict. In fact, I volunteered for this war because they are entirely in sync. A sniper without a God is a mercenary at best, and quite possibly, just a cold-blooded killer."

"Oh, *I* pray to God. But *I* don't need to go to a church to do that."

"I can respect that, Sir. But that is not how I worship."

Not realizing he was getting outgunned, the Lieutenant said, "I don't go to church, anymore. My parents forced me to and punished me when I didn't go."

Moran thought, "Why's he telling me this? Just re-schedule the fucking interview or say *no.*"

But he said, "With respect, Sir, they must have also taught you to brush your teeth, use silverware, and wipe your ass. I hope you haven't rejected those habits as well."

From the crowd, "Ah, Sir, aagh, uhhmm. He can have my eleven o'clock and I'll take his at two."

"Fine, then. I don't really care what you do."

Moran tried not to look victorious or smug. He didn't feel that way anyway. He felt cheap and silly for his dramatic soliloquy about God and Country. He'd have known better if he hadn't been so tired. He was practiced in better ways to handle the Mass/training conflict. He went through it with someone every seven days. He had grown tired, though, of defending his going to Mass every Sunday.

He, along with the other three soldiers from his platoon, had ended up in the seventy-two left standing. They headed back to the barracks together. It was a mile walk and they still had their rucks, so they expected to walk it rather than go through the stressful and undependable process of calling transportation. The base shuttle was inefficient when it was running and often it wasn't running.

While discussing this, however, the younger soldiers decided that Moran was dying. He feebly denied this, hoping they would come to their senses and call the damned shuttle anyway. They did, and during the wait they were kind enough not to mention that, but for the old man, they "could all have walked home by now." When the shuttle arrived, Moran staggered a bit getting the pack off and into the trunk, so during the ride, they argued that he should go to the dispensary, that he could really be, in fact, dying.

"I am not dying. I am simply old. This is what *old* looks like."

"Dude, how many classes you gotta go to before you know what heat exhaustion is?"

"Not one more, I hope. I *know* I have heat exhaustion and, like you, I *know* how to treat it."

"Yeah, with the tub and the needle."

"Perfect ending to a perfect day. Fuck you. No way."

"I heard the tub is so cold you can get *permanent* shrinkage."

"I heard that too. Your balls can get sucked right up into your stomach."

"That's ridiculous."

"No, really! I heard it happened to one of the guys from artillery."

"Did you see the guy?"

"No, but I heard."

"Shut up. This did not happen. Shrinkage is what happens to the brains of artillery guys. Their brains get so rattled from the explosions, they get stupid, then they can't find their balls and they just think they shrunk."

"You sure it was the stomach? 'Cause I don't think it can get in there that way."

"*Please* shut up. You are giving me a headache."

"Well, you are staying in your rack when we get back then."

"Oh no. Don't throw me in *that* briar patch!"

"Briar patch? What the fuck is a briar patch?"

"I *will* die if you don't shut up."

"He's delirious already, talking gibberish."

"That's right. There's no such thing as a bristle patch or whatever he said."

"Oh, God, SHUT UP!"

When they got to the barracks, Sergeant Boyd grabbed Moran's ruck and Sergeant Dieterrick walked alongside of him.

"You okay? Gonna make it, Old Man?"

"I sure hope so. I know you can't carry me. Not today."

"That's right, but I can roll you in the door if I have to."

"Comforting thought."

"Hey, Moran, are all Marines as fucked up as those guys?"

"Yup."

"No wonder you're such a stubborn idiot."

"I was a stubborn idiot before I joined the Marines."

"Christ, you're a trip."

"And look who's talking stubborn, Herr Dieterrick! We're the Master Race; we want your country and we're not gonna stop goose-stepping till we get it."

"Damned straight, my people wouldn't throw you in the tub. We'd go straight for the oven with the rest of the old and infirm."

"You're a sick bastard."

"Keep talking like that and I'll have to see my therapist. You are definitely fucking with my self-esteem."

"Now I heard everything, a German with a self-esteem problem."

When Moran got inside, Sergeant Boyd had already filled a gallon jug with water and put it on the footlocker by Moran's bunk. "It is now 7:00 PM. You will drink this whole gallon of water by 10:00. You will not leave the immediate area of your bunk without an escort."

"Is that an order?"

"It *can* be."

"Tough love; I'm getting misty."

"It's only your cataracts, Pappy."

"Did you say you were getting me an escort? You said something about an escort?"

Moran drank the whole gallon of water. He got up one time to empty his bladder before falling asleep and then slept through the night. Very little of that water went to waste. His body needed all of it.

The next day, he felt as though he had concrete in his veins. He was stone stiff. Getting out of bed was a real struggle. The other guys were hurting as well, and they didn't bother trying to hide it. But they didn't complain much either. The story of all the pain was an old one.

"I'm going to the shower. Who wants to escort me?"

"The president of GLAD, but he's not here. We'll have to draw straws."

They went together, and they each labored through the rigors of washing, shaving, and brushing their teeth. This last task was particularly difficult. To brush his teeth, Moran had to keep one arm up and moving for

two or three minutes. He had to switch hands; his right
arm cramped up right at the inside of the bicep, where
the tendons meet the muscle. It hurt like hell. Brushing
his teeth with his left hand had toothpaste flying everywhere. When enough had made it to his teeth, he surrendered and struggled through the rigors of washing and
storing his toiletries back in his shaving kit. He was already exhausted at this point in what he knew was going
to be another long day.

They all went to their interviews together, even
though their times were far apart. They were still babysit-
ting Pappy, as Moran was increasingly being called, and
protesting was going to do him no good. What the hell,
he was dizzy and these guys made no effort to hide that
they were only marginally less beat up than Moran.

When Moran's turn came, he entered the room,
marched smartly to the table where the four interviewers
sat abreast, came to attention and announced himself.

"Specialist Moran reporting for his interview, as ordered, Sir!"

He stared at the wall over their heads and listened to
the silence for about a minute. Great, they were still doing
that tough-guy thing. "Finally, we haven't had enough of
the tough-guy shit lately," he thought to himself. "What
we need here is some good old-fashioned hazing."

"At ease, Specialist. Sit down."

At the center of the board sat the Lieutenant who
Moran had had the run-in with about Mass the day
before. That trick of knocking him off guard yesterday
was a little-known interviewing technique, where the

interviewee intimidates the interviewing officer into submission. The Lieutenant, apparently, had not heard of
this technique.

"Let's get down to business. Why do you want to be
a sniper?"

"It's a tough job and I can do it. It is one of the few
ways in the Army that I can stand out as an individual
rather than as just part of a group. I can succeed or fail on
my own. No excuses."

"Yes, I can see you are an independent thinker. I
learned that yesterday. Yes, Specialist, you are a true individual. First Sergeant, do you have any questions for
the professor?"

The First Sergeant took over, "Here's the situation.
You are sent on a mission to kill a known terrorist leader.
While you are sitting in your nest, you see the terrorist arriving, just where he is supposed to arrive, dressed
exactly as intelligence says he would be, and surrounded
by the expected entourage. There is no doubt that this is
your target. As you look through your scope, you see that
the target is, in fact, your brother. What do you do?"

"Call our mother. I'm telling on him."

Thoroughly thrilled with himself, Moran burst into
a belly laugh and was pleased as punch that two of the
board members seemed to think it was a riot too. But
they stopped short when the Lieutenant glared at them.
Apparently, at Officer Candidate School, there was some
procedure that involved the surgical removal of the candidate's sense of humor. Moran knew he was toast, that
the interview was over before it began, so he made no real
effort to stifle a good laugh. He was still giggling when
the Lieutenant barked, "I am glad you think this is so

funny, Specialist. I would have thought that with the deficiencies your age presents, you might make up for it with a bit of maturity."

"Now," Moran thought, "he has pissed me off."

"Sir, with respect, that is an absolutely ridiculous hypothesis. It *deserves* to be laughed at. It just can't be taken seriously."

"And why is that?"

"Well, for one, my brother's a pussy. He'd never be a terrorist—too dangerous."

Standing and yelling, "I take it seriously and *you* will take it seriously! I *order* you to answer the question, and if I detect the slightest bit of mirth, I will charge you with disobeying a direct order."

"Don't ever think I don't know when I'm beat," Moran thought.

"Sir, I would radio my commander and tell him the situation. Without even the tiniest hint of mirth I would ask for permission to abort the mission."

"Okay, Smartass. He denies your request and orders you to complete the mission. You are to take the shot."

"I would, respectfully and as mirthlessly as possible, refuse to follow that order."

He came around the table and put the tip of his nose to the tip of Moran's nose. Moran was about four inches shorter, so he stood on his toes just to make it fun for everyone.

Realizing how silly he looked, the Lieutenant took a step backwards.

"Are you saying that you would simply refuse to follow a direct order?"

"Yes, Sir."

"Just like that?"

"Yes, Sir. Just like that."

"That's it? Fuck the mission? Fuck your buddies?"

"Fuck the whole country! I'm not shooting my brother. There are just some things that one does not do and this would be one of them."

Without breaking his glare or turning his head, he asked the board members behind him, "Do you men have any more questions for Specialist Moran? I think I've learned enough to make my decision."

In unison, "No, Sir."

"We will notify you of our decision. You are dismissed."

Moran didn't share the particulars of his interview with Boyd and Dieterrick, so when they were notified of the decisions, they were surprised to find that Moran had not even been given the courtesy of being notified.

"Why do you think they didn't even let you know?"

"Don't know for sure. Maybe it was something I said."

An Army of One

"You cain't come in heya. Dis whole area's off limits to ever'body who don' work heya." The soldier made a performance of standing his ground. He spread his legs apart, jamming his balled fists to his hips.

From the two dozen soldiers who were his audience came a representative. The group parted as their platoon sergeant stepped from the rear to confront the obstacle. The soldiers leaned forward as one, anticipating a confrontation—hopefully, some violence. After all, Sergeant First Class Mulcahy gave no quarter when it came to standing up for his troops. If they wanted to get into the building, then the Platoon Sergeant would see that they got into the building, and this rear-end "pogue" ("pogue" is a derogatory term used to describe non-field personnel in the Army and Marine Corps), certainly wasn't going to stop them. The only question was whether Mulcahy'd bother having a conversation with the "pogue" before he teed off on him.

Instead, Sergeant Mulcahy slowed down as he approached the man, even placing his own hands limply along the seams of his pants, offering the universal symbol of submission and respect in the warrior world. "Can we have a word offline, Sergeant?"

The soldier's face relaxed as he turned it toward an open space alongside the front door and nodded at it. His own arms even dropped from his sides as he led the platoon sergeant to his "office." He turned to face Mulcahy even as he was arriving just one step behind him, "Look Sarn't, I can appreciate that you wanna to see the body, but da rules on dis is clear. Rules is rules."

"Hey, I know how it is. We're in the same Army after all. It's just that my boys are really upset and they need to see him. They never saw him fall and never saw him carried away. I can't begin to help them till we get past the first part, seeing him dead. I need you to help me with this, Sergeant."

"Dis ain't nuttin' new fo' us, S'arnt. Dis what we do. We takes dese bloody messes and we box 'em up and ship 'em home soon as we can. We don't fix 'em up much. Soldiers come in here and starts crazy shit when dey sees 'em like dis."

"That 'bloody mess' in there is one of my men," Mulcahy's posture change indicated that he might be having second thoughts about his initial docility.

"Oh, I know! I know! Das jes da point. See, dat's jes it. He don' look so good, ya know. Soldiers get crazy when dey sees dey's buddies all busted up. We got a tuff 'nuff job as it is."

"Well, they lost a buddy and this is the only funeral they'll get to go to for him. They'll be out in the shit again before that kid in there is buried. I give my word that my men will not cause a disturbance. I know them and I will take full responsibility."

"Uh, I dunno . . . ."

"Five minutes. Not one second more. We will be in and out in five minutes."

"What if the Cap'n come by?"

"More than just the Captain is coming by if my soldiers don't get a chance to see their buddy. We're both going to have a problem that only a platoon of MPs will solve. The fastest way to make this go away is to give us the five minutes."

"Okay. Okay. Five minutes an' no mo'! Not one secon' mo'! An' you got to give me a minute to get 'im ready."

"Thanks, Man. Thanks a lot. I'll talk to the men while you're inside. We will be in and out in five minutes and no one will ever know we were here. I owe you a big one, Sergeant."

The men parted to allow the mortuary sergeant to disappear inside the building; Mulcahy turned to his troops. Mulcahy's eyes moved from one soldier to the other, seeking and getting eye contact with them all. "Okay, we can go in. Listen carefully. We will go in together, each man with his battle buddy. We will *say* nothing while inside. We will *do* nothing while inside. We will *touch* nothing while inside. We will see Robinson. We will say our good-byes, and when I give the word, we will leave together. Got it?"

After the mixture of loud assurances and murmurs of assent from his men, Mulcahy said, "We are soldiers. We are men. We will act like soldiers. We will act like men. Maintain your discipline and military bearing."

All nodded their assent in unison, the anxiety over not being able to see PFC Robinson being replaced by the fear that they would. The front door opened and the mortuary sergeant waved them in. Sergeant Mulcahy moved to the lead, just like he always did, and the troops fell in behind him, just like they always did, shoulders back, chins up, and jaws clenched. Battle buddies—pairs of men assigned to stick with each other, no matter what, during battle—found each other for this task as well.

They filed through the front door, each man having to hold the door for the man behind him. Like almost all of the doors in Iraq, this one had broken hinges and twisted metal, thanks to the first soldiers who came through it during the initial assault. The glass had been replaced by plywood which also served as a sign board. This one had the words *Mortuary Affairs* stenciled on it with black spray paint.

They followed each other down the corridor, respecting its silence with all but their boot steps. The empty stone walls echoed the sounds of their progress as they followed each other around two corners and down the last hall to another set of doors. These doors were made entirely of plywood and crudely fastened to the remnants of the original metal door frame. These doors had the words *Do Not Enter* posted in foot-high red letters across them; there was no attempt at neat stenciling, clarity and authority being the only goal.

The implements of the mortician's trade were situated along the walls of the brightly lit stone room. At one end were three makeshift cubicles, rectangles of sheets suspended from rings that brought to mind a hospital room. It was ice cold. The soldiers' attention was directed to the gurney that had been pulled to the middle of the room. Curiously, the mortuary sergeant put his index finger to his lips as his wide and urgent eyes looked for theirs. He was a different man now from the stern gatekeeper they had first met. This reverential persona did much to explain his other self though. These fallen soldiers with whom he spent his days were to be allowed the final peace they deserved. For the short time they'd be with him, he cared for them. His other hand waved at them, inviting them forward.

Each man had, in his own way, prepared himself for the scene. After all, few were strangers to battle death and most knew what to expect. Robinson would be on the gurney, bloodied and broken. Mulcahy quickly moved around the gurney to the side across from where his troops were gathering. From there, he could view all of them, as well as see his fallen soldier. He'd be able to anticipate immediate problems, of course, but more than that, he'd get a sense of who might need his broad shoulders later on. Prepared as they might think they were, there are some heartbreaks that no one can ever really prepare for. He'd find out now.

All business now, the mortician pulled the sheet off. Robinson was on his back, naked except for the towel covering his midsection. The blackened chest was the most obvious wound, though it had been the least serious and had not caused his death. All the soldiers looked—and ate the horror. Some continued to look while most quietly averted their eyes, another duty done. One soldier in particular did less looking and more hurting than the others. Jack Becker had been the first to see the fallen boy in the early dark hours of that very day. His unspeakable pain came from the certain knowledge that he'd had the power to stop this horror from happening. That knowledge was his alone, sitting in its own little place in his guts, kept company by his shame.

The platoon had left on a route-recon mission the night before. These missions were not the most dangerous and were often accomplished without a shot being fired, but they were wildly unpredictable. After all, a successful reconnaissance mission requires that the troopers cover the route, gaining information and identifying obstacles and opportunities and bringing this information back to the commanders. Getting in and out unseen is the goal. Contact with the enemy is to be avoided, but something had gone terribly wrong on this mission.

Traveling past a small village, where there had up to this time been no terrorist activity at all, they came under small-arms fire. Instinctively, all the drivers turned the vehicles toward the village and raced directly at it, all on line, gunners firing in continual six-round bursts. This procedure was choreographed and rehearsed so often that the evening's martial ballet went off without a hitch or a thought. Usually, when this wave of machine guns raced towards the village, the enemy who weren't instantly killed took off running, their war being a hit-run-and-hide affair. But last night, it hadn't gone that way at all. By the time the trucks hit the village line, the men were still seeing the muzzle flashes of automatic weapons in the upper stories of some of the buildings. They buttoned up the hatches and fired from the small ports along the sides of the trucks, but each man knew that this wasn't going to solve the problem and they dreaded what came next. The enemy was entrenched behind concrete, darkness, and civilians.

Over the radio, Mulcahy called for all but the drivers to dismount, to leave the security of the armored trucks, go inside the buildings and hunt and kill the attackers. A split second after the radio clicked off, Mulcahy was the first one out the door. Silently and immediately, the soldiers opened their doors and poured out from their Humvees, streaking for the closest cover. No one said a word, each man knowing where each other soldier was, looking to see each man but avoiding eye contact at the same time. Pouring the sweat that only the combination of desert and fear can produce, each man grabbed some cover. Under trucks and in alleyways, they waited for Mulcahy who ran from team to team, assigning each their target building to be secured. The last instruction to each team leader was that they were to attack on his signal.

"I'll drop a smoke grenade in the middle of the intersection. This'll give us cover. As soon as you see the smoke, run through it to your objectives. Don't lose your battle buddies!"

Mulcahy disappeared into the darkness. Seconds later, they heard the hiss of a smoke grenade warming up. As the smoke filled the intersection, the men raced towards its protection, each knowing where they were to exit its cloud and how they'd get to their buildings from there.

This enemy was just as resourceful as they were. They tore out of those buildings and into the street the minute they saw the smoke. They knew the American's procedures better than the Americans had learned theirs. Their odds were better in the chaos of a street fight than they were with their backs against the walls of their lairs. The enemies clashed, even amid the smoke and chaos.

Confusion and terror ruled these moments as man slammed into man, each not knowing if the warm sweating obstacle was friend or foe.

It only took a few minutes for the smoke that changed their world to begin dissipating and when it did, both sides were scattered, each man looking for a hole he could climb into, a comrade to join or an enemy to kill. Becker was on all fours in the doorway of a house, gasping for air and groping for his rifle. Finding both, he lay down to survey the scene.

Grinding the side of his face into the pavement, smelling the urine and tasting the dust, he could see parts of the street and a half dozen pairs of feet still searching for life-saving cover. Identifying an armed enemy, he rolled over onto his back, then sitting up, raised his M-4 carbine rifle to his cheek. Firing two three-round bursts at the fleeing man, he watched the flaming tracer rounds disappear into the smoke along with the man. He had no idea if he had hit him.

Jerking his head all around, trying to see everything at once, his eyes met Robinson's. The cockstrong Robinson was a study in contrasts. His wide eyes yelled his fear and his clenched jaw told of his resolve. He was gathering courage for something. Crouching in a doorway across the street, Robinson first waved to get Becker's attention, and then began talking in the hand signals that had become the soldiers' second language. He signaled that he'd be leaving the doorway and heading down the alleyway halfway up the street. He wanted Becker to provide cover fire for the move and then follow him into the alley as soon as he turned the corner.

Becker vigorously shook his head, signaling that they should wait for reinforcements; Robinson's idea was risky as hell for such an uncertain objective. When it became clear that his hand signals were being ignored, Becker screamed at the top of lungs, "Hell no! You stay put!"

Robinson repeated his intentions and Becker waved him off.

"Stay put, you stupid bastard!"

Specialist Becker was two ranks higher and six years older than the twenty-year-old PFC Robinson, and he knew he ought to beat feet across that street and collar that kid before he could make his stupidly brave move. If he cut diagonally across, Becker could head him off before Robinson made it to the alley. But that too was a dangerously stupid move and Becker wasn't going to compound stupidity with stupidity. He vigorously shook his head and lowered his weapon to his lap. He wanted it made perfectly clear to Robinson that he was not supporting his cowboy horseshit.

"That kid's got more balls than brains. He knows we work in teams," Becker said to himself as he signaled again to stay put. Robinson shook him off again. Becker knew he could order him to stay put or he could race over and sit on him, and that he probably should, but in a decision that would change him forever, he decided he wasn't going to baby-sit this dumb-ass kid if he didn't want to be baby-sat.

Becker saw the end before he heard it. Seconds after Robinson turned the corner into the alley, the alley was lit up, yellow-orange flashes splattering against the buildings, darkness returning just as fast. Then there were the sounds, the distinctive staccato of an AK-47 firing on full burst, the sound of the bullets ricocheting, and ricocheting again, turning the tiny alleyway into a blender. And after that, things falling, thudding and rolling. Then silence. Horrible silence, the silence of the alley louder than the din of the battle around it.

Becker raced straight for the alleyway, stopping just short of the entrance where he hit the ground again, his whole body in the dirt. He heard voices and moving feet, fast-moving feet. Sticking his head around the corner, he saw some cans and crates scattered about and only one man, lying against the wall in a heap of desert-patterned clothing and equipment. The moving feet had carried the voices away, the voices of those who had done this.

He was up and at Robinson's side in a minute, pulling his equipment off and tearing his clothing away. Robinson had died instantly, taking the full blast of the Russian made assault rifle. Most of the bullets had hit the vest; the material covering the plates was torn and shredded. The bulletproof plates had held fast, keeping the bullets from entering the body but still delivering their impact. The kinetic energy of the speeding bullets had spread across the whole breastplate, slamming it onto Robinson's chest, almost certainly knocking him down breathless. It wouldn't have killed him though; the two bullets that had hit above the vest had done that.

Becker was reliving that moment now as he looked at the same chest on the mortician's gurney. The bruises somehow looked less ghastly on the corpse. Wounds on the living look worse than wounds on the dead, their being out of place on a live body. Becker looked to the head next, grateful that the mortician had already fixed some of that damage. He remembered what his head had looked like on the alley floor. One bullet had entered Robinson's neck leaving a neat hole. Not hitting anything hard, it had exited at the back through a hole only slightly bigger. The bullet that hit Robinson in the face had behaved quite differently. As soon as the 7.62 round hit his cheekbone, it spread itself outward at supersonic speed, making the hole bigger and bigger as it tore through his skull. When this round exited the back of his head, along with a chunk of skull and a stream of brain tissue, it left a ghastly three-inch hole. Becker had found this place with his hand as he tried to pick up Robinson's head in the alley.

As he was trying to place his head back down gently, the pool of blood surrounded them both, spreading Robinson's life in the dirt of an alleyway eight thousand miles from home, in a town whose name he'd never learned and whose inhabitants he'd never met. Becker was ashamed to have left a pool of his own vomit in that sacred place.

The smoke had cleared and the gunfire had died by the time Becker left the alley. The street was a busy scene as soldiers searched out their battle buddies, relieved faces sporting wide grins as the living met the living. There were four bodies lying side by side on one sidewalk. These enemy dead had been searched for documents and then "dressed," which is to say they were left with their feet crossed at the ankles, their arms folded across their chests and some article of their own clothing covering each face. This is SOP for the American Army that never misses an opportunity to show the world they are a civilized and humane bunch. The enemy dead are "dressed."

On the sidewalk across the street were grouped the American wounded. All the wounds were minor. Kilmer had smashed into a market stand while running through the smoke. He was holding a pressure bandage to a nasty tear on his forehead, enduring the good-natured ribbing of his fellows about the sheer dopiness of such a combat wound. Danner had a burn on his face from the muzzle flash of an enemy AK-47. Going through the darkened doorway of his target building, an enemy soldier had fired a full burst at him. Danner had sped past him by the time he fired, the burst being his first notice that his enemy was there at all. With his cheek burning and his ears ringing, he'd spun around as he raised his own rifle to the other cheek, muscle memory and instinct pulling the trigger and dropping his would-be killer in a heap in the dark.

It fell to Becker to kill the celebration that was brewing as the men surveyed their low-cost combat victory.

"Robinson's dead! Over there!" He pointed to the alley using the rifle in his right hand.

"Dead?!" freezing in place.

"Are you sure?" knowing the answer even as the question was asked.

"Where? Over here?" as the soldiers ran in the direction Becker pointed.

Kilmer entered the alley first, but Mulcahy sprinted by him at the entrance, slowing down as the body came into view. "Stop. Don't let anyone come down the alley. Keep them out!" he yelled to Kilmer without turning to look at him. Kilmer had only caught a glimpse of the carnage, so he understood the reason for the commands immediately. Turning on the ball of one foot, he streaked back up the alley, running into the crowd of soldiers coming down.

"Get back! Get the hell back! Sergeant Mulcahy's with Robinson now and he says for everyone to stay out."

The crowd stopped, some looking past Kilmer's shoulder. Anticipating this, Mulcahy had positioned his body between Robinson and the alley opening. He turned his head around, not speaking until all the men were gone.

"Kilmer, get on the radio. Call a Medevac. You know the format. One KIA. Two ambulatory wounded. LZ is the open field we dismounted. We'll mark with vehicle headlights. Got it?"

"Roger, Sergeant."

"Do it now."

The next hour passed in labor, the men mostly silent as they worked. The field was marked. The choppers came in, one for Robinson, another for the wounded. The Army never transports the KIAs on the same chopper as the WIAs. Mulcahy rolled Robinson's body onto a litter and wrapped a poncho around it. Only when it was fully concealed did he call Kilmer back to help him carry the dead soldier to the helicopter. The men were all at their vehicles now, each one solemnly watching the camouflaged tragedy pass by. When the body was loaded and secured on the one chopper and the two wounded soldiers were on board the other, Mulcahy waved them both off and returned to his men.

"We all feel bad, but right now we have to do what we

are doing right now. Focus on getting back to base. Think of nothing else, or we'll have another casualty. Mount up and fire your engines on my radio command countdown. Do it."

The crews were silent on the way home, and on returning, they dragged through the process that checked the equipment back into storage, the weapons back to the armory, and the vehicles to their garage. They received word that their after-action review would be in the headquarters building with the Colonel rather than in the barracks with Mulcahy, as it usually was. On arriving there, they found the Colonel at the door, holding it open for them to enter. This reversal of military courtesy was as much a ritual of condolences as the whispered regrets he offered each soldier as they passed him. He directed them to his conference room, another windowless tomb like all the other rooms in all the other buildings in this god-awful country.

The Colonel followed them into his conference room, walking to the front where an oversized map of their area of operations covered the wall.

"I am terribly sorry for your loss. I know you'll all need time to deal with this and get some things done for PFC Robinson, so I will make this as brief and painless as I can. As you know, the quicker we can get the facts from you, the better the information will be and the better the chances are that we can make use of it. First, Sergeant Mulcahy, would you brief me on the whole mission up to the contact with the enemy?"

Coming to his feet, Mulcahy faced the Colonel and

told him of the events of the previous night, starting with their being assigned the route-recon mission, all the way up to the smoke grenade. The Colonel stopped him there, "You mean . . . they counterattacked through the smoke?"

"Yes, Sir. They ran right out into us."

"That's new for them, isn't it, Sergeant?" It was more of an invitation to agree than it was a question.

"First time I ever saw it, Sir."

"I will need you to speak with Major Botteck in my S-2 shop. He needs to know about this change in the enemy's tactics. But not today; take care of your men first. I'll tell him you will be by to see him tomorrow. Now, tell me about Robinson."

"Sir, I didn't see him. It happened in the dark. Everyone lost their battle buddies in the smoke. We were all fighting alone and no one seems to have seen him fall. Specialist Becker found him dead and came and told me."

"Becker?"

Taking his eyes from the floor and slowly rising, "Sir, I never saw him alive. When the smoke cleared, I started looking around for someone, anyone, and when I looked down that alley I saw him there, already dead." The first lie was easier than he'd thought it would be and he knew there'd be more to come now. (But he thought to himself, "Why lie? Why not just tell the truth? I didn't do anything wrong. Robinson got himself killed.")

"You never saw him enter that alley, then."

"No, Sir." He said as he moved deeper into the world of his own creation.

To the group, "Anyone? Did anyone see Robinson alive after the smoke?" A flurry of *No, Sirs* formed a dead end for the Colonel.

Turning to Mulcahy, he said, "I want you to talk some more about this and speak with each man individually to see if we can jar something loose that might help us, but I'll let you do that as you see fit, Sergeant. Let me know if you need anything."

Then, to the group, "Men, once again I am sorry for your loss. If anyone should remember anything that might be helpful in getting an explanation, get with your Platoon Sergeant immediately. I know that each and every one of you did your absolute best out there and would have done everything and anything in his power to save Robinson's life. I am grateful."

Becker thought, "Is he looking at me?"

"In the meantime, you are secured for a few days. You did a great job for us tonight. Don't forget that you took four more bad guys out of the game. You uncovered a terrorist hiding place and we got tons of weapons. It didn't come cheaply. Nothing's worth the loss of a good man. Thank you."

Mulcahy walked to the door first, and spoke over his shoulder, "Back to the barracks. We need to inventory Robinson's stuff." The men filed out behind Mulcahy, anxious to perform the work of charity that this "inventory" actually was.

A man's belongings, both issued and personal, are inventoried as soon as practical after his death, and the

Army insists that this process be diligent and complete, even designing specific forms for the task. The true comrades will get to the soldier's stuff before the guys from the back office come up to do the job. The Army will inventory everything it sees and place it in boxes to be sent to the deceased's next of kin. Pornography, letters from lovers, evidence of drug or alcohol abuse, etc.—anything and everything is boxed and sent, with no discretion or prejudice.

The guy's buddies get to the stuff first to make sure there are no girlfriend's letters mixed in with the wife's, skin mags, ticket stubs to a strip club, or worse. Anything at all that might present the impression that the soldier was not a prayerful warrior of virtuous soul and stout heart is destroyed, forever, on the spot. And no one ever mentions it again, ever. If anything like this is found while they are searching, the discoverer will destroy it then and there—being careful not to even let the others in the room see it. Each hidden fault can be seen by only one person, who takes it to his own grave.

In a world where each man's faults and foibles are laid bare for the edification as well as the entertainment of his fellows, this ritual sanitizing is the soldiers' obligation and privilege. There are no pretensions in the lives of men who live so vulnerably close to each other. That is, there are no pretensions until now, at the moment of death. The inventorying is taken very, very seriously, its secrets scrupulously guarded.

Becker stood on the edge of these men as they sifted through Robinson's belongings, each lost in his private pain. There was no confessing it, but neither could it be doubted. He had let Robinson down. He had been slow, lazy, and selfish. He could have intervened and didn't. Of course he knew he didn't kill him, but neither did he save his life and it had been in his power to do so. He had been weak where so many others had found strength. He had been passive when he needed to lead. He had failed a fellow soldier, and now that soldier was dead.

Robinson was dead to him in a much worse way than he was dead to everyone else. Because, even dead, Robinson was a bigger part of the company and camaraderie of these soldiers than a live Becker would ever be again.

Mulcahy stood at the open wall locker where the things of Robinson's life waited for his return. Becker's section leader, Sergeant Pulowski, took each item out, first selecting the uniforms and equipment that were Army issued. These were placed in a large box by themselves. The Army would check them against the records it kept to see that Robinson returned their property. Anything missing would likely be written off as depleted or lost, but the records needed to account for them in some way. Dead or alive, each soldier owed the Army a final accounting.

When "Ski" finished with the green and tan stuff, he reverently picked up each item of Robinson's more personal property. CDs and DVDs, letters, civilian clothes and personal hygiene items were all inspected and, if they passed the "okay for a mother to see" test, were placed in another box, apart from the Army stuff. There was little in the young soldier's life to indict him, save for a few CDs with language-warning labels on them.

Each item made its way to the box while the barracks filled with the soldiers' covering banter. Some items invoked some memory from the living soldiers and each soldier was eager to share that memory. There was the T-shirt from the Crawfish Shack in Gulfport, Mississippi where Robinson had gone on a two-day pass with Johnson. When he saw the shirt, Johnson shared the story of that holiday, the success they'd had in overeating and overdrinking, their failure at finding romance.

At the sight of a Flogging Mollies CD, Kilmer recalled the affinity that he and Robinson had for Irish punk music and their hatred for gangsta rap. Musical taste was something these two soldiers had shared, along with their lives in the heat and sweat.

A fishing hat, with elaborate lures attached to the crown incited the laughter of the group as they recalled Robinson making it. He hadn't fished a day in his life and he'd had no desire to. He had made the hat in order to impress the fishing fanatic father of a girl who had caught his eye. They all recalled Robinson's telling them about the conversation he'd had with the girl's father, how the father had been onto him from the start. Seems Robinson had been unable to tell freshwater lures from saltwater lures and that he couldn't carry on the simplest conversation about fishing with anyone. The old man, on discovering his deceit, had let him off the hook. Over a beer weeks later, the father had told him that he had been honored to see the soldier go through the trouble of impressing him. He had said that he was glad that his daughter was seeing him. The father had even come with the girl to see the soldier off when he shipped out to Iraq.

"Come back in one piece; we'll go fishing," he had teased. The father had shaken his hand and walked back to the parking lot, leaving his daughter and his newfound friend to share their goodbyes in the manner of the young in love.

Becker felt a sudden stab of pain as a Harley-Davidson belt buckle was produced. He recalled Robinson's briefly flirting with the idea of buying one of the greatly discounted motorcycles that Harley-Davidson had reserved for American troops in combat zones. Robinson had asked Becker to go with him to talk with the Harley sales rep since Becker had mentioned he had once owned a Harley. Robinson didn't buy that day but he was thrilled with the belt buckle the rep had given him. He reprised the Harley dream with Becker often. Becker watched silently as the buckle was tossed into the box.

A contraband bottle of Jack Daniels was making its way through the crowd of broken brothers, the soldiers often commenting on how such strong whiskey made the eyes water. Tongues loosened and hearts opened as the brothers lay to rest the things of their friend. They were together in this task as strongly as they had been in other tasks. They were all living through a common grief and holding each other up in a common pain.

And Becker stood at the edge of this crowd, his memories of Robinson's last minutes conquering all the other memories he had shared with these men. He could find no comfort in their brotherhood, in their tears or laughs. He belonged in that world he had created, where private pain lives alone, denied the benefit of fraternity.

No one heard the barracks door open or the Chaplain enter, so lost were they in their common effort. It was only when they heard him ask for a pull from the bottle that they turned to notice Father Devlin, their spiritual guide, U.S. Army captain and occasional drinking buddy. Today, he was Father Joe, drinking buddy and crutch.

"So sorry to hear about our losing Robinson." He whispered to them, his throat tight and dry from a healthy hit of the Jack Daniels. "How you fellas doin'?"

They stopped picking through the wall locker and turned to Father Devlin. They were all glad to see him and they all knew, even the agnostics among them, that he might be a help to them now.

"It was fu . . . I mean screwed up, Father. Just smoke and sh . . . stuff and uh, then he was dead. I don't know. Shit happens."

"Shit does indeed happen then, doesn't it? I understand that no one was with him when he fell. Is that right?"

"Yes, Sir. I was his battle buddy. We got separated in the smoke. I ran straight into a building and got knocked on my ass. Next thing I knew I was alone in the smoke. I feel like shit, Father."

"You can't blame yourself, Danny." Danny hadn't. Father Devlin looked directly into the young soldier's eyes and said, "I know, and everyone here knows, that you would have done all you could for your battle buddy. You got separated and it was not your fault. In fact, each and every man here would have done all he could to save each other man here. Isn't that right, Sergeant Mulcahy?"

Becker struggled to keep his eyes down and his ears shut. "They'll look to Danny for answers. After all he was his battle buddy. They won't blame me. They can't blame me," he thought. The lonely world he kept returning to was still warmer than the company of these good men—men who still thought of him as a soldier and a brother.

"You bet, Father. I have all good soldiers here, each and every one." Mulcahy tried to make eye contact with each of them as he said this.

Becker thought to himself, "No one suspects."

The priest invited the soldiers to pray. Each of them bowed his head as Father Devlin talked to God for them. As a Roman Catholic priest to a mixed group, he had learned long before to avoid the strict rubrics of Catholic liturgy when he could. Instead, he adopted the familiar conversational tone of the Evangelicals, and this is how he led them in prayer now. He asked God to keep Robinson close to Him, to help his brothers here and his family at home to endure the grief. He asked for peace and he asked that those that remained be spared this fate. Lastly, he thanked God for the camaraderie they shared, leaving each man with the idea that their healing was to be found here, in each other's company.

When he had finished, the men all raised their heads and waited. Father Devlin motioned for the bottle, and when he had it in his hand, he raised it above the center of the group.

"To PFC Robinson, a brave soldier and a good friend. May he rest in peace." To the muffled heaves and stifled sobs of the men, he tilted the bottle to his head and took a perfunctory pull, his own eyes watering at the assault on his senses. He passed the bottle to the man beside him and reminded them all that his door was always open to each of them, but that its invitation was especially offered now. He suggested they write a letter for Robinson's folks. He advised that he would share with them any information he could get about arrangements regarding Robinson's transport home and interment. Then he left them to their task.

No one looked any other man in the eye as each of them recovered his military bearing and waited for the bottle to come his way. But when it reached Becker, he quickly passed it along to the man beside him, somehow repulsed at the thought of sharing a drink from the bottle. Normally not one to turn down a drink, he was afraid of his own emotion, his own loose tongue.

When the packing was done, the boxes were taken to the end of the squad bay to await the office POG who'd be coming by to do the official inventory.

The men drifted away from Robinson's locker. Some left in groups of two or three to find more liquor and to finish the drunk. Others settled into their own bunk areas, talking about Robinson, the day's events, or anything else that might keep them with each other. Three or four formed a group for prayer. Becker drifted to his bunk and locker alone, saying nothing to anyone, avoiding their attention.

The men who had gone in search of more booze would return to their home here soon enough. No one but Becker wanted to be anywhere else but with his team.

Some drank. Some talked. Some prayed. Individually or in groups, they were still doing this together. Robinson's death was the only thing in each of their lives.

Becker opened his locker and pulled his folding chair in front of it. Sitting down, he looked at the things that were his life now and imagined his platoon mates standing in this same spot, inventorying his gear. The thought of his own death did not alarm or frighten him. He wasn't suicidal by any means and he certainly didn't want to die, but he couldn't help wondering about the peace that death brings.

"Rest in peace. Rest in peace, Robinson," he said under his breath. He was talking to Robinson directly now, talking to the other man who had left the platoon that day.

The Shavetail

"Put a little *ass* into that, L-T! Don't tap it, for chrissakes. Kick it!"

Sergeant Ryan turned—to tune in to the excitement. The platoon leader, Lieutenant Mendez, was kicking at something embedded in the ground. He had the complete attention of the soldiers circled around him, their circle rapidly expanding as they backed away from him. The lone voice belonged to Private Dyson.

Damned Dyson.

The Lieutenant stopped in mid-kick to face Dyson. "Private Dyson, my rank is that of a Second Lieutenant in the United States Army. You will address me with the proper respect and courtesy due a commissioned officer. I am a Lieutenant or I am a Sir. Is that clear?"

"Uh, yes *Lieutenant*! Yes, *Sir*!" Dyson answered the Lieutenant's chastisement by snapping to an exaggerated position of attention and rendering an even further exaggerated salute.

"At *ease*, Private Dyson! Stop saluting! Right *now*!" The Lieutenant began advancing on Dyson, stopping only when Dyson stood at ease, this new position as exaggerated as his attention and salute were. He was now slouching and shuffling around.

The Lieutenant understood that he was being mocked but wasn't quite sure how to respond. His confusion showed on his face and he was left standing there with only that confused look to keep him company. The rest of the men followed Dyson as he slithered away. They were sticking with the winner and in the contest of Dyson vs. Mendez, Dyson was the winner, again. He was undefeated in his contest of wills with the Lieutenant.

"You men get back to the trucks! Drink some water!" said Sergeant Ryan as he trotted towards the Lieutenant. He was eager to get between Dyson and Mendez before Dyson drew any more blood. Resolving to torture Dyson at the next opportunity, he turned his attention to his leader, "Lieutenant, did you find something, Sir?"

"Find something? Uh, um, did you see Private Dyson just now? He was *saluting* me! He was saluting me in a *combat* zone!"

"Yes, Sir. I did and I will deal with Dyson later. You can count on that. Now what was it you were kicking at?"

"Oh, yes! Yes! Over there. There's something in the ground over there. It could be a claymore," said Mendez with the breathy intensity of a child who has just discovered where the Christmas presents are hidden and is sharing that precious news with a younger sibling.

A claymore is an anti-personnel mine. It is contained in a hard rubber block, its harmless appearance disguising its vicious mission. Real claymores will kill everyone within a hundred meters. It was named after the Claymore Sword, a medieval weapon wielded by the stronger warriors of the clan. The man would take the weapon in both hands, hold it extended at shoulder height and spin around, wading into the ranks of the enemy. Depending on his strength and endurance, he could cut a wider and wider circle, killing indiscriminately. Claymore mines did this as well, only today's soldier didn't have to work as hard; he just pressed the trigger located at the other end of a long wire attached to the mine.

"Let's take a look, sir"

The middle-aged Sergeant followed the Lieutenant for a few steps till the newfound treasure was in his view. "We better hold on right here, Sir. Let me use the glasses." Sergeant Ryan raised the binoculars strung around his neck and looked to where the Lieutenant was pointing. After taking a few seconds to adjust the focus, he was able to see that the object was actually a track pad from a tank, half buried in the hard-packed sand. This was an easy mistake to make, but he kept his revelation to himself. Tank track pads are hard rubber blocks about the same size and shape as a claymore. "I see it, Sir. Let's go take a look. *Carefully*, Sir."

Ryan walked ahead of the Lieutenant as he retrieved the plastic spoon in his pocket. He was in the habit of carrying a spoon from his MRE rations. There always seemed to be some new use for it. High tech, the U.S. Army's pride and joy, was not always the answer for the soldier in the field. American ingenuity filled in the gaps. The spoon's purpose now would be to function as a training aid in the education of the newest addition to the Officer Corps of the United States Army.

The twenty-two-year-old officer watched his Platoon Sergeant's every move as Ryan slowly bent towards the black rubber pad. Ryan spooned the dirt from around the pad, slowly, gently. His movements were as exaggerated now as Dyson's had been before. He knew the pad was harmless but this exercise was for educating lieutenants, not uncovering mines.

"Sergeant Ryan, would you like to use my knife?"

"Sir, I like to use plastic or wood, whichever is handy. The metal knife can set off the mine if it's magnetic or electronic. These spoons are pretty tough. They'll do the job, Sir." When Ryan was sure the Lieutenant had seen enough of the process to remember it, he announced his discovery.

Relieved, "Looks like a track pad from a tank, Sir." Safe now, he dug aggressively so as to prove his conclusion and in no time the track pad was disinterred for both of them to inspect.

"Well, thank goodness for that, Sergeant," said the Lieutenant, a little disappointed.

"You bet, Sir. I usually try to use the binoculars to take a close look at a suspected IED. I don't like to get close to it unless I absolutely have to, and then I use the spoon. You don't want to yank it loose or hit it in any way."

"I guess we don't want to kick it either then," said Mendez, his eyes finding Ryan's.

"Definitely not, Sir. Kicking would be a bad idea." Ryan made sure Mendez saw his collegial grin.

"Then why would Private Dyson . . . ?"

Abruptly, "I'll deal with Dyson, Sir." It was almost, but not quite, a command.

The two men walked toward their troops in silence,

Ryan's eyes searching for Dyson, the Lieutenant's for the safety of his command truck at the rear of the line. He had seen Sergeant Ryan discipline wayward soldiers before and he was terrified to even be within hearing distance. He was concerned about it. The Sergeant's methods were not in keeping with the modern mainstream philosophy regarding leadership. Ryan was a retread from another era and as such, had maintained some harsh, even brutal methods from a less enlightened era.

Lieutenant Mendez had been gathering some course materials and other information regarding the new management methods that the Army was learning from Corporate America. He intended to begin regular counseling sessions with his Platoon Sergeant about changing his methods. Sergeant Ryan should learn to rely more on motivation exercises, self-esteem building, and positive reinforcement to lead his troops. Studies had shown that these approaches would yield better results than the old tactics of fear and force. Until he could get that going though, he'd resolved to stay out of the Sergeant's way.

Ryan collected his thoughts on the way. Dyson had been encouraging the Lieutenant to kick the pad. If Dyson knew the suspected IED was a harmless track pad, then he was trying to humiliate the Lieutenant for the entertainment of the rest of the troops. If he thought it was a mine, as the Lieutenant did, then he was trying to get him killed. As for his saluting the Lieutenant out in the middle of a hostile fire zone, this was certainly a dangerous act of aggression. Nobody salutes anybody when in the enemy's territory. Snipers lie in wait, trying to identify the leaders. A salute is a clear indicator to an enemy sniper. There were snipers all over Iraq. Dyson was reckless, malicious, or murderous.

New lieutenants like Mendez and shitbird soldiers like Dyson have been having this contest for as long as there have been shitbird soldiers and new lieutenants. Both these soldiers were countrymen of the same age, the Lieutenant just starting out and on his way up, the shitbird stopping in the Army just long enough to do some damage before resuming his decline into a wasted life.

Some shitbirds actually have managed to get lieutenants killed, even taking an active hand. The Viet-Nam experience records countless incidents of second lieutenants being fragged within days of their arrival in country. The newer a lieutenant was, the more vulnerable he was. He was also the most ignorant and therefore the most dangerous officer in the company.

Veteran soldiers, not eager to be used as tools on which new lieutenants practiced their skills, would toss a grenade in the direction of the new platoon leader at the onset of a battle. Fragmentation grenades don't leave prints and in the confusion of battle, it is impossible to identify which grenade or mortar shell or artillery round turned the young man's body into an unidentifiable mess. In the Viet-Nam era, when the draft pulled too many miscreants into its ranks, fragging was all too common.

Dyson was a pure pain in the ass. In the Army more than three years, he had only risen to the rank of PV2. This rank, E2 on the Army's pay scale, was normally achieved in about six months. He should have been a specialist (E4), working his way towards the central leadership position, that of sergeant (E5). If a soldier was promoted to sergeant in three or four years, he was doing very well. If he was a private after even a single year, he had had some trouble. Dyson was still a private after more than three years in the Army and he *was* trouble.

The tragedy was that Dyson was a natural leader and a charismatic comrade. He had the frustrating ability to lead good men in the wrong direction. More than one soldier in Ryan's platoon had gotten into his first bit of trouble in the Army when they had been with Dyson. Most learned from their mistakes, corrected them (with a little help from the Sergeant Ryans of the world) and moved up. Some, too many, joined Dyson in the exciting life of making everyone else's life miserable. He was a leader all right, and since his humiliating of the Lieutenant was done before an audience, he would be corrected before that same audience. It was the Army way.

Ryan set a course for Dyson's truck, watching his troops as they watched him approach. They all turned their eyes away as he arrived, not wanting to make eye contact with a provoked Sergeant Ryan. Ryan's eyes found Dyson's though.

"GET YOUR ASS DOWN HERE, YOU MISERABLE SHIT!"

Dyson struggled to get past the legs, rifles, and tons of gear soldiers have to carry that was now littering the floorbed of the truck. He stumbled twice, each falling accompanied by louder yells from the red-faced sergeant.

"GET DOWN HERE! GET DOWN HERE! GODDAMNIT! GET THE FUCK *DOWN* HERE!

Ryan barely let Dyson's feet find the ground before he

ordered him to start doing pushups. "START PUSH-ING, PUKE!"

As soon as Dyson started doing pushups, Ryan was lying on the ground in front of him, so that the two could maintain eye contact. "Push, you bastard! Push this miserable country *down*, and *down*, and *down*, until you move it to below sea level! You're gonna keep pushing till I see the ocean coming across that desert! Push!"

Ryan regained his feet, standing over the soldier, waiting for him to get muscle exhaustion. He found his moment somewhere around thirty-five pushups. It was there that Dyson started to tremble, stopping in between each pushup.

Ryan squatted down beside the struggling soldier and began his period of instruction. Calmly now, "Who told you to stop pushing?"

"Uh . . . no . . . ugh . . . one . . . uh."

"Well, keep pushing. You seem to be having trouble. You know, I'm old enough to be your father and *I* do more pushups than that. Hey! You know what? I bet the Lieutenant can do more than both of us! Huh? What do you think? Think the Lieutenant can do lots of pushups?"

Dyson was on his belly now, unable to push up a single time, yet without the order to cease doing pushups. "Uh . . . dunno . . . aaarrgghh."

"Well, I guess that's not important. KEEP PUSH-ING! I don't even want to deal with you but I can't get rid of you. We've taken all your rank, all your privileges, and most of your money, but still you live. You are a vampire. I cannot seem to kill you. The only option I have left is to court-martial you. And by the way, I have no doubt that

that little bullshit with the little Lieutenant is worthy of
a court-martial. KEEP PUSHING! KEEP PUSHING,
YOU LITTLE SHIT!"

"Gasp . . . uh . . . oh . . . Saaar."

"Where was I? Oh, yeah, your court-martial. Yeah,
we gotta forget about that. You might get off, and in the
time it would take for your court date to come, you would
be in some safe cool jail in Kuwait. You might like that.
Nope. No sir. I'm gonna keep you right here with *me*.

"Christ, you're miserable. Get on your feet."

Dyson struggled to stand up, his arms now useless
to even help him do that. Gasping for air, he squatted in
front of Ryan and glared.

"You . . . GASP . . . um . . . GASP . . . uh . . . ."

"Shut up, Dyson. Listen to me. You fuck with the
Lieutenant one more time and I will kill you right here
and leave you under this desert. He's got a lot to learn,
but at least he knows how to learn. You, on the other
hand, are a terminal idiot and will never learn. You think
the Lieutenant is some sort of joke, do you? Well, he's a
better man than you are. He has brains. He has balls.
You have neither. Know what else he's got, Dyson?"

By now, Dyson had recovered both his wind and his
sneer. "No. What?"

"He's got honor, Dipshit—something you know
nothing about. The Lieutenant has character. You got
shit. He's teachable and you are not. Ignorance can be
fixed, but moron? Well, moron lasts forever. Get on the
truck, Dyson."

Ryan waited for Dyson to regain his seat on the truck,
a tougher task now that his arms were useless. When

Dyson finally found his seat, Ryan fired his best shot, the one he'd been saving so that he could be sure the whole platoon heard it. "Oh yeah, Dyson, there is one more thing the Lieutenant has that you don't. Know what that is? I *said* do you know what the Lieutenant has that *you* don't have?"

"No, Sergeant."

"*Me*, Dyson. He's got *me!*"

Looking away from Dyson and toward the whole group, "You guys make sure you're drinking plenty of water and make sure Dyson gets some too. Look how hard he's sweating. Looks like the heat's really giving him an asskicking."

"You gotta get in better shape, Dyson."

He walked up the line to his truck at the lead and found his second-in-command waiting there. Jones was a decent soldier and a brand-new sergeant. "Hey, Sergeant Jones, I want to ride back with the Lieutenant. I think you can handle the lead. Can you?"

Eager to begin his first opportunity solo, "Yeah, sure! You left the maps and stuff in the cab?"

"I left them right on the seat. Pick one of the specialists to ride shotgun with you. I'll give you a radio check when I'm set, then we'll move out. Okay?"

"Roger that, Sergeant, and thanks for the shot."

"No problem. And you'll do fine."

Sergeant Ryan had been out of the Army for almost twenty years, after spending four years in the infantry immediately after graduating from high school in 1984. He first became a sergeant then and was always proud of this accomplishment, though he'd had little time to enjoy it. He was promoted about three months before his enlistment expired, and when it did, he couldn't leave the Army fast enough. It wasn't that he didn't like the Army. He did, but he'd had enough by then and it had been time to move on.

He traded Army life for married life. He married the girl who had waited for him and they bought a house together. He started working in a factory in Hillsboro, Illinois that made glass bottles. He used his GI-Bill benefits to study business administration in the evenings. When he finally achieved his bachelor's degree in 1996, he was pleased to see his two sons and one daughter sitting with his wife at his commencement. Between his getting a good education and his outstanding production on the factory floor, he was promoted to the administrative offices after about two years, and by 2001, he had become the Assistant Controller for the entire organization. He was living the American dream and he was smart enough to know it and be grateful for it.

When the World Trade Center was attacked on September 11, he was at his desk at the plant when his wife called him. She was crying hysterically, telling him to find a TV and see the tragedy. When he got to the factory's only TV, the one in the company cafeteria, he found a crowd there already. Many were crying; most were silent. By 11:00 AM, all work had ceased and anyone who hadn't left for home was in the cafeteria in front of the TV. He found long-lost tears while in the car on the ride home, and wiped his eyes on the sleeve of his suit jacket. Negotiating the route home caused him to realize that he did not know how to drive while crying. He had never faced that challenge before. He should have pulled over, but he wanted only to get home to his wife and children.

He tried to re-enlist the next morning, but the Army told him that at thirty-nine he was already too old. Try the Guard, they said, and when he got to the National Guard recruiter, he found that office hectic. They were getting up to speed on age waivers, hearing waivers, vision waivers, weight waivers and any other waiver that might be required to enlist the scores of former active-duty, now middle-aged men who provided continual traffic through their doors. Sergeant Ryan enlisted in the Illinois Army National Guard, the "Lincoln Division," and was told he was to drill one weekend a month and two weeks per year and that he could expect to be mobilized and deployed in the near future. Most of the Guard would be deployed at some time or another in the next few years. Well, that would be fine with him. Deployment or not, the events of September 11 simply demanded that he do something—anything. It was that damned "Honor, Duty, Country" thing. For guys like him, Duty wasn't a choice. Duty meant you had no choice.

On his way back to the last vehicle, he saw Lieutenant Mendez before the L-T saw *him*. He was sitting in the passenger seat, reviewing the maps and the operation order for the day's mission. He was deep in thought, writing notes in the margins and on the blank backs of the pages. Ryan needed to interrupt him. Mendez needed to get his head out of his papers and into the world, this world.

He decided he'd make the conversation about his

changing seats a very short one. With the L-T, this was done by simply speaking first, speaking aggressively and allowing no gaps for questions or comments. He'd made the decision and that was that. He opened the door and jumped into the driver's seat.

"Hey, Lieutenant! I decided to give Jones a shot at the lead. I'm going to stay back here with you. We'll both move up if he needs us. Ready to go?"

"Well, yes, Sergeant. That'll be fine."

"No shit, it'll be fine," Ryan thought.

Ryan contacted Jones on the radio, and after a short discussion about the route and the condition of the troops and trucks, told him to move out. "I want fifty meters between each truck. I am back here if you need me. If anyone falls out, I'll let you know right away and we'll decide what to do then. Let's do it. Out."

The lightly armored Humvees started simultaneously, on Jones's radio command. Convoys start their engines this way so that an enemy who might be listening won't be able to count the engines. All that can be heard is one big roar—could be three trucks or thirty. One by one, the trucks started off, allowing fifty meters between them. It was three minutes until the second-to-last truck started moving forward and Jones waited till it was fifty meters ahead, then he pressed the gas pedal and took off. Pressing the button on the radio handset, "I'm away, Jones. By the way, we did three minutes. Looks like we're learning how to do this."

"Did Private Dyson get a medevac or is he still with us?" The L-T had put his Op Order away and was giving Ryan his best command face.

"He'll live, sir. We shared our differing views on a few

things and I think I was able to have him see a thing or two our way."

"*Our* way? Or *your* way?"

"Our way. You and I are on the same page. One thing, Sir. Calling a Lieutenant an L-T doesn't sit very well with me either, but the fact is, that it has become part of the Army culture. Everybody does it and I don't think we can change it. They don't mean any disrespect. We have bigger problems to deal with anyway. Let's save that one for another day."

"Well, I still don't like it."

"Well, neither do I, L-T." He made sure the Lieutenant saw he was smiling.

"Fine, Sarge . . . S-G." They laughed together.

"Good. Laughing's good," thought Ryan.

Sergeant Ryan was busy for the first half hour of the convoy. As the long line of Army vehicles, painted desert tan or olive green, made their way home, he took advantage of each small curve in the road to view the vehicles ahead. He checked to see that they were maintaining proper intervals, that each turret gunner was seated low enough to have the protection of the vehicle's armor, yet high enough to see his surroundings. He made sure the windows were closed, that all exposed soldiers were wearing their Kevlar helmets and body armor. He looked for vehicle problems like unusual exhaust or flattening tires.

He looked and looked and checked and checked. He radioed each vehicle commander to make corrections, always letting him know that it was his, the vehicle commander's job to see these problems before he, the platoon sergeant did. Looking, checking, communication, it was a constant cycle of leading and caring. He was training. He was leading. He was worried sick.

The Lieutenant was in awe of Ryan's sheer comprehensive competence. He had a hundred things in his brain that were labeled *top priority*, and seemed to take care of them all. He was tough on the men and often too tough, the Lieutenant thought. He knew them all, really *knew* them. He knew their family situations, what they did for a living in civilian life, their individual idiosyncrasies. He knew who were the drinkers, the womanizers, the Bible thumpers, the intellectuals, and the poor in spirit. He knew who the degenerates were and who were here in search of martial glory. This last category comprised the most dangerous.

In the citizen Army that is the National Guard, the diversity is staggering and the Guard sergeant has a much more complicated job than the active-duty U.S. Army sergeant. These guys are *complicated*. They are not fooled, will not accept poor leadership, won't do pointless tasks, and they challenge authority easily. They have Palm Pilots that contain, among other things, the phone numbers of lawyers and newspapers. They are difficult to manage and high-maintenance. All of this requires that their leaders be the very best and give them the very best. Those leaders that are not up to speed are disobeyed, or simply ignored.

"Lieutenant, we're gonna speed it up on the way back. I think, if we haul ass, we can make evening chow."

The Lieutenant, studying his wristwatch, frowned.

"Chow hall closes at twenty-hundred. We can make

it, but we won't be able to put up the guns and ammo. We'll keep them in our cans overnight, load them back up tomorrow and we'll be set for tomorrow's mission." The soldiers lived in "cans," metal boxes adapted from over-the-road trailers. They were heated, ventilated, air-conditioned and, when reinforced with a few sandbags, damned good protection from mortars, grenades, and bullets.

"Sergeant, you know we can't do that! Battalion is adamant. We are not to keep weapons and ammunition in our quarters, at *any* time, for *any* reason."

"Battalion doesn't run this platoon. I do. I mean, *we* do."

"Yeah, and *we're* supposed to run the platoon the way the Colonel says *we* run the platoon." The Lieutenant was angry, turning his reddening face towards Ryan as he spoke. This delighted the Sergeant. One thing he wanted to see in his Platoon Leader was some guts. Without guts, a little anger and volume, he would become moot. He thought a little human emotion from this guy wouldn't hurt either.

"Act normal, for chrissakes!" Ryan thought to himself.

"Yeah, well the Colonel can come out and run the platoon *his* way if he doesn't like the way we run it. The men have been out for two days and they are heading out again tomorrow at 0400 for another two. That will mean four-plus days without a decent meal or a cool drink. With all due respect, Sir, not if I can help it."

"I know, Sergeant. You think I don't care? I do, but regulations are regulations."

"And men are men, and these are *our* men. What

good are regulations if they don't take the men into account? No, Sir. These men need a good meal, a shower, and a full night in a real bed. If we turn in the weapons, by the time those assholes from Battalion get the armory opened, check the guns in, count the rounds, process the paperwork, it'll be 2300. You can bet your ass on that. Then, we'll have to be back to them at 0300 to check all the same stuff out again. At best, they get four hours sleep and no food. No way, Sir. No way!"

"Sergeant, what'll I tell the Colonel if he finds out?"

"Tell him you took care of your men, Sir."

"Yes, but just the same . . . ."

Ryan cut the L-T short by picking up the radio handset and showing it to him. "I'd like to let the men know we're going to try to make chow. With your permission, Sir." He waited.

"Fuck it, go ahead. I'll just toss these gold bars away now. Seems like I'm not using them anyway. Yeah, go ahead and send them to chow." He slumped and stared out the window.

Ryan picked up the mike. "Hell, sir. You just *did* use them. Thanks." He keyed the mike.

"Listen up, warriors! I don't want to see any NAS-CAR tryouts here, but if we make some speed, we can get to chow before it closes. I'm worried about the engines in this heat, but the Lieutenant insisted, so that's the way it's gonna be. Put the weapons and ammo in your cans overnight. Team leaders take charge of that. Over."

They arrived at their camp in time to get the last of the hot food. They were grateful to get a hot meal on a plate and it showed in their energy and laughter. Ryan went with them, eating last as always. The Lieutenant disappeared during the initial confusion and reappeared about the time Ryan was sitting down. Only then did Mendez go to the food line to try his luck.

In the American Army, when there is any chance that food might be scarce, the lowest ranking man eats first. The officers wait till all the men are fed before even making an appearance. Tonight, as is the case so often, the young soldiers got full meals and the Lieutenant made do with much less. The great officers truly don't care, as long as the men are fed. Mendez wolfed down his three PB&Js while he watched his tired soldiers destroy daunting piles of burgers, fries, and cobbler with ice cream, and he thought that his meal was the best he'd ever had.

The next morning, the Lieutenant was in front of Sergeant Ryan's can at 0300. He wanted to make sure that Ryan was taking care of everything for the day's mission. When he arrived, Ryan let him in and it was apparent that he had been up for some time. He had the maps in front of him and had acquired the latest intelligence reports. He had gotten his junior sergeants up and assured Mendez that they were tasked with getting the guns, ammo, and other equipment on the trucks thirty minutes before the start time. The Platoon Leader couldn't come up with a thing that Ryan hadn't already thought of.

At 0350, Ryan was in his vehicle at the front of the line. He keyed the radio, "Truck commanders, are we ready? Let me hear you. Over." At this, the radios came to life.

"Scout one is up. Out."

"Scout two is up. Out."

And so it went, trucks reporting they were ready, one at time, in order. The one exception was Scout six, Sergeant Derrick's vehicle. He was concerned about a transmission leak he had been developing.

"Scout six still has that leak in the tranny. I don't think it's any worse than it was yesterday, so I think we're in good shape. I stocked extra fluid and tow ropes just in case. Over."

"Good work, Sergeant. Way to stay on top of it. No bullshit now. Are you up for today's mission? Your call. Over."

"My call? I'm in. Over."

"Okay. Keep an eye on it, and if you change your mind, let me know. Out."

"Sergeant, you *can't* be thinking of letting that vehicle out on this mission?" The Lieutenant had been walking from his vehicle at the end of the line to Ryan's vehicle during the radio exchange.

"I have to, Sir."

"Why do you *have* to, Sergeant?"

"Because I delegated the authority to the truck commanders. They know what I expect, and I have to let them do the job. Part of the job is making those kinds of decisions. For the record, I think Derrick made the right one. The leak is slow enough that he can stay ahead of it by adding some fluid now and then. We need his truck and we need his guns and we need his soldiers."

"That may be, Sergeant. But Battalion regulations are quite clear on this. No vehicle with a leak of that type may leave the pool. He needs to be deadlined."

"Oh no, not that again," thought Ryan.

"Yes, Sir. And if we followed that directive, half our vehicles would be deadlined for one reason or another. Tell the Colonel that if he is so concerned about our having safe vehicles, he ought to stop writing directives and order some damned parts."

"Damn it, it's too late to argue. Let's get moving."

At that, Ryan took the hand mike and had his trucks started and on the road by 0404. They followed the route he had outlined and given to the truck commanders. They moved across the desert in a single file, with the full moon their only light. It was enough. They arrived at their first checkpoint and scattered into hiding places in the rocks and hills. They were turning their engines off just as the sun came up. This was the plan: they were to be in place, overlooking the intersection of two highways before sunrise. They had made it. This intersection was the scene of repeated vehicle bombings and they had decided to put an end to it. They watched and waited.

By noon, it was apparent that today was not going to be the day to catch these particular Ali Babbas—the nickname the troops had given the insurgents. They came out of their hides and met by the roadside to eat and get new instructions for the afternoon's portion of the mission. They sat or lay about, scattered on the ground. Some napped. Some smoked. They all drank water.

"Sergeant Ryan, why aren't the men wearing their body armor?"

"Sir, they're only off for a few minutes while they eat and take a break."

"They have to have their armor on *at all times* while on patrol! You know this!"

"Yessir, and I also know that we'll be putting these guys on choppers and sending them to the hospital if we don't give them a chance to rest. Look at them. They are all drenched. It's over 120 degrees and there's still plenty of day, and sun, left. They won't make it if you don't relax the rule a bit."

"What about snipers then? Did you think about that?"

"Yup. See that bluff over my shoulder? I don't want to point. Do you see it?"

"The one with the rock pile on the top?"

"That's it, Sir. We got two guardian angels up there now, with sniper rifles of their own. They have binoculars, thermal scopes, and infrared goggles. They can see every living thing within a thousand meters. I put Kilian and Scotsman up there before we broke hiding."

Ryan ended the conversation by yelling to the soldiers around the area. "Okay, guys. That's it! Suit up! Mount up! It's back into the shit in five minutes. *Do it!*"

Then to the Lieutenant, matter-of-factly, "The guys who made the rule about having all that body armor on at all times haven't worn it for five minutes, not in this heat anyway."

They grunted, groaned, whined, and bitched, but they all moved as one. Wet armor went back on top of soaked shirts. Weapons were retrieved, inspected, and shouldered. Kevlars found their places on the correct heads. The men moved towards their vehicles and in no time, the line of trucks was again on its way. They covered thirty-five kilometers that afternoon, patrolling along known insurgent routes, hoping to find them before they themselves were found. That was what this was, a game won by the side that sees the other first. It was inefficient, dangerous as hell, and nerve-wracking. But no one had come up with a better way to find them.

Evening found the platoon at a safe house. These buildings dotted the landscape of Iraq and were used by the Americans as way stations. They were manned by American soldiers around the clock. They were constantly covered by air surveillance and were used mostly to grab a few hours of sleep. Nobody ever stayed longer than that. The Lieutenant and the Platoon Sergeant waited outside for all the men to be under cover before they spread the maps on the hood of the truck and planned the next step. Both exhausted, they agreed to be on the road at 0200, six hours later.

They walked into the house together to find that an impromptu congregation had formed. One soldier was standing before the group, Bible in hand, preparing to read to his fellows. The two leaders stopped still, one out of respect, the other knew better. Ryan tensed to see what would follow.

The soldier began, "'Whoa ho *ho*,' sayeth the Lord! 'Woe to the evildoers who now inhabit the land I gave to Adam.'" The Lieutenant's mouth dropped and Ryan bit his tongue to stop from laughing.

"I warneth thee! Just as I smited Adam when he fucked up, so shall I smite *you*!" The soldiers roared with glee.

"And since drowning your dumb asses did not drive you to repent, I now sendeth the world police to do my smiting. Prepare ye, ye evildoers, to feel the vengeance of Team America!"

"I will place the mark of *W* on your heads so that you and yours will never forget the days of shock and awe!"

"Sergeant! Outside please."

Ryan stopped laughing soon enough and was on the Lieutenant's heels, both of them through the door and in the yard instantly.

"Sergeant, I will not have this sort of blasphemy! There are some things that are just not done. If the Colonel ever saw this, he'd be furious!"

"Yes, Sir. I will put a stop to it immediately." Ryan decided he'd have to let the Lieutenant win one occasionally and, he admitted to himself, he was not comfortable that this would be the time or place for taking God's sense of humor for granted.

He stepped back inside and ordered his men to eat and sleep—the stated purpose for their being where they were. "And that'll be enough preaching. I don't want to see that again. We're here to rest. You still got energy? Then we can head out *now*."

He and the Lieutenant took turns sleeping. The Lieutenant slept for the first three hours and Ryan woke him at 11:00 for his turn. "Sir, please make sure I'm up by 0130 so that we can take off by 0200."

"Sure, Sergeant."

The Lieutenant was troubled, his doubts about himself jaded all his thoughts. He paced the house, inside and out, listening to the snoring, teeth-grinding, and restless grunting of his men. He thought they looked like a den of canines, sleeping soundly in the middle of danger, the company of each other providing the security necessary. They slept deeply when in the same room.

He thought that it must always have been this way with soldiers. In so many ways, their fellowship becomes their greatest weapon, their most secure armor, and the thing they owe their allegiance to. He thought that he could never be part of the pack, not this pack. All he could do was to lead them and care for them, and he couldn't even do this were it not for Sergeant Ryan.

He woke Ryan at 3:30, careful to keep a safe distance from the violence that often accompanies the wakening of a soldier in a combat zone. In an instant, Ryan took it all in: the Lieutenant, the safe house, himself, the war. Glancing at his watch, "What time is it?"—forgetting the "Sir."

"It's 3:30, Sergeant and before you fly off the handle, let me inform you that I have reviewed our plan for the day and determined that we can get the mission accomplished and still get the extra two hours sleep. We'll just have to make some adjustments is all."

"Why the extra two hours?"

"The men needed it. *You* needed it."

"And the adjustments we're going to make?"

"We'll skip two of the most distant checkpoints on the long-range portion of the patrol."

"What'll the Colonel say?"

"I'll just tell them it couldn't be done, not without an unacceptable amount of wear on the men. They are my men, I will tell the Colonel, and I need to take care of them *first.*"

"He'll piss a bitch, Sir."

"Let him. Now, turn to, Sergeant. I have a platoon that needs readying for the field."

"Yes, Lieutenant. You can count on me." Ryan headed straight for the sleeping soldiers.

I'm *a* Soldier, *Too*

"Wow, that's a beautiful drawing! You're really good!"

The young artist, sitting in the sand, legs crossed underneath her, continued shading the slope on the face of the mountain range that was taking shape on the sketchpad in her lap. She ignored the voice but it didn't go away. She turned her head just long enough to get a glance at the soldier who'd demanded her attention, then returned her attention to her work.

"Are you a draftsman?"

"No."

"Maybe an art student?"

"Definitely not," this time with a chuckle.

"Do you know what you're looking at?"

With as much charm as he'd managed to gather in his twenty-one years, the soldier took a step closer, and lowered his athletic frame to a squatting position so that he could look directly into her eyes, their faces on the same level. Maintaining his eye contact and with the most sincerity he could fake, he cooed, "You. I am looking at you."

Deliberately, she set the pad down on the ground beside her, first clipping her pencil to the pad's edge. Raising her body up by pushing against the ground with her hands, she turned herself to face him directly. Leaning

~ 97 ~

closer and waiting for his cheeks to flush, she responded with the command voice that the Army had trained into her. "So what you really want is to hook up, right?"

"Huh? Well, uh . . . I mean," the soldier stammered as he fell backwards.

"You're just hitting on me, Soldier," she said. "You haven't the faintest idea what I'm doing, do you?"

"Look," he said, "I'm just trying to be friendly. Why the attitude?"

"I'm working. This is work. Good-bye."

Having secured the attention of the remainder of the soldier's squad, the eleven men inside the nearby tent who'd been watching the entire episode, she continued to talk to him, even as he walked away. "You don't give a shit about what you call my 'drawing.' You don't even know what you're looking at, right?"

"What do you want to be such a bitch for? I was just trying to be nice."

"Yeah, I know. We females need you males to be nice to us 'cause we're just girls and you are the big, strong, *real* soldiers. Thank God you're here to protect us." Satisfied, she returned to her work.

He returned to the relative safety of his squad and managed to project the required air of indifference and muse the usual musings about the girl being a "dyke" or a "bitch" or just plain crazy.

The artist returned to her drawing. The Neanderthal had gotten under her skin. She was madder at herself than she was at him. She took pride in her ability to keep these cads out of her head as well as her bed. Ordinarily, she'd dismiss these guys with less vitriol, but this last one wore an arrogant look on his face as well as a wedding ring on his finger. Constantly having to fend off the sophomoric advances of married men was tiresome enough, but to be dealing with this crap while she was trying to work on something so critical was infuriating. While it was the conventional wisdom that most girls joined the Army in order to get guys, she, like so many others, had other motivations.

The reality was that the Army *was* loaded with girls who wanted to get guys. The Army was a place where the homeliest girl in high school, the girl who'd never had a date, could be surrounded by dozens of attentive men. The attention multiplied when a unit was deployed, when the male/female ratio soared into the stratosphere, when there were no other alternatives for female company. "Deployment Queens," they were laughingly called by the men who used them. There were many, many whores in the Army, and for each one of these there could be found a dozen girls who were just promiscuous. The women who were professionals and patriots could easily get lost in the dysfunction.

She was angrier at her sisters than she was at this latest soldier. He, after all, was just being a guy. His expectation of who she was and what he might expect from her came from the experience of the many girls he'd known who were her peers. Men should behave better and it was women's job to see that they do. What the hell is a decent girl supposed to do when every woman around her is acting like a rutting bitch? Don't these bitches know that they are making the lives of *all* the women in the Army pure hell? "The girls are filthy and the men are morons," she thought.

She shaded the depressions of the mountain range that was taking form on her lap. She knew her drawing was hardly beautiful, but it wasn't meant to be. It was functional, useful, and valuable, worth much more to a soldier in the field than mere beauty. An intelligence specialist, she had been given the assignment of sketching landscapes for the soldiers' use. This would be a large part of her duties when she deployed to Iraq with this combat team, and she was constantly striving to improve her product before then.

She worked in the "S-2 shop." This is where a select staff of officers, along with some exceptionally able enlisted soldiers, gathered information and tried to make some sense of it, so that the combat soldiers could use it. The sources of this information were numerous. Certain soldiers, like cavalry scouts and artillery forward observers, have the formal job requirement of gathering information for the spooks at S-2. These soldiers travel well ahead of the main body of troops in order to identify the best routes for the rest of the force to take. They carefully search so that they can identify obstacles and dangers as well as target opportunities and resources. Since they are trained to observe, record, and report these things, their information is meant to be useful and comprehensible. Beautiful is never the objective.

There were some other sources of information that were equally as valuable but much more difficult to process. The dozens of informal sources included other types of soldiers, enemy prisoners, local tribesmen, and businessmen. All information gathered from these is suspect as to its reliability and accuracy and this has to be taken into account as it is processed. All information goes into a data base of sorts called the ISR matrix or Intelligence Security Requirements Matrix. Each bit of information is graded as to its usefulness as well as to its reliability and is then placed into the matrix. There, it is studied and cross-checked and the intelligence product that results will be produced for the use of the line officers.

The format of the product takes many forms, one of which is the drawing or rendering, like the one she was now creating. Such renderings are of use in open areas where there are no street signs or highway markings. The drawing will simply function as one aid for the soldier who uses it to make sure he is in the place where he is supposed to be. Having a picture of the battlefield beforehand is also a big help for the line soldiers while they are in their planning stages. So, if the information is scarce or difficult to understand, she would fit it to a picture if she could. She often acted as a fortune teller, filling in the unknown areas with the details thought "most likely."

If the men in the field were doing their job well, she'd be able to draw tomorrow's vista with some accuracy. Esthetic beauty was of no consequence, with accuracy and usefulness being the currency of her trade. "Wow, that's a beautiful drawing!" she murmured to herself, sarcastically mimicking the vanquished soldier's lame line. She still managed to take great enjoyment in the irony of her role being so critical in keeping dumb-asses like him alive and in one piece.

Since arriving at the Army's National Training Center in the Mohave Desert, she and her colleagues at S-2 were sketching landscapes, as well as constructing the 3-D equivalent, the sand table, all day, every day. Her commanding officer, a major in the Army National Guard, was a police detective in his civilian career. As such, he brought a wealth of skill to the shop. Like so many Guardsmen, he was able to bring his civilian experiences to the Army, arguably making him that much more qualified than his regular Army counterparts whose entire frame of reference was likely to be Army training. He treated her well, though with more practiced courtesy and distance than he afforded her male counterparts. He continually pressed her to improve her skills and pursue excellence.

"A little better intelligence product means a little less American blood gets left in Iraq. We are never good enough until all the bleeding stops," he regularly chanted, often in response to the gripes and grumbles from his troops about their living conditions or work hours. "The line soldiers have it far worse than we do. Hell, you got it easy! If you think working here is so tough, I can find you a seat in a Humvee if you like."

She looked up to the Major and was grateful for his leadership, but even *he* couldn't completely exorcise his own testosterone-fed demons. Men are, after all, men. While she couldn't even imagine him making an unsavory suggestion or fumbling a stupid pass like the young soldier, it could not be fairly said that he treated her like the other soldiers either. He treated her like a girl. Sure, he respected her work ethic, product, and professionalism, but she was still a girl and this attitude was evident in every single interaction between them.

He spoke the same words to her that he used with the men but she always got a gentler tone, even an occasional smile, not unlike that of the Don Juan of the sands she had so handily dispatched earlier. It was always such a disappointment to catch the Major looking at her in *that* way, rare as it was. In this world so sorely short of gentlemen, she suffered to have her hero tarnish himself by being a guy.

When they first arrived at the training center, a week earlier, they were setting up their new work spaces when she caught him leering at her. She had been standing on a chair, putting a box of printer ribbons on a high shelf when she sensed the look. The Major was across the room, on his knees putting folders in the lowest drawer of a filing cabinet. While his hands were efficiently moving the files from the cardboard box to the file drawer, his eyes were fixed squarely on her bare thighs and they had "the look."

In an effort to adapt to the intense heat of the desert, the Major had authorized his staff to wear their Army-issued PT gear, rather than the heavier work uniforms, while they were doing the heavy work of moving in and setting up. The PT uniform is black baggy shorts and a gray cotton T-shirt, with white socks and running shoes. She had remembered to wear a sports bra as well, even though she would have been more comfortable without it, but she cursed herself for having omitted her black bicycle shorts. Most female soldiers wore these biking shorts under their Army-issued shorts while they were exercising alongside the men or using one of the many coed gyms found on Army bases. They provided a measure of extra protection for modesty, as rigorous physical activity tended to cause material to flow, bounce, and shift aside, resulting in embarrassing unwanted exposures. Of course, the men knew this and it seemed as though they never, ever stopped looking for it.

She had not considered that moving into the offices would require the same degree of care because it would only be her and her office mates, her buddies. Now here was the Major, with that same stupid stare. So focused was he on her shorts that she could observe him observing her without his detecting that he was caught.

She finished stocking the ribbons and descended the ladder, breaking the Major's trance as she did so. She thought to herself that for her, a woman in uniform, just wearing PT gear could be a major event. Men would never have to think something like this through. They'd never have to calculate the effect of each clothing choice, word spoken, expression presented, or posture assumed. For the woman in desert camouflage, absolutely *everything* had the potential of inciting lust, disrespect, or that stupid "look."

She carefully put the finishing touches on her sketch. Procedures required that she record the compass direction, the scale, the topographies, legends, and symbols that are the mapmaker's language. She titled the sketch, relating it to its map location, and penned her name and the date on the bottom. She rose and dusted herself off, anxious to deliver the sketch to the Major.

She had gotten better at her craft under his guidance. She was satisfied now that he'd be pleased with this product, all of the key features identified and clearly visible, properly located and proportioned. The drawing was decidedly not beautiful, she thought. It was however, useful, valuable, and professional—like her.

Returning to the S-2 shop, she found the Major reviewing the other soldiers' drawings. He looked up at her and smiled when she entered the tent, eagerly accepting the sketch she offered him.

"Good work as usual, Specialist. In fact, this is excellent work. I see that you've drawn the wadis and flood ruts the way we discussed. Good. Good work."

"Thank you, Sir. I appreciate your instructions on that. I can see how it helps." She was careful to avoid any familiarity with her facial expression or body language. She waited.

"There's a supply truck heading for Fort Irwin at 1800 tonight. I want you and your tentmate on it. You'll get a chance to clean up, but make sure you're on that truck when it returns at 2100."

"Roger that, Sir," she said as she turned and headed for the door. Grateful as she was for the chance to shower and wash the desert grit from her scalp, this once-each-72-hours ritual was a cause of tension. Army regulations required that all female soldiers were to be afforded an opportunity to shower at least once every three days. The men might go weeks without seeing a shower if there were none available, but the women would be shuttled to the rear every third day for their showers.

A man, on the other hand, would live in the field with the dirt for as long as the mission required that he do so. Soldiers brushed their teeth often enough, most having experienced the long-term problems caused by skipping it. Each man had to shave daily, a smooth face being necessary for the gas mask to seal properly. He cut his hair very short, or simply shaved his head before a long field exercise, denying the crust and critters a home. He took enough socks with him so that he could change these each day. He wore one uniform per week, and changed his T-shirt every other day. As for his skivvies, or at least for those soldiers that wore them, they were discarded when they became intolerably dirty. No washing machine on the market could completely clean a pair of shorts, once they were made filthy, inside and out, by the lifestyle of a field soldier. It was common practice to buy the cheapest underwear available, wear them once for a few days, and throw them out.

This was the field soldier's lot until God created baby wipes. These commercially available, disposable wash cloths, designed and marketed for cleaning a baby during a diaper change, have seen duty as a soldier's "bath in a box" since their invention. Each day, a soldier uses one on each of his feet, finishing them off with medicated foot powder before putting on his clean socks. He uses another baby wipe on each armpit and applies deodorant afterwards. He uses one on his junk and another on the area for which it was designed. That is the extent of his daily personal hygiene regimen.

If women were present in the field, he had to add the inconvenience of performing this tedious ritual "out of sight." If it was a male-only environment, he could do this almost anywhere, stripping naked wherever he might be. In the coed environment, he headed for the tree line, or in the case of the desert, he walked into the darkness till there was enough night to cover him. The morning sun would reveal a ring of baby wipes around the camp, about a hundred yards away from the perimeter.

She returned to the tent to gather her roommate and her things and together they left for the motor pool to meet their ride. She and her roommate shared a tent designed for twelve men, they being the only females in the battalion. Women were quartered apart from the men and if only two were present, they were assigned their own tent—the smallest being a twelve-man tent. The tent was erected well apart from the male soldiers' tents. It stood conspicuously alone across the camp from the thirty-six male tents, which were grouped together and bursting at their seams with an oversupply of soldiers.

The two women met their truck and driver, the driver waiting for them at the truck's tailgate. He stood by and enjoyed himself while he watched them struggle up the gate into the bed of the truck. The five-foot climb was difficult for anyone and was best negotiated with a leg-up from another soldier or two. The portly sergeant stood motionless as the two women partnered each other aboard. He made sure they caught his smirk as he lifted the tailgate behind them and secured it with a bolt on each side.

"There're two Kevlars for you. Make sure they're on your head. The last thing I need is for you to split your skulls open and for me to get charged with damaging such precious cargo." The Army's new helmets are named for the material from which they are manufactured. Kevlar is lightweight, bulletproof, and stronger than steel. They are molded into the soldiers' helmets which are the required headwear for all passengers in all Army field vehicles at all times.

"You're a real prince, Sergeant. I can see you've attended to all our comforts. Thanks for making us feel so at home."

Challenged now, he had to remember to maintain his smirk. "Hey, mind if I ask you a personal question?" Not waiting for an answer, he pursued, "What's a yeast infection, anyway?"

"You got a wife? Maybe a girlfriend?"

"Yeah, I got both," he smugly lied.

"How lucky for them both! It would probably be better then, if you asked one of them about yeast infections."

Ignoring her response, he continued, "It's just that I was asking the Captain why it was that females got to shower every seventy-two hours and that real soldiers don't get to. He says it's 'cause you get yeast infections if you don't. You don't have a yeast infection, do you?"

"Sergeant, first of all I *am* a real soldier. Secondly, I am not discussing yeast infections or anything else with you. You'd better stick to your truck. That's about the right speed for you."

Both women laughed and the Sergeant, angry at his wounding, charged, "Well, is it any different than jungle rot, athlete's foot, jock itch, crotch rot, or diaper rash, 'cause we get them all the time."

"I'll bet you do!" she squealed, both women laughing again.

"Bitches! Fuckin' bitches!" he growled as he retreated, stomping towards the driver's cabin. Not having learned his lesson, he yelled over his shoulder into the troop compartment as he was cranking the engine, "Field soldiers got to live with the mud and the blood. You women get special treatment."

"Sergeant, when was the last time *you* lived in the field?"

Motor transport sergeants lived pretty soft lives themselves. They transported troops and supplies to and from the field. They usually managed to schedule their trips so that the last trip of the day ended in the rear where they availed themselves of the showers and bunks of the comparatively civilized garrison area. They lived in the rear, with the beer and the gear. Before women became a part of this society, truck drivers, cooks, and office workers were the targets of the sarcastic comments of the field soldiers. The soldiers call them POGs—it rhymes with *rogues*, not *dogs*, and stands for "person other than grunt." And they are resented for the comparative safety and comfort of their lives. But in today's Army, where women get the softest treatment, POGs pretending to a life of rigor did not go over well with the soldiers—male or female. A POG is still a POG, whether the Army has women in its ranks or not.

The truck started moving, its gears grinding and its metal groaning as it made its way through the trails to the paved road. Swaying and bouncing, and with both hands gripping the bench on which she was trying to sit, she leaned forward to speak with her roommate. Anxious to change the mood and the subject, she said, "I can't wait to get this crud out of my hair."

"Roger that! Let's get done quickly though so we can make a PX run while we're here. I'm out of cigarettes and I have to stock up on Snickers and Skittles, too."

"You go ahead. I'll meet you back here."

"Are you kidding? You're not going to go to the PX?"

"This trip is for personal hygiene purposes. Let's not take advantage."

"Screw that! This place sucks and I'm taking any bennies I can get when I can get 'em. I don't see how picking up some candy and cigarettes can be hurting anybody."

Purposely meeting her eyes, "The guys don't get to—that's all."

Annoyed and indicted, she said, "Well, if you want to be Ms. High-Speed Soldier, go right ahead and wait while I go to the PX. What did 'the guys' ever do for you anyway?"

"I'll be here." There was no sense in trying to get the younger soldier to see it her way; they'd had this conversation before. She harbored hope that the chasm between the men and the women could be and would be shrunk. She knew she couldn't outshoot the men, or outrun them, or outfight them. And for that matter, she probably was less suited to the rigors of the field than the average man was. But what of it? She could outthink, outwork and outproduce most of the men, in her own skill. In this manner then, she would make her contribution to the cause that they all had embraced. What she did, and did well, would ultimately save many of their lives and help them all achieve victory. What she contributed was not as easily replaced as the efforts of just another foot soldier would be.

And she took a back seat to no one in her dedication to the Army values. The seven character traits that the Army had adopted as its values were taught to all soldiers and the principles of loyalty, duty, respect, selfless service, honor, integrity, and personal courage were reinforced in each of them, every day. They were posted somewhere in every building in the Army and each soldier wore a tag, with the dog tags, on which they were inscribed. And as for her, she thrilled to the sound of them. For her, they never got stale. She loved the Army values and she loved the Army, too. After all, where else in the "me, me, me" world that was her America could she find a life centered on such high ideals? The PX issue was simply another "integrity check" in the life of a soldier who strived to live up to these ideals.

Arriving at the female latrine, she was pleased to find an empty shower stall in the otherwise crowded facility. She hung the clean uniform she brought with her on the hook across from her stall. Placing her gym bag on the bench, she retrieved her soap, shampoo, towel, and shower shoes from it. She undressed quickly, dumping her filthy uniform, socks and underwear in a heap on the floor, and kicked the resulting pile against the wall, out of the way. She wrapped her towel around her body and stepped into her shower shoes, quickly darting for the privacy of the stall. She closed the plastic curtain and pulled her towel off, hanging it over the shower rod behind her.

Then, she was under the shower, luxuriating in the warm, steaming spray. She stood motionless in its therapy for a few minutes before finally grabbing her shampoo and going to work on the mess. Like most of the females, she combed her hair straight, then knotted it in a tight bun at the base of her scalp. This seemed to be the best way to get the hair out of the way but it made the wearing of certain headgear uncomfortable. The Kevlar would rest on the bun, pulling the hair too tight or tearing at the bun. Helmets were not designed to accommodate a bun.

Cleaning her hair took a full ten minutes—untangling the knots, scraping the grit from her scalp, and getting a comb completely through each section. Looking down as she worked, she could see the dirt from her body running down her legs and across the concrete floor to the drain. The dirty water washed past the bugs and chunks of hair that were once hers and were now imprisoned on the screen.

After thoroughly scrubbing the rest of her body, she perfunctorily shaved her armpits and legs. She dried off in the stall, re-wrapped herself with the towel and left the precious privacy of the shower to join the company of the others in the shower room.

The high energy conversation among the six women present was about their upcoming leave. After the

California portion of the train-up to deployment to Iraq, in about two weeks, they'd return to their mobilization site at Camp Shelby, Mississippi for another few days, then it would be a glorious ten days at home. Friends and family and food and fun awaited the hard-worked soldiers, an uneasy respite before spending a year in combat.

Like all soldiers in all wars, they talked about mom's cooking and great places to hang out at home. They talked about parents and children, siblings and friends, husbands and lovers. She had a boyfriend at home herself. She had enlisted alone two years before, her boyfriend from high school having rejected her entreaties to join along with her, under the Army's "Buddy Plan."

On the night before she was to leave for boot camp, they had made a commitment to be faithful to each other. They would wait for her hitch to be over. In the meantime, he was to get established in some way and then make a life for them. As for his getting established, she didn't care how and he didn't know how.

"Why not go to college?" she challenged.

"Nah, I just finished with school. No more of that crap for me. I'm not a book smart person; I am good with my hands though."

"Well, how about trade school?"

"No money."

"Why not get a full-time job so that you can have the money to go to the trade school part time?"

"Yeah, maybe I'll do that," he said, without a trace of conviction. Both knew there had been nothing resolved. She suffered that he had no ambition, no sense of the future. He had no goals or dreams. He got easily bored when she talked about hers or tried to encourage him to find some.

In the two years since, they both told each other that they were still an "us." But for her, he and her whole life at home were becoming a shrinking dot in the rearview mirror of her life. She was learning and growing, developing skills as well as developing herself. She was serious about the business of living her life and he had not even considered the questions she was working so hard to answer.

On the night when they had made their commitment, she knew she was talking to a boy who was far less mature than she was. She knew that the commitment wouldn't last. Her time in the Army had only exaggerated the situation and made their differences more obvious. In his rare letters to her, he told of his escapades with his buddies and with the friends they had had in common. Drinking, music, road trips, and fun had formed a full-time lifestyle for those she had left behind.

Her boyfriend had become less attractive to her as she moved forward. He had the looks, the laughter, and the energy that he had always had, but now she knew this would never be enough. There could be so much more to a man. The men who were her comrades now were an entirely different breed. The same age as her boyfriend, the soldiers had met challenges, becoming resourceful and competent. These men had purpose and confidence and strength, real strength behind the phony machismo. As she mulled over the upcoming reunion at home, she sullenly accepted that on this leave, like the last one, she'd spend much of her time with her boyfriend, silently missing the company of the male soldiers with whom she served. She would be bored.

She was saddened to know that real love was not possible when one person viewed the other as being inadequate, when respect was too hard to hold. Still alone in her thoughts, she grinned at the irony. She'd finally found a world where she could respect the men, where real men could be found, and in this place, she'd never have *their* respect.

She had come to respect her brother soldiers as the epitome of manhood, but had never known anyone who could be so frustrating and as vexing as the average soldier could be. They infuriated her daily with their testosterone-addled, genital-centric, chauvinistic insensitivity. She loved them though, every thick-skulled one of them.

It had grown dark while she was showering, and night covered her as she left the rowdy noise of the female's latrine. Across the way stood the empty and silent men's latrine and she found herself fighting the urge to check it out, while no one was around. Externally, the male and female latrines were identical, but the interiors were said to be different.

Losing the fight with her curiosity, she entered the building and flicked on the light switch. The first obvious difference was the absence of walls and private places. There was one long urinal along a wall, a trough twelve feet long and a foot deep, with a slow and steady stream of water running along it, keeping it clean. The toilet room was purely functional, with toilets lined along each wall, no stalls or walls or curtains. Two rows of identical toilets, in silent, sterile, soldierly rows. No pretensions or secrets in this culture. It was impossible for a soldier to take himself too seriously in this world.

Similarly, the showers had no stalls or curtains. Instead the shower was a single room with a dozen shower heads on each wall. Like the toilets, the showers were identical and contained nothing between them but air.

Relieved to find the truck empty, she climbed aboard to enjoy the time with the brilliant stars and cooling breeze that was the desert night. The clean air moving against her clean body was delightful and the dust she would accumulate on the ride back would ruin this. This time to enjoy her cleanliness, as yet unspoiled, was to be a short-lived luxury.

Back at the camp, she first made her way through the sand to the tent that served as the S-2 shop. She was required to sign back in at the log book on the Major's desk. On entering the tent, she greeted the specialist who was on duty there. Someone is always on duty in the tent, the safeguarding of its contents being critical. His rifle across his lap and handgun strapped to his right thigh, he sat at the Major's desk with orders to use any amount of deadly force that he thought necessary to protect the information and equipment contained in the shop. This, of course, was unlikely here in the Mojave but would be a serious issue in Iraq. In the Army, soldiers "train as they fight" and an armed guard is part of the fighting for which they were training.

He had been looking at the sketches on the Major's desk, trying to learn what he could about his own craft. He was a Specialist like she was, and he too was tasked with the processing of raw data into products that were useful to the war fighters.

On top of the stack was her drawing and this is what he was admiring when she entered. Not expecting her, he started at her passing through the tent flap. She saw him and greeted him as she approached the desk. Scanning for the log, she found it and pulled it towards the desk's edge.

As she bent forward to sign, he could smell the soap and shampoo and he could see the clean white part in the center of her auburn hair. He thought again, that she was wonderful, carefully keeping his eyes on her hair so as to avoid looking down the front of her blouse. His peripheral vision had caught her blouse front falling forward as she leaned to sign the log. He wanted to make sure he didn't embarrass her by seeing what was not his to see. He knew how much of a lady she was and how she would be embarrassed by any breech of her modesty. Besides, her scent and her presence were pleasure enough for him. To be near her was to be happy.

He struggled for something to say that would keep her there, if only for a few minutes longer. She had, as she often had, an affect on his body. His heart sped up; his breathing got short and shallow. His chest tightened and his cheeks reddened. He saw the hair on his own forearms stand on end, the visible part of the goose bumps that covered his body.

She was wonderful. She was capable and mature, nothing like the girls he had known in high school and who were becoming rapidly fading memories of his own life. He thought she was truly beautiful, though he seemed to be the only soldier who thought so. His friends couldn't see what he could see, he thought. For him, she was simply lovely.

He had been longing to spend some time with her but she was so difficult to talk to; she was all business when dealing with him. Working near her was a pure joy, though he suffered for the longing. He became a stammering idiot as well as remarkably accident prone each and every time he sought to engage her. His soldierly armor was unequal to the task of protecting him from her power.

He looked at the desktop and saw his opportunity. Her landscape was right there and, after all, it was good, really good. When she finished signing, she lifted her head to look at him before straightening her body. In that quick instant, as he looked into her eyes, this close for the first time, he thought that he might actually be in love with her. Ridiculous, he knew, but the heart wants what the heart wants. Her eyes betrayed nothing but a hint of heaven as he looked deeply into them.

Now! He had to think of something to say now, before she was gone, leaving him alone with his dreams of her. "Say something, you idiot!" his brain screamed.

His hand quivered only slightly as he managed to lift it and point it in the general direction of her rendering.

"Um . . . you know . . . this is a beautiful drawing. You're really good."

The Grappling Hook

The soldiers were anxious. The day of their first mission had arrived. This first mission had taken on the air of some sort of gala event. The soldiers had trained for months, and then spent two weeks in Kuwait drawing equipment and getting used to the hellish heat. Then, after a four-hundred-mile convoy trip to this air base in the desert on the western frontier of Iraq, they spent a month manning towers and gates. This initial duty was meant to "acculturize" the soldier, getting him used to the reality of his new place in this old world. In the towers and on the gates he would get a sense of the layout of the base, gain a flavor for how things ran, and get used to the climate that no human being could possibly get used to.

Working the towers and gates was supposed to settle the soldiers down some. In the month-long period of routine work, NCOs could identify those that were too shaky for the tougher missions to come. Soldiers who were likely to become undependable identified themselves by missing the guard truck or sleeping on duty. NCOs could then determine if these weak links were salvageable by training or discipline, or if they were best re-assigned to some less critical duty within the perimeter of the base.

During the time between tours, the soldiers would

be in classes. They had gotten firsthand information as to what to expect on the roads when they finally got assigned to patrolling and escorting convoys. The instructors were NCOs with recent experience on those same roads. The classes would be informal and lively, the soldiers' eager anticipation coupling with the instructors' natural tendencies to exaggerate their own war experiences. The training gave the soldiers a sense of what they could expect and a confidence in their own preparation and knowledge.

This morning, they had met at the scout shed. The scout shed was a garage the Iraqis had used as a maintenance facility. The thick concrete walls provided some relief from the sun and the interior of the cool room was stocked with the scouts' equipment. The walls were adorned with tactical maps and charts of IEDs, local custom and language posters, Army regulations and base procedures. A workbench ran the length of the back wall and was heavy enough to accommodate the radios, water jugs, binoculars, night sights, and other tools of the scout trade. Under the bench, food and water were stored. Water came in boxes of six bottles, each containing a liter and a half. Food was MREs, boxes of twelve meals each. There was always plenty of food and water. Man-high pallets of both were always found wherever the soldiers were housed or working.

The front corner of the shack, just inside the door, was equipped with a cage made of scrap-metal grating, welded together into a medieval-looking box and bolted to the wall. The machine guns and ammo were stored in there and the platoon sergeant had the only key. A sign-out log was affixed by a chain and contained the history of these men in this place. Each time a soldier checked out a gun or returned it, he made an entry in the log. So surreal, this soldier's world—fill out the paperwork to check out a machine gun, go kill the enemy with it, clean it and properly fill out the paperwork when it's returned, being sure to properly stow it away for the next soldier. The accountability and order of the civilized world was juxtaposed to this barbaric business in this primitive world. Dot the i's and cross the t's.

The opposite corner had a makeshift podium and desk. There was a coffee maker on the desk and, depending on what was going on at the moment, a clipboard or two with the necessary information for the upcoming missions or training evolutions. Sometimes there'd be a dismantled IED that had been found before it had a chance to detonate. At other times, there'd be some piece of equipment or some literature that had been confiscated from a local suspect. These were often useful in reminding the soldiers how little equipment his enemy needed to kill him. The discarded pager turned into a detonation device or the washing machine dial turned into a timer were silent reminders of the havoc they could have caused. The soldiers came from a throwaway world and were now living in a hostile land where just about anything could be used as a weapon. It doesn't take long for American-soldier savvy to kick in, and all the classroom time in the world couldn't impress him any more than the dismantled bomb itself could, sitting inert on the table, constructed in significant places with the trash of American soldiers.

The wall behind the desk contained the largest map in the room. It was the official Department of Defense tactical map for the area extending from Syria's eastern border on its left to the center of Baghdad on the right margin. Running horizontally through the center of the map were highlighted the roads the scouts would be patrolling. Their area of operation centered on a long stretch of desert leading from the eastern perimeter of Al Asad, the airbase where they were sitting, and running east. The most conspicuous features were the two main highways that would be their constant concern.

There are a dozen or so gates on the perimeter of Al Asad, but only one leads out to a paved road. The rest open to desert roads. The easternmost gate that opens to the paved road has the most sophisticated security. It's named *Flea*, and a soldier doesn't have to ask why it's named that after he's been there an hour. The ground is thick with tiny carnivores who quickly find the rare opening in a soldier's uniform. It's no mystery why new guys are called *fresh meat*.

The road through the gate at Flea extends about three miles out to a dangerous intersection with MSR (Main Supply Route) Bronze. Most convoys make the right onto Bronze and cover the desolate and shell-pocked thirty kilometers to MSR Uranium. They'll make another right turn and be on a *real* highway. Uranium is a hundred and fifty kilometers to Baghdad, but the traveler will first pass through Ramadi, Fallujah, and Abu Graibe. Uranium is more interesting if you are in Iraq to see the sights, but it's the thirty-kilometer stretch on Bronze that's of the most interest to the soldier. The insurgents on Bronze are as numerous at the insects at Flea and just as invisible. They could have named it *MSR Adrenaline*.

This day, the soldiers would be clearing MSR Bronze. Clearing a road before a convoy is a natural task for a scout. A scout section heads out about an hour ahead of the convoy. It proceeds slowly along the road, looking for IEDs and scanning the horizon for ambushes. Presumably, the soldiers will find the IEDs and dismantle them before they can do any damage, and they'll kill any enemy combatants who might be waiting in ambush. The idea is to make the road safe for the convoy, a long line of trucks carrying building supplies, food, and water, or just about anything that might be needed to rebuild and restock the devastated country.

When the scouts arrived at the shed, they immediately set about preparing for the mission. The first task was to find the four Humvees that the scout section would need. The drivers walked or hitched a ride to the maintenance shed, signed out the vehicles, and drove them to the fuel depot. They got the tanks filled, signing the requisite forms and logs that no one would ever read.

The drivers then headed to the scout shack, parked the vehicles and topped off all the other fluids. Any discrepancies were noted on a vehicle's log book and inside the shed in the Platoon Sergeant's log. It is a rare thing indeed to find a Humvee that has no discrepancies. In fact, it is an oddity to find one that is combat worthy, at least according to the Army's explicit standards as to what constitutes combat worthiness. At the scout shack, there's certainly concern about combat worthiness—but there are different standards.

The Army insists that each seat have a working seat belt and that each vehicle have a serviceable fire extinguisher. At the small-unit level, in a unit like the scout section, concern for these minutiae disappears immediately, but concentration on the real elements of combat worthiness increases. First the driver, then the vehicle commander, then finally the Platoon Sergeant—checks each vehicle to ensure that the engine runs well, it has four sound tires, and the turret will turn when the gunner needs it to.

While this was going on, the gunners secured their machine guns in the turrets. The care for the operation of the gun is even more important than for that of the vehicle. The gunner carefully inspects each part and runs the gun through its functions. He slides the bolt back and forth to see that it locks and unlocks when it is supposed to. He opens and reopens the cover to see that it is functioning properly. He removes the barrel and carefully inspects it, along with the spare barrel he carries, to see that both are clean and ready. He checks his sights to see that they move easily, and looks at a dozen other small places where only an experienced gunner knows to look.

This morning, following SOP, each gunner also loaded the frequencies into the radios and checked to see that he had contact with all the critical communication stations. He conducted radio checks with Battalion Headquarters, Artillery Command, and the guys in the air. He double-checked his frequency with the Medevac folks, and—most important of all—he checked to see that he had contact with each of the other three vehicles and the Platoon Sergeant.

By mid-afternoon, the scouts were all assembled at the shed. They sat in the relative coolness of the darkened concrete structure and passed the time. They ate constantly, either from the official Army food in the MRE packs, or from the boxes of care packages sent from family and friends and hoarded there. The younger soldiers could eat the candy, cookies, and beef jerky without consequence. The older men avoided the junk food; even here, the middle-aged were calorie counters.

Political correctness has found its way all the way to Southwest Asia as well. Half the soldiers smoke, and they are required to go outside to do it. There's no smoking in the scout shack. After all, we wouldn't want to expose our soldiers to any dangerous second-hand smoke—that juxtaposition again.

A first lieutenant from the Intelligence Section arrived, armed with the latest information about MSR Bronze. There had been other patrols and convoy activity and a lot of the information came from the pilots who patrol the skies above the road—and the desert for miles on either side of it. Marine pilots in Cobra helicopters and Army pilots in Apache choppers are the main air support in Iraq's western desert. They are dependable and professional men piloting attack helicopters with awesomely destructive capabilities. The information-gathering capabilities of these men and machines are less awesome, though. They do what they can, but the insurgents have learned to make themselves part of the desert when they hear the gunships coming.

Lieutenant Payton didn't have to ask the men for their attention when, after some quick greetings, he headed toward the map. He turned to the map and, because he was blocking the soldiers' view of it, he moved as close to the left edge as possible and extended his arm to the map. He ran his finger along the familiar red line that showed MSR Bronze.

"Your mission today is the one we've been talking about. You'll be clearing Bronze. The convoy will be leaving from Flea at 1700, and you'll leave precisely at 1600. All of your support elements—air, artillery, medevac—have coordinated their operations to the time of your leaving."

The Lieutenant looked to the Platoon Sergeant, Sergeant Seidel, in anticipation of the question the Sergeant was expected to ask.

"Can we expect any enemy contact, Sir?"

"*Always* expect enemy contact, every minute of every mission. On this particular mission, be looking for two- or three-man teams in the desert. The pilots have seen people on the road. This road is supposed to be off limits to all civilians and there's nothing for miles around on either side of this route, so there's no good reason for anybody to be walking on that road. If you come across anyone, anyone at all, treat them as hostiles until you are convinced they are not."

"Can't we just shoot them?" asked a PFC who could always be counted on to say something stupid. Everyone knew this wasn't funny, but most laughed anyway—a good way to project "cool" or "cold" and cover up being scared.

Making the mistake of treating the question as legitimate, the Lieutenant had begun to explain why the preemptive shooting of civilians is not allowed when the Platoon Sergeant rescued him.

"For PFC Johnson's benefit, we will review the Rules of Engagement once more before we leave. Any more questions for the Lieutenant?" Sergeant Seidel's glare made it clear that he did not expect, and would not appreciate, any more stupid questions. To the Lieutenant, "Thank you for coming, Sir. We can handle it from here."

With more ceremony than was necessary, the Lieutenant turned on his heels and marched out. The room was now back in the Platoon Sergeant's hands.

"Crew Chiefs, make sure you double-check everything once more and make sure you and your crews are ready to move in fifteen minutes." Without waiting for any more instructions, all the soldiers got off the floor and headed out to the Humvees. There was very little checking and double-checking at this point as each man had treated his raw nerves by scrupulously checking out his equipment a number of times already. They moved to their positions, anxious to get started. Gunners climbed over the hoods of their Humvees and dropped down into their hatches. Drivers got in and started the vehicles while vehicle commanders got in on the passenger side and immediately brought the radios online.

The vehicles were pulled out from their parking spaces and lined up on the pavement in front of the shack. All four Humvees took their assigned positions in the order in which they would patrol, the Platoon Sergeant's vehicle first, the following vehicles placed in respect of their experience and ability. As per this platoon sergeant, the talent was up front with weaker leaders to the rear. Sergeant Seidel was the last to leave the shack and the last to mount up. A few minutes after he disappeared inside the passenger seat of the lead vehicle, he could be heard on the radio. "Proceed to the Flea gate. Stay online. Maintain fifty-meter intervals. Move out."

The two sentries manning the gate moved it out of the way. The gate was a large iron pipe rigged across two roadside pylons and weighted down. The weights had to be removed and the pipe moved out of the way before the road was clear. This took the full effort of both sentries because of its size and weight, but no one was misled to believe that this jury-rigged security post could hold up against a car bomber in a truck or even a small car. That's why the sandbagged machine gun stations, on either side of the gate, were always manned and ready.

The fort on the left had two men, each armed with the light B240 Belgian-made .30-caliber gun. This dependable and efficient weapon is a low-maintenance producer that is exponentially better than the cumbersome, finicky M-60 machine gun it replaced. The M-60, or pig as it was affectionately nicknamed, was heavy, difficult to assemble and disassemble, and usually worn out, most of them remaining in the American arsenal left over from Viet-Nam service. Worse still, the M-60 was entirely undependable. It jammed continually. Soldiers had a nickname for the 240 Bravo as well. They called it the *wetback*. It would always work no matter how badly you treated it.

On the right side was a .50-caliber gun. It was as old as the 240 was young. Having joined the Army in between the two World Wars, it is the oldest weapon in the arsenal of the U.S. military. The younger soldiers like it because it is big and loud, but the older guys will reach for the light machine gun when given a choice. The .50-cal is four feet long and weighs about seventy pounds, even before you add the ammunition. It needs solid support to be fired, whether that is a gun mount or a tripod. It can rip through buildings and vehicles and is extremely dependable. It is a perfect gun to place on a road to deny access.

The trucks proceeded down the road to the Flea/Bronze intersection, about a mile out. This four-way intersection, within binocular sight of the back gate and the guard towers, was a common site for IED placements. They could only be placed there by one man, or a two-man team, who crawled out to the roadside in the middle of the night. Any more men or anything more conspicuous, like a vehicle, and the operation would have been observed from the towers and gate. And the insurgents would have been killed, probably by an attack helicopter. One way or another, helicopter or not, they would have been killed.

At the intersection, the trucks raced through, each of the four trucks taking security positions on their pre-assigned "bases." The troopers name road directions after the bases on a baseball diamond. It is efficient and understandable and even fun, but best of all, the enemy doesn't understand the system if he's listening on the radio. At a four-way intersection, the truck that makes a left is "covering third." The next truck moves straight through and covers the opposite side of the intersection. He's "safe at second." The truck making the right is "on first" and the last truck stays at home.

All the gunners knew to face their muzzles outward and had them moved into position, facing down their respective roads, even before the drivers had the trucks settled into place. When the trucks had the hasty 360-degree security ring set around the intersection, all the soldiers who were not either drivers or gunners left their vehicles and began to walk along the sides of the road. They had been trained to look for IEDs on the shoulders of the road. The nervous soldiers recalled every bit of their training as they stared at small piles of gravel, looked behind every rock, and carefully checked each bag of garbage in this land where the language has no words for *litter* or *recycle*.

Iraq is a big landfill, with garbage everywhere you look. And for these soldiers, each of these discarded bags, boxes, or cans could hide a bomb that might kill them. They all had to be checked out. The task is tedious and nerve-wracking. The benefit of doing this scrupulously the first time out is that the men will get to know every inch of this road, so that when they head out the next day, they will more easily know when something is out of place, when something just doesn't belong there.

Later on in the tour, instinct would replace rote training, and these roadside stops would take less time and cause less stress. But for this first mission, it was all new and terrifying.

The road surface at the intersection had been blown up so many times that there were huge chunks of pavement missing. All the road shoulders had been destroyed as well. At intersections like this, insurgents have the advantage. It is easier to bury a bomb in the sand and gravel of a pothole than it is to place it under a road surface that is intact. Army and Marine engineers, as well as civilian workers, are regularly sent out to fill in the potholes. Then the soldiers or marines have to stay for a day or so until the concrete sets, otherwise Hajji will put an IED into the soft surface.

After about twenty minutes, the consensus developed that they'd done the best that could be done and Sergeant Seidel waved them all back to their trucks. The four trucks headed to the right, each one assuming its previous place in line. But there was no real sense of relief when they got through all this with no crashing explosion. There were countless more intersections, potholes, and wadis still to come. The convoy that would come by after them had to get through without an explosion. That is the mission. That is the scouts' job. The convoy would have between forty and eighty full-size tractor-trailers, each one fully loaded with goods of all kinds and manned by civilians—both those who are unusually brave and those who are too poor to pass up the lucrative job of being a convoy driver.

The line of Humvees headed down MSR Bronze. It traveled about fifteen miles an hour at its fastest, but often at little more than walking speed. The gunners, and especially the gunner in the first truck, scanned the roadside and road surfaces intently, staring at anything that had any possibility at all of being the home of a killer IED. The constantly changing speed made the maintaining of the prescribed fifty-meter intervals impossible, so the familiar voice on the radio, Sergeant Seidel's, advised the drivers to open the interval to a hundred meters.

The lead vehicle came to a complete stop whenever there was a pothole or other break in the road surface itself, the gunner leaning out of the turret and peering down past the front hood at the gravel and sand hole in the spot where blacktop used to be. When he was satisfied that the pothole didn't contain a threat, he slapped his hand down on the windshield and yelled for the driver to continue on. The waving, slapping, and yelling are still forms of communication that prove to be the most effective sometimes, even in the world of million-dollar communications systems.

About three miles down the road from the intersection, they came upon a portion of the road surface that was severely broken up. Well past the pothole category, this section of the road had been completely broken up for about thirty feet, shoulder to shoulder. The lead vehicle was ordered to leave the road surface, travel well wide of the broken road and return to the road one hundred meters down the road on the opposite side. The second and third vehicles headed out on either side for about a hundred yards and took up defensive positions facing out. The last vehicle moved up to a position about a hundred yards away from the hole. The scouts had posted the four vehicles in a defensive position in the shape of a baseball diamond again, but this time it was *off* the road.

A man from each of the two vehicles still on the road

surface exited his vehicle and headed toward the hole. The soldier from the vehicle at 12:00 o'clock (second base), SPC Mignutt, stopped suddenly. Frozen, he was staring at the edge of the broken road and as suddenly as he had stopped before, he burst into frenetic action.

"IED! IED! Get back!" Though he could be heard and seen by everyone, his attention was on his counterpart coming towards the hole from the opposite end. He was making the agreed upon hand signal for an IED sighting, chopping at the front of his helmet with his hand fully extended as in a salute.

"Get the fuck back! IED! IED!" he screamed at the top of his lungs, his right arm chopping at his helmeted forehead repeatedly. He didn't make a move to get out of the way himself until he was certain that the other soldier understood him. He was satisfied when the other soldier, PFC Roberts, froze, and without sticking around to confirm Mignutt's diagnosis, turned on his heels and ran back to his vehicle—chopping at his own head and screaming "IED" all the way. Between the two of them, Mignutt and Roberts managed to alert everyone to the danger. Soldiers were jumping back into Humvees and hatches and doors were slamming behind them, as the group tried to gather their wits and figure out how to do the next right thing.

The chaos and confusion began to subside as Sergeant Seidel's voice came over the radio.

"What'd you see?" he asked over the open net. He skipped the formalities of radio protocol and dropped the soldierspeak. He didn't even identify himself or the man to whom the question was directed. No need to.

Mignutt answered with the same lack of formality and procedure.

"A piece of metal sticking out of the ground, with wires running from it."

"Just one piece of metal?"

"Yes, it was about three inches long and an inch wide, sticking up at an angle."

"The wires. Did you see them connected? What color were they?"

"Two black wires but definitely connected at the bottom of the piece of metal, right where it goes down into the dirt."

"What about the other end of the wires?"

"They lead right back into the ground about a foot away from the piece of metal."

"Wait one. Everybody stay where you are and keep your eyes open—360 security."

Sergeant Seidel reached inside his body armor and retrieved the IED smart card from the chest pocket on his shirt. He studied it for a minute while he fingered the trigger on the radio handset. There is an exact procedure to be followed when calling in a potential IED. It contains nine lines of information about the IED suspect and they must be delivered over the radio in that order. There are nine bits of information required. Not eight, not ten, but nine.

"Raven, Raven, this is Dagger Two," he began.

"Dagger, this is Raven. Go," came the reply.

Sergeant Seidel delivered the required nine lines of information. He told the guys at headquarters where the bomb was, what it looked like and that the mission was stopped until the situation could be cleared. He was confident he'd made his case and waited for the confirmation that a bomb squad was on its way or that he should blow it in place by using a machine gun and then continue the mission.

But not so fast.

"What kind of explosive do the wires connect to?" crackled the voice over the radio—the voice coming from the safe bunker in the rear, a bunker with an air conditioner and coffee maker. Sergeant Seidel didn't move but for his head which turned to look out the window. His intention was to hide any hint of disgust or distrust on his face from the troops. He was dealing with the famous Major Weathers—the Officer of the Day, a copier salesman turned Battalion Operations Officer—an incredible pain in the ass.

He was a thoughtful, thoughtful man. Major Weathers thought so much that his war, the war in which he was supposed to be leading operations, was entirely in his head. He'd been a thorn in the side of the troops from day one and was the quintessential commanding officer of all things petty, small, and insignificant. And he stood between these twelve soldiers and the bomb squad. There are commanders who place themselves between their soldiers and a bomb, and then there are those who place themselves between their soldiers and the bomb squad. Major Weathers was one of the latter.

"Major Weathers," the measured voice came from Sergeant Seidel as he raised the hand mike to his mouth. He changed his tone just as he keyed the mike to tell the Major, once again, the obvious. "The explosive device is not visible. The wires lead into the ground. Only the trigger is visible."

"How do you know it's a trigger if you can't see any explosive?" The Major's voice was that of a curious student inquiring about an experiment; it had an air of innocence even. Sergeant Groff, Seidel's driver, was also one of his best friends. Groff and Seidel broke up laughing as they exchanged looks of incredulity.

Seidel was still laughing as he keyed the mike to respond. "I can't really think of any other reason there'd be a trigger right there."

"How do you even know it's a trigger?"

"It looks like a trigger. It looks a lot like a trigger. In fact, I can't imagine what else it might possibly be. No, Sir. It's a trigger."

The Major heard the sarcasm and decided to counter the soldier's lack of appreciation for the Major's amazing powers of intellect by walking them through the steps—by the numbers. "Tell me what it looks like. Tell me *exactly* what you see." And so it began. The state trooper turned platoon sergeant described the metal tab sticking out of the sand and gravel. He told the Major it was at a 45-degree angle, that it was shiny and new metal, that the wires attached to it led directly into the ground.

Weathers asked about the surface of the ground. "Does it look like it's recently excavated? Can you see shovel marks?"

"Okay now, this is getting strange," said Seidel to Groff. Then to the Major, into the keyed mike, "I can't see any marks on the ground. We are too far away for that sort of detail."

"Did you use your binoculars?"

"That's affirmative." Then under his breath to Groff, "Well, no shit, Moron."

"Wait one."

Sergeant Seidel switched the frequency so that only his soldiers on this patrol can hear him and he advised them that the Major was thinking things over and they ought to be getting the bomb guys any minute. But in his gut, Seidel knew this wasn't going to be that easy. After a few minutes of silence the radio came alive and Major Weathers was in command.

"Dagger, this is Raven. We are going to need visual confirmation."

"What the fuck does *that* mean?" Seidel thought.

"Say again."

"We are going to need visual confirmation. Someone needs to get closer and see for sure that this is not just some debris or other nonlethal object. How copy?"

"Loud and clear . . . but . . . aren't the bomb guys the ones who would be best at confirming this?"

"We don't want to bother them with a false alarm. Let's make sure we have a bomb before we call the bomb guys," said the Major, as though he were talking to a small child.

Seidel knew that to debate the Major at this point would only make things worse. From the first time that Sergeant Seidel tangled with the Major, back at the train-up in Mississippi, he had marked their association with one inane conversation after another. Direct confrontation was never the best way to deal with this particular major. Logic, linear thinking, and common sense weren't particularly effective tools either. This guy was all Army when he put down his copier catalogs and donned his utilities. Never mind that Seidel had been on active duty deployment in combat zones three times. Forget that Seidel was an experienced state trooper when not in the Army. None of that mattered to Weathers. *He* was a major; Seidel was a sergeant and needed to be shown his place. Seidel had learned to humor him and ignore him when he could, but in this situation, Seidel knew that none of the tricks he had learned would help him.

Looking at Groff, "Any ideas?"

Groff, who had considerably less at stake, could nonetheless be counted on to have the Platoon Sergeant's—his friend's—interest at heart, not to mention the rest of the team.

"Shoot the Major." He grinned.

"Any *good* ideas?"

"We sit here and lie. We make up a story about how we walked right up to the IED and checked it out. We just picked it and poked it and turned it over. When we found the label that clearly said, *Hey, this is a bomb,* we felt confident we had some sort of explosive device."

"And while we are calling in this story, we are just sitting here?"

"Roger that."

Sergeant Seidel considered all of this. He was concerned about lying in front of his men. He was not concerned about getting caught at it and losing his job. This concern had nothing to do with his affection for the work so much as he knew these soldiers needed protection from the Major Weatherses of the world and he wanted to be there to do that protecting for the rest of the tour.

He decided he couldn't risk it, and with only a glance at Groff, who knew that Seidel would not take his advice anyway, he keyed the mike on the internal frequency.

"BDOC wants visual confirmation. We need someone to get a closer look at the IED."

Seidel didn't need to use the radios to hear the collective groan and the shrieks of disbelief. The entire platoon reacted at once and the din poured through the windows and open turrets. They were going to have to leave their vehicles and walk up to the suspected IED and confirm its lethal nature. Hopefully that confirmation could be achieved without an actual demonstration from the beast. Everyone knew no one would have to be ordered, that someone would volunteer, and half the men were relieved that the other half spoke up immediately.

The choice quickly whittled down to the two new sergeants, Bedel and McMann. This was one of the jobs that would rightly fall to an NCO, and these men needed to prove they were up to the new stripes. Besides, no self-respecting NCO sends a junior man out in front on a dangerous assignment, not in the American Army anyway. NCOs are taught to lead from the front and when, in the future, Sergeants McMann and Bedel had to order a soldier to perform some mundane or distasteful task, any complaints from the soldier would be quickly crushed. Somebody's got to go right up to a bomb and look at it? Sounds like an NCO's job to me, says the private.

The two sergeants left their trucks and walked up to Sergeant Seidel to work out a game plan. They'd have the entire area covered with fire from all the other soldiers.

Sergeant Seidel got on the mike and ordered all soldiers, except for the machine gunner in each truck, to find a high spot, get some cover, and scan the desert. With a dozen sets of eyes constantly scanning the desert around the site, they hoped they could spot any threat (sniper? vehicle-born IED?) before it became a problem.

When the men were placed, Seidel and the two sergeants got down to business. It was decided that the men would circle outwards and approach the IED from the desert on either side. Each side had a dirt mound running along it about ten feet from the edge of the road. This dirt had been there since the desert had been moved out of the way for the road, thirty years before. Up to this moment, the soldiers and marines had complained that these running hills provided too much cover and concealment to the enemy, and that the roadsides needed to be cleared for at least a hundred feet out on either side. They were right about these concerns, and the engineers had the berm-removal project on its to-do list. For this duty, though, the offending berms would be useful cover.

The men approached the roadside from the desert and used the berms for cover the whole way. They were not to cross over the berm onto the road surface but rather, were to lie on the berm and look with their binoculars at the trigger and wires. From ten meters away, using 25X-power binoculars, the soldiers would be able to see plenty of detail.

McMann and Bedel checked and double-checked their own gear and each other's. They pulled the bolts on their M-16s and looked to see that their rounds were properly situated. They tapped the bases of their magazines to see that each was properly seated. Each man checked his extra magazine pouches, touched and looked at his fighting knife, first-aid kit, and the half-dozen other things they each carried affixed to their body armor. All of this was perfunctory as each item had been carefully checked and re-checked before, but the ritual was still necessary, though no one could tell you why. Lastly, McMann took the binoculars that Seidel offered him and he peered through them, making sure they were properly focused. Bedel took the hand radio that would connect them to the Platoon Sergeant.

With Sergeant Seidel standing outside his truck and watching each man's every step, the Sergeants walked out into the desert on either side of the road. They walked carefully and slowly, the exaggerated caution a function of the constant warning that one couldn't be too careful. Taking each step with deliberate care and only occasionally taking their eyes off the ground immediately in front of them, the men made their ways out from the road about fifty meters and then walked parallel to the road until they were alongside the IED.

With two berms between them, the two sergeants had lost sight of each other as well as the road surface itself. Each could see Sergeant Seidel though, who supervised the entire operation from his perch atop the Humvee's roof. He waved each man toward the road when they came alongside the IED; each man made the 90-degree turn and headed to the road.

When they got closer to the berms, Seidel's voice came over the radio, "Stay down behind the berm. Climb up to get a look but keep as much of yourself behind the berm as you can."

McMann and Bedel lay on the scorched dirt and

slithered up the mound until they could each see over the top. Each man focused immediately on the exposed trigger and wires and then looked at each other. They both knew this was an IED, that an IED was the only thing it could be. The ground around it was clearly turned over and the new dirt hadn't taken on the dried tan coloring of the ancient ground around it. The dirt had been carefully replaced and leveled.

From the vantage point of the berms on the sides, the soldiers could peer down at the IED and this view provided a new bit of information that escaped the initial soldier's attention. The piece of metal sticking out of the ground was positioned over another piece of metal that was lying flat on the ground. This was a contact-detonated IED, situated so that the wheel of a Humvee would depress the top piece of metal so that it would make contact with the bottom piece of metal. On contact, the circuit would be completed and the IED would detonate. Boom.

"I have eyes on the IED. Definitely a trigger and wires," said Bedel, into the hand mike.

"And the ground?"

"Newly turned over and then flattened out around the wires."

"Sounds like there might be something buried there," said Seidel with triumphant sarcasm.

"That would be my guess." Relieved, the atmosphere became that of playful kids rather than wary and scared soldiers. They should have known better.

Sergeant Seidel called into the radio, "Raven, Raven, this is Dagger. Come in."

"Dagger, this is Raven. Send it."

"We have eyes on the IED. It is definitely a trigger and wires. The ground is new. There's got to be an IED under there."

Seidel's relaxed smile faded instantly when Major *Weathers's* voice killed the mood. "How close are your 'eyes on'?"

"There are two sets of eyes on. One set on either side of the road, behind the berms."

"So they are ten meters or so away?"

"About that."

"Well we need a little closer confirmation. We can't have our IED asset off on a wild-goose chase. Can you get some eyes on the issue a little closer?"

Annoyed and urgent, "Negative, Sir. The men are behind cover now and will lose all cover if they get a single meter closer."

Seidel thought he had the Major boxed in. He was going to hold his ground on this. Politics or no politics, he was not allowing his men to move to the IED side of the berm. If and when the IED detonated, both men would be vaporized.

The Major heard the resolve in Seidel's voice, so he made sure that the Sergeant heard the resolve in his. "Do you have your grappling hooks with you?"

(Oh shit, the grappling hooks! He didn't say the grappling hooks, did he?)

Seidel was stunned. He searched his mind furiously looking for a way to reverse the direction of this conversation and was entirely without success when the Major, stronger now, pressed on.

"Do you have a grappling hook with you? You were

issued grappling hooks and trained on their use back at Mississippi."

"Well, yes we were but we didn't think you were being serious."

"Watch what you say over the net! Hajji is listening!"

(Hajji? Grappling hooks? This isn't happening.)

The scouts had been issued grappling hooks and ropes. The day they were trained on them back at Camp Shelby was one of the funniest days they spent there. The "trainers," back-office brainy types without a day's field experience, had devised an ingenious way to deal with roadside IEDs. Scouts were to hook the wires and triggers with their grappling hooks and then, from the other end of a hundred-foot rope, drag the IED from its hole. The practicing of this skill, which involved the throwing of the grappling hook at a dummy bomb ten meters away, was good sport. The soldiers had enjoyed the day competing with each other and betting on the results. The laughing and grab-assing that accompanied the training would never have occurred had they thought for one minute that they'd actually do something this freakin' stupid. Hook a bomb with a grappling hook? No goddamned way.

Each soldier knew that, should the need to get up close and personal with an IED ever arise, they'd simply pull back a hundred meters or so and light it up with the .50-caliber machine gun. This was strictly forbidden by the corporate types in the Army, their concern being that they might actually not detonate the bomb but make it more dangerous by dislodging it and damaging the detonation mechanism. A damaged detonation mechanism is harder to dismantle.

Your red-blooded American soldier wasn't concerned about those things. He knew he could destroy the IED with a .50-cal at a hundred meters, and that's what everyone planned on doing when the time came. Except for one thing. That one thing was Major Weathers, and he was at the other end of the radio only a few miles away. Major Weathers had had a cabinet meeting with the crazies in his head and they had decided that they just loved the whole grappling-hook thing.

Shit.

Sergeant Seidel had had enough though. His men were not going to do this and he was not about to go head to head with a Major on it either. He decided to take Groff's earlier suggestion and simply lie to the Major. The troops would more easily forgive a lie at this point than they'd forgive him putting them in harm's way unnecessarily.

He motioned to the two roadside soldiers to stay put and moved around to the back of his truck. Opening the hood with one hand, he reached in with the other and started throwing rucksacks, parts, boxes of MREs and water all around the back till he found his own ruck. He tore it open and reached in to get a hand on his grappling hook. The heaviest item, it was the easiest to find but hardest to get to.

He ended up dumping his whole ruck on the pavement behind the vehicle as he watched the grappling hook fall out last and roll down the pile of gear, coming to a rattling rest on the pavement. Like most of the soldiers' grappling hooks, his was still wrapped in plastic and the attached rope was bound with tape. Seidel unwrapped and untaped the big hook and jogged around to the back of the berm with it. He chose Bedel's side and scurried up to him, flopping down in the dirt next to him.

Bedel watched Seidel coming the whole time, curious and amused as Seidel tried to negotiate—but at twice the speed—the same treacherous roadside that Bedel had crossed. He saw what Seidel had in his hand just as he dropped down next to him. Looking first at the grappling hook, then at Seidel, he burst out, "You're fucking kidding me."

"Actually I am kidding you, but Major Weathers is not kidding. He expects us to use the grappling hook to retrieve the IED."

"Why?"

"Major Weathers. . . . Get it?"

"Yeah." Then with a long sigh, "What a moron."

"Right. But we have to play along a bit. I want you to throw the grappling hook at the IED. But *first*, make sure you are tucked down behind the berm. Just throw the fucking thing blind."

"What if I hit it?"

"*Don't* hit it! That's the point. We just want to be able to say we attempted to hook it. We definitely do *not* want to succeed in hooking it."

"Whew! Glad we cleared that up. I'll toss it as soon as you're back at the truck."

"Back at the truck? I'm staying right here with you."

"Why?"

"'Cause that's what platoon daddies do."

"No use arguing with a high-speed hero."

"Good. And I'm glad we're agreed. Let me make sure McMann knows to stay down."

"Good idea. That old bastard will take about an hour to get his old ass out of the way so you better start talking now."

"McMann, can you hear me?" yelled the fearless leader, opting for the ancient basic way of soldier communication.

"Saddam Hussein can hear you in Baghdad. What are we doing?"

With a wink at Bedel, Seidel yelled, "We are going to hook the IED with a grappling hook."

Bedel and Seidel grinned and chuckled together as they waited for this to kick in. McMann was a 40-year-old retread—a volunteer, as are all retreads, but no Rambo.

"Is that your best idea? Twenty years in the Army and you decide that blowing yourself up makes the most sense?"

"No, you dope. Major Weathers thinks it makes sense."

"Since when do we listen to Major Weathers?"

"He's got the radio on his side now. The troops have heard him. So if he says to throw the grappling hook, the troops got to see us throw the grappling hook."

"Just once. Right?"

"Exactly. So keep your head down. Understand?"

"Roger that. Keeping my head down. You

don't have to tell me twice. By the way, keep your head down as well."

"Roger. We're on it. Don't move till we tell you."

Sergeant Bedel unfurled the cord and made a coil out of it. Holding the coil in his left hand, he took the hook in his right hand—his arm cocked and ready. Taking one last look at Seidel and McMann to make sure he couldn't see them, he tossed the hook and dropped to the ground. He was completely flattened out well before the sound of metal clanging on pavement announced that the hook had landed. All three men lay completely flattened out for a good minute, ensuring there was no delayed fuse or any other problem with the IED.

Bedel began to get up when Seidel grabbed him by the flack jacket and pulled him back down. "I'll check," he said, as he first did a pushup, then pulled his leg up beneath him to get some traction. Then he was up in a crouch, peering over the berm at the IED.

"You missed it by ten feet."

"Shit that was close!"

"I'll say. Next time put a little more distance between the hook and the IED."

"*Next time?*"

Seidel, louder now and across the berms, "Mc-Mann, you still there?" The soft cloud of cigarette smoke rising above the opposite berm gave him his answer before he even spoke.

"Yeah fine. We hangin' out?"

"For a bit. Just to let the Major think we've suffered enough."

"He's gonna be pissed we didn't get blown up."

"He's not *that* bad."

"Don't bet on it. The guy's a freak. Count on it."

The three NCOs lay out in the desert sun for about fifteen minutes. They could hear the radio chatter from the Major in the BDOC to the men in the trucks, the Major asking about the progress on the IED and the soldiers keeping him posted. The soldiers had to keep reminding the Major that the NCOs were not visible, that the IED was too far away for the men in the trucks to see fine detail, and that the grappling hook had indeed been deployed. The silent conspiracy that developed involved just how many times the grappling hook had been deployed. While the sergeants had thrown it once and only once, the Major was under the impression that this time was being spent by repeated attempts to hook the bomb. No one tried to disabuse him of that notion.

Sergeant Bedel crushed out his third cigarette and drained the bottom of his 1.5-liter water bottle, the sound of the bottle hitting the desert floor coming only a second after it gave up its last glug. Iraq is one big landfill. Garbage stays where it is the minute it becomes garbage.

"Let's head back," said Bedel. And when there was no immediate objection, he leaned his head back and yelled at the sky, "McMann . . . ready to head back?"

"Roger." McMann drained the last of his water bottle, tossed it to one side and rolled down the berm in the opposite direction. He headed toward the truck and saw Seidel and Bedel across the road walking in the same direction. All three walked with their eyes to the deck, carefully scanning the ground immediately in front of them. It became second nature to everyone here, the constant vigilance about roadside IEDs, vehicle-born IEDs, and booby-trapped IEDs. Everywhere, at all times, soldiers scanned for IEDs.

The men in the trucks were lethargic. The heat made inactivity the default status for everyone in this miserable country, so unfit for human habitation. The Platoon Sergeant never discouraged this lying about until it was absolutely necessary. The men had the armored doors on the Humvees closed. This made them safer of course, but maximized the heat inside. So the men were seated perfectly still except for the occasional smoke break or piss break and the methodical drinking from liter water bottles.

All the Humvees had music coming from them except for the lead vehicle that requires silence because of its constant radio contact with the BDOC. The trucks that had music employed IPODs with battery-operated speakers. The technology was wonderful—hours and hours of too-loud music that could be carried in one man's cargo pocket, though he'd have to shift his day's supply of cigarettes, candy, and batteries to the other.

Sergeant Seidel took a long pull from the new water bottle he'd retrieved from the back hatch, then spoke into the radio.

"Raven, Raven, this is Dagger Two."

"Dagger Two, this is Raven. Go."

"Be advised we were unable to hook the IED. Request EOD at our POS."

"Why couldn't it be hooked?"

"Be advised we were unable to get the hooks into the hard dirt." Seidel was proud of this half-lie. Though the real reason they were unable to hook the IED was that they hadn't tried, it only just occurred to him that repeated tries were unlikely to ever succeed in hooking the IED anyway. The grappling hook had simply bounced off the ground.

"What about hooking the wires?"

"*Is this idiot kidding? Nobody* can be this clueless. Screw this; the truth is just going to have to do." Taking a moment to collect himself, Seidel spoke into the mike, "I thought hooking the wires would absolutely detonate the IED. It had a pressure detonator on it. That's the way they work." He was angry and determined and the Major heard it.

The two minutes of silence that followed was the longest part of the day so far. Then came Major Weathers, impatience in his voice. "I am going to call EOD for you. I hope you understand how valuable their time is and that you'll be able to make the case to them that you did everything you could to take care of this yourselves."

"Roger. Out." Then to the men, "After all, we wouldn't want to disturb the bomb squad, would we? They probably got tons of shit to do. They might have to go dismantle an IED somewhere. Jeeeeeez."

Seidel took his seat in the Humvee and joined in the waiting. Major Weathers's despicable voice came over the radio once more, this time to advise that he had succeeded in contacting EOD and was getting a mission arranged. He, Major Weathers—the heroic Major Weathers—was now going to take credit for any possible success in the day's mission.

The wait along the roadside could take hours, and sometimes it did. But on this day, they could see and hear the EOD guys within about a half hour. From the direction of the base, first could be seen a dust cloud on the horizon, then the EOD vehicle. There was some excitement when the soldiers recognized the Marine EOD truck. It was a much better day when the Marine EOD guys came instead of the Army EOD guys. The soldiers were technology-dependent, methodical, corporate. They had robots, and screens, and bomb suits. They planned, discussed, strategized, and sometimes, just sometimes, all this crap could actually dismantle or destroy a bomb.

The Marines had Marines and that, as they say, is an entirely different thing altogether. The Marines were fearless, or crazy, or both. They had designed their vehicle from an old 6X6 and had welded onto it as much steel plating as it could handle. The soldiers had nicknamed the huge lumbering box of steel *Mammoth* and then had to explain to about half the Marines what a mammoth was. Appreciative of the moniker, the jarheads had spray painted *Mammoth* along the steel plates on the side.

When the vehicle pulled up, a familiar man jumped down from the passenger side of the front cab. "Jesus Christ! Can't you guys do *anything* without our help?"

The 6-foot-3-inch Marine Sergeant was serenaded with the familiar enthusiastic reception as he pulled on his Kevlar helmet and flak jacket. He was still basking in the attention as he arrived at the lead vehicle, Kevlar unsnapped on his head, flak jacket open and flapping wildly.

Sergeant McCarthy was one of two Marine EOD team leaders at Al Asad and had become fast friends with these soldiers in the short months they'd been training together. On his third tour in Iraq, he had come to like the oddballs of the National Guard. Guardsmen were anything but Marines, in terms of toughness, training, and discipline, but this didn't lower Mac's esteem one bit. Rather, he appreciated that these civilians in uniform, these teachers, janitors, and store clerks gave a hundred percent, never accepting lesser duties, obligations, and dangers than the Marines with whom they served.

Mac knew how tough the Marine's life was. Marines were training for war 24 hours a day, 365 days a year. These Guardsmen trained for one weekend a month and for two weeks during the summer and came to this same miserable place determined that no Marine would think them second-best. Slower, weaker, and softer than Marines, they had matched them pound for pound in humor, courage, loyalty, and devotion to duty. Like most of the Marines here, Mac liked the Guardsmen and he was always glad when they called.

"Hey, Mac, sorry to interrupt the card game."

"No problem, I was losing anyway. What do we have here?" he said as he fumbled for a cigarette in the sweat-soaked utility coat under his flak jacket. He took the binoculars that Seidel handed him and spent only seconds looking through them before handing them back and announcing to Seidel that the "suspected" IED was now a convicted IED, that the pressure plate and wires could mean nothing else.

"But what's with that hook thing? Is that yours?"

"We were trying to hook it with the grappling hook," said Seidel, just remembering that they'd left the hook and rope strewn across the road.

"What the fuck? A grappling hook? Like fuckin' Batman? A fuckin' Batman grappling hook? Are you fucking nuts? Fuck!"

"Orders. Major Weathers in the BDOC, our operations guy. He wouldn't call you until we tried the hook first."

The humor and youth left the Marine's face as he let this news settle. Glaring directly at Seidel, who was two ranks senior to him, he growled through gritted teeth, "That is insane, just fucking nuts. I'll make sure that I get someone with enough juice to handle the Major, but *you* should have known better anyway. What are we going to do about *you*?"

"We didn't *really* try to hook it. We just tossed it once to make the Major happy. We *did* know better."

"Well, now I feel better," said Mac with complete sincerity, the teeth returning to a smile and the slits in his head becoming eyes again. "'Cause I didn't know what I was going to do if I found out that the Scout Platoon Sergeant was as stupid as this Major. I can live with stupid majors, but us NCOs gotta know better."

Mac walked back to the Mammoth and climbed the ladder in the back that led up to the truck's bed. He returned a few minutes later with wire, explosives, and a

PFC. He had a block of C-4 in each cargo pocket and a coil of wire in his left hand. The PFC had the bullet-sized blasting caps in his left hand, preparing them with the pliers in his right.

Mac handed the coil of wire to Seidel and pressed the blasting caps into the C-4 blocks he'd retrieved from his pocket, one cap in each block as each cap was handed to him by the PFC. He then returned each block of C-4 to his pockets, took the wire from Seidel, and handed it to the PFC. He lit another cigarette, then took one end of the wire from the coil in the PFC's hand and headed down the road toward the IED. The PFC fed the wire from the coil at the speed Mac walked.

Usually, a pressure-detonated bomb was safe unless someone detonated the trigger. There was no danger standing next to it as long as you did not trip the trigger. Later on in the war this would change. The insurgents were never far from the IEDs they'd placed so lovingly. They watched all the time. Each man knew that some-where out through the hazy heat of the desert, they were being watched. Later on in the war, Hajji would place two detonators on his bomb, the pressure detonator so that it would go off when run over by a truck and an electronic detonator underneath the bomb so that the watcher could detonate the IED from a distance if, as in this case, it was discovered. The bad guys would kill a couple of bomb squad guys as a consolation prize if they couldn't get a whole truck. Killing the bomb squad was a good day's work for an insurgent. Nice guys, these Hajjis.

But on this day, the Hajjis hadn't gotten smart yet, so Mac was safe. He squatted over the hole where the IED was and dug a trench on either side of it, using the Kabar fighting knife he'd retrieved from the scabbard on his belt. When he was satisfied with the size of the holes, he placed the prepared C-4 blocks in them, attached the wires to the blasting caps, and stood to survey the result. In a few seconds he was satisfied with his work and headed back to the men by the trucks.

When he got there, he sent the PFC back to the truck for the detonator. This box had two wire posts on the outside, a battery on the inside, and a plunger handle on the top. It looked like an olive-drab version of the mining detonators from the movies of the Old West—and with good reason. The technology at the plunger end was almost unchanged since then—although the explosives at the other end were light-years ahead of the dynamite those plungers were originally made for. The C-4 is lightweight, safe to handle, and makes one hell of a boom.

Mac was in the habit of leaving the detonator in the truck until he had the C-4 placed and he had returned to the rear. PFCs were famous for doing stupid things, and he was not going to have that detonator in a PFC's hands at one end of a wire while he was handling the explosives on the other end. The Marine placed it at Mac's feet and Mac knelt beside it to connect the wires. This entire step took only a minute or two and Mac stood up to take one last look around.

"Mount up and button up." This was one order that was universally and immediately followed as soldiers and marines alike scrambled for the inside of the nearest armored vehicle. Seidel stayed with Mac—these two

NCOs, the leaders of their respective units—and stared down the road at the IED as Mac positioned himself over the plunger. Holding the base of the plunger with his left hand, he slammed the plunger down with his right. A second or two later (there's a discernable delay in this type of technology) all hell broke loose. Both C-4 blocks exploded and there was some sort of synergy to the combined power. There was an immediate tower of flame, debris, desert, and road extending a hundred yards into the air and bending outward at the top. The soldiers could watch the tower turn into a cone as the exploded matter slowed down and spread out in all directions.

There was so much power behind the explosion that the top of the cone kept spreading out as gravity and wind began to affect it. The soldiers watched the cloud of debris spreading over their heads with awed fascination. Many were looking up at the sky with eyes and mouths open when the debris began to fall. An area the size of two or three football fields was pelted with dirt and rocks and road. Some men screamed and others laughed and some shrieked like kids as they ran for cover from the dirt storm. Mac simply put his helmet on and stood there, confident he'd only get dirty, and not hurt.

When the dust cleared, Mac turned to Seidel and said, "Let's check it out," as he headed down the road without waiting for an answer. When they arrived at the hole, Mac stood at the edge and stared down into the crater. It was the biggest one he'd seen on this, his second tour in Iraq. The crater was four feet deep and about twelve feet across.

"Two blocks of C-4 didn't do *this*."

"What do you think it was?"

"I dunno. Something big though."

"'Ya think?"

The humor took a bit of the edge off. These hardened grunts were scared right now. This had been a huge IED, and if only one man had not done his job correctly, from Mignutt to Mac, the IED would have hit men and machines, not just road.

Mac walked around the crater, jumped in, and dug around in the dirt. He climbed out of the hole and walked around the crater some more. In increasingly larger circles, he walked around ground zero and picked up debris. About twenty minutes passed and he and Seidel returned to the trucks with cargo pockets full of bits of metal and wire. Mac got on the radio and told the BDOC that the IED had been destroyed in place, and that the road was almost entirely gone and would need repair. He told them that he was confident that the IED had been at least three 155mm artillery shells, but probably more.

"Say again your last. Did you say *three* one-five-five-Mike-Mikes?" The voice crackled over the radio.

"I say, the IED was *at least* three one-five-five-Mike-Mike artillery shells. The hole is big enough for more than three but I only have physical evidence of three distinct shells."

"What's your sit-rep?"

"Echo Oscar Delta returning to base. The Dagger detail will continue mission." Mac eyed Seidel as he volunteered his assumption to their commanders. Seidel nodded affirmatively as Mac spoke. He yelled to all the soldiers to prepare to mount up and continue their mission as he accompanied Mac back to the truck.

Mac stopped and pointedly looked through Seidel's eyes, hoping his words would penetrate and stick in his brain. "Listen. Serious business. Don't ever fuck around with this stuff. You call us immediately when you even *think* you got something. Okay?"

"You bet. And I'll just fill the Major in with some fantasy story while you're enroute."

"Exactly. And don't worry about your asshole major. I got a major too and he's gonna love straightening yours out for you. See, my major doesn't like it when one of you civilians gets blown to pieces on his watch."

"Tell your major I love him."

"He won't go for that. He's not in the Army; he's all Marine. Doesn't swing that way. Get it?" Mac grinned.

"Thanks for getting here. Safe back, Buddy." Seidel grinned back.

"No problem. That's what they pay me for."

"They don't pay you enough."

"True dat. But you know, the last time I was home, people kept asking me how many people I killed. Ain't that funny? That's all they want to know. I used to tell them that my job was about saving lives and that I hadn't killed anyone at all. Then they sort of look at you disappointed. They don't get their jollies and they don't think I'm a real Marine anymore. So they walk away looking for the 'killer' in the bar who'll entertain 'em."

"I guess they figure you got it easy."

"Yup, just like you—driving around in a Hummer all day, listening to tunes, catching great rays."

"You got that right. We got the life, don't we?"

With that, Seidel waved once more, turned on his heels and returned to his men to continue the mission of clearing the rest of the road for the convoy that followed.

The Weapons Cache

The Humvees were positioned outwards, like the four points on a compass, forming the familiar 360-degree-security posture. Each truck had a man in the turret, constantly scanning the horizon. The soldiers had come to rely on these four gunners for their security, when in daylight. The rest were milling around, smoking and joking, a testament to their confidence in the turret gunners. They were about ten miles down the road on MSR Bronze, the only road that leads from the main gate at Al Asad Airbase in the western Iraqi desert to just about anywhere else in Iraq.

They'd stopped here about a half hour before, having found an IED in a roadside bag of trash. The diligent gunner in the front vehicle saw the IED before the vehicle came upon it. After spreading the alarm and ensuring that the men had all taken their positions for security, the soldiers began the wait that always followed. The platoon sergeant got on the radio to the BDOC (Staff Headquarters) and requested that the Marines from EOD (bomb squad) come out and blow the thing up. The soldiers had been through this a few dozen times before.

There was always a sense of victory when an IED was found in time. After all, that was becoming the major measurement of success for them. Not dying was important, too. In this war, they never got around to tracking enemy KIA very often as was common in most wars. This enemy avoided personal contact, preferring to fight with booby traps, bombs, and any other sneaky thing they could come up with. The Hajjis in Iraq fought the Americans, and their own countrymen—who drove the trucks that carried the building materials to their other countrymen who were trying to build a civilization in this stinking desert—by planting bombs in their way. So when these Americans find an IED before it finds them, it is a good day. When the bomb finds them, it is a bad day. Simple as that. There are no office politics or ambiguities in the life of a soldier or a Marine. The sheer black-and-white simplicity of the profession was what attracted many men to it.

This part, the waiting, was a problem. The soldiers would wait for the men from EOD to come out and blow the thing up. This delay would mean that that much more of the trip would be conducted in the dark. Dark deserts are dangerous places and the return mission would usually have to be driven more slowly, with frequent stops to scan the desert with infrared or thermal goggles. The goggles are a product of the amazing technological advances and the production capabilities of America. In this war, just like in every other war America had fought, the Great Satan's industrial machine was providing the edge.

The pitch black desert came alive through those goggles. More than one ambush was thwarted by soldiers who'd looked through the goggles and seen the man-shaped neon-green shadows setting up the kill zone.

There was ol' Hajji, thinking he was snooping and poop-
ing around in the darkest of deserts when, all of a sudden,
all hell breaks loose from above. Soldiers call for air support in these situations. The men in the choppers don't
miss.

So, if the Marines or soldiers from EOD could get
here soon, they could use the daylight getting the mission accomplished and avoid the shenanigans of the Iraqi
night. If the Marine EOD team was on duty, they'd haul
ass to get there. They didn't like leaving soldiers or Marines on roadsides waiting for them. Besides, they loved
it, this job of finding bombs and blowing them up. Marines get into EOD because they love to blow things up.
If it was an Army EOD team, it could take some time.

The soldiers were different from the Marines in this
area, as in most. The Army EOD did everything they
could think of to *not* blow the damned thing up. They
had robots and special tools and handbooks and experts,
and when they arrived on the site, they would assess, deliberate, diagnose, plan, and finally, execute. It could take
hours for them to deal with the bomb. The Marines arrived, blew it sky-high, and headed off into the sunset,
war whoops and all.

This particular day was in mid-August. The temperature had reached 100 degrees before 9:00 AM and
kept climbing—hitting 125 by early afternoon. There
was no need for weathermen in Iraq because this was the
way it was every day. The blinding sun burning from the
cloudless sky cooked this country so that the dirt on the
ground would be 140 degrees by midday, every day. The
soldiers lived in this oven completely covered by layers of

clothing. The direct rays of the sun were so lethal that soldiers were ordered to wear their shirts buttoned to the collar, sleeves rolled down, and trousers bloused around their ankles.

Kevlar helmets were *never* to be removed and the two inches above the collar on the back of the neck was covered by a kerchief. The men all wore wraparound goggles. They slathered sunscreen on the six square inches of face left exposed, and the sun mocked the sunscreen, burning it completely off in minutes. This place was hot.

They wore Nomex gloves. If a soldier touched just about anything, he'd burn his hand, hence the fireproof gloves. There wasn't a soldier who served in the field in Iraq who didn't have a dozen anecdotes about the heat. He suffered a third-degree burn from leaning on a Humvee that had been sitting in the sun. The skin on the balls of the feet burnt completely off from the heat coming off the desert floor. The rookie's metal-framed sunglasses burned blisters around his eyes. Everybody had to learn; this place was hot, not fit for humans. It did a lot to explain the disposition of the local population. They were damned irritable, and crazy as hell.

To be fair, the commanders who ordered the uniform and equipment regulations were keeping the welfare of the troops in mind, but then again, they came up with their grand schemes from inside air-conditioned buildings on base. The men in the field lived on an entirely different planet, just a few miles from the front doors of the brass. All soldiers and Marines wore body armor on top of the uniform. This modern addition to the battlefield has its roots in the armies of antiquity. Like the men who carried swords for the Persians, Greeks, and Romans, the twenty-first-century warrior covered his body with hard, heavy things meant to stop hot, sharp things from entering his body. The modern body armor weighed about twenty-five pounds when it had the thick Kevlar plates in the front and back. An enterprising soldier could double that weight by adding the accessories—deltoid covers, groin flap, neck roll, and hip pads.

On the body armor was an endless supply of hooks and straps where the soldier was required to affix his seven magazines of M-16 ammunition, his compass, fighting knife, first-aid kit, flashlight, and night-vision goggles. If he could find the room, he put on an extra pouch for his cigarettes and one for his IPOD. He carried his Gerber, or multipurpose tool, on his pants belt just so he could find it and it wouldn't get lost in the tons of crap he had on his vest. When he was done, he'd sometimes have added eighty pounds to his well-worn body, and all of it combined to block even the tiniest air bubble from hitting his skin.

He drank a liter and a half of water an hour in this oven. He had to keep track of it because his mouth never sent thirst signals fast enough that were strong enough to relay the accelerated dehydration his body was going through. He measured his water consumption against his watch, writing it down in ink on the inside of his forearm where the medic would know to look for it if he were unconscious.

The one universal measurement of proper hydration was his urine. Each soldier knew to watch his urine stream. He'd be looking for at least one clear urine stream each day. He was taught that this was a good indicator that he'd maintained the proper minimum hydration. The medics told him that, when standing still and exerting no energy at all, he was losing more than a liter of water an hour. The medics told him what his body couldn't. The soldiers never felt a drop of perspiration; with the intense sun in the bone dry air, even sweat died.

These soldiers were in touch with the news from home, at least with the national news. So was the enemy. Hardly a day went by that there wasn't another congressman or mother or somebody complaining about there not being enough body armor for the troops. It was crazy. Most of these guys would have tossed it all in the dunes and risked the shrapnel in order to get a free breath of air and to walk without having to lean on their rifle, their vehicle, or a hot rock. Everybody had plenty of body armor. Of course, it was effective protection against shrapnel but it was also heavy and hot, God-awful hot.

"Sar'nt! Sar'nt! There's somebody out there!" The young gunner off the left side of the road was screaming the alarm and pointing out towards the desert. All eyes turned to the soldier, then out towards the desert to see what had the gunner so excited. The Platoon Sergeant ran to the gunner's Humvee and leapt up top to the turret where the gunner was focusing his binoculars. The gunner gave them to the Platoon Sergeant as soon as he arrived. The Platoon Sergeant, SFC Kramer, looked through the binoculars and saw the two men that had gotten the gunner's attention.

All the crew chiefs had eyes on the men now. They had

returned to their own vehicles and retrieved the binoculars from their own gunners, training them immediately out on the desert. Two men were running away from the road, toward Baghdadi, the small village located on the Euphrates. There was no reason to believe the two men running were not bad guys because there was no reason for them to be out in the desert by the road. No reason that is, except for that IED. If they got to the town before being apprehended, they'd disappear into the population and you can bet that not a soul would know a thing about them.

Two of the crew chiefs, Sergeants Wallace and Reeves ran toward Kramer's vehicle. "We'll get them. We're on our way." They didn't wait for an answer as they chugged away and Kramer had to scream at them and wave them back. He'd already figured the terrain that he'd been looking at was not going to easily accommodate the Humvees. There were too many deep and steep ditches. He knew he'd probably have to send someone on foot, but he was wracking his brain for other ideas before he'd let these men go. It was sloppy and dangerous and the Hajjis had a decent head start. Also, the Hajjis had no body armor. They were moving.

"Take a walkie-talkie. I'll be right behind you, but don't get too far ahead. If we lose them to the village, so be it. It is better than watching you guys getting beheaded on Al Jazeera." Like so many of the NCOs, Kramer was a cop. In many ways, this instinct made him better than the full-time Army NCOs who were his peers. He smelled the threat of a trap and was most wary of the soldiers being separated from the main body. In Iraq, where the job of a soldier often looked a lot like the job of a policeman, having cops as platoon sergeants was a great asset.

"Roger that, Sar'nt," both crew chiefs barked in unison as they headed out on the heels of the bad guys.

The desert, which looks flat from the road surface, isn't. Since everything is the same ugly brown and there are no rocks, trees, or creeks to break up the horizon, it all seems like one big expanse of dirt. The heat waves coming off the desert floor complete the picture—no discernable break in the ground. The Iraqi desert in mid-August resembles an impressionist painting, without the color.

As the soldiers moved out, they got an entirely different picture. The ground was an obstacle course. There were ditches, mounds, and rocks, and traversing the distance would be hard work for anyone. The weight of the body armor and equipment made it grueling, and both of these young men were huffing and puffing within seconds.

The soldiers were in great shape and there was no doubt they'd be able to cover the distance, but it was slow going. The insurgents and their decision to keep running—even after Kramer had ordered them, in bad Arabic through the bullhorn, to stop—erased any doubt that they were, in fact, insurgents. They were looking over their shoulders and moving closer to the town as the minutes ground by. They were unburdened by equipment and they were used to the heat and terrain, but they were still losing ground to the two relentless soldiers who followed.

The Hajjis were running for their lives, but the soldiers were *competing*. They were American boys and in this theater of war, as in all theaters that Americans have served in before, the Americanism played a significant part. They loved to compete, especially athletically, and they loved to innovate. They functioned best in the chaos of war where ingenuity and flexibility were at a premium and where the competitive spirit could whip the fanatic any day. The Americans were eager and motivated and they closed the distance, each step closer won at supreme effort.

Wallace and Reeves both sensed they might win this and they ran as a team, each man pacing himself to the other, each man encouraging the other when he could spare the wind. They were in the hunt and had finally gotten a chance to fight a real enemy combatant face to face.

Running across the desert, they would lose sight of their prey when they had to drop into ditches and chug up the other side. They'd scramble to an open area then. When they had a hill to climb, they'd slow down as they reached the summit, trying each time to get a new and better view of the big picture while scouting for the fastest route. The view and the route changed constantly as each new terrain feature changed the field for them.

It was on one of these summits that they spied the Hajji's destination. There was a brick building out in the middle of the desert. It was a square building, twenty-four feet on each side. It had one steel door and no roof. It was used to house a pumping station for the well water that the townspeople used. These men had seen this type of building before, and they had a pretty good idea what it was and what it would look like inside. What they couldn't figure out was why the Hajjis were heading for it.

The soldiers were about a hundred yards from the building when the Hajjis disappeared around the far side of it. This was an entirely different situation if the two men could get behind steel and brick; the soldiers began to feel fear for the first time. Wordlessly, they both circled out to the left side so that they'd approach the building from the other side, the side not visible now.

As they swung left they came within sight of the two guard dogs—mutts really. The Iraqis trained all their dogs to bark and bite. These particular dogs were small and ordinarily would be considered harmless anywhere else in the world. Skittish and nervous, they'd be driven away with some noise or a quick kick. But these soldiers couldn't afford that luxury. Every dog in Iraq—every single dog—is diseased. Even if a bite wasn't fatal, the soldier might end up spending weeks fighting a nasty infection. These mangy mutts were walking, growling Petri dishes, incubating colonies of every know germ in the Middle East.

"Hold up, Man." It was Reeves. Picking his rifle up to his right shoulder and taking a stance to shoot the dogs, he extended his left up and out, looking as he did so to make sure that Wallace had indeed heard him and wouldn't run into his line of fire. Both men liked dogs and both winced at the yelp that came from the first one immediately after the fourth crack of the rifle. Reeves had to fire four times to kill the dog. He was gasping so hard for air, he couldn't get a decent sight picture, so he threw lead until something hit the dog. Moving the rifle just an inch or two, Reeves found the second dog in his sights and again he fired four times. The second dog, confused by the disposition of his canine partner, just stood and stared as he was felled by Reeves's second shot.

The soldiers were still catching their breath, the dry, swollen, and dusty condition of their mouths worsening as they dragged the hot filthy Iraqi air past their lips. The platoon sergeant had sent two of his four vehicles after the men and they could see them laboring over the terrain, still a hundred yards away. Looking back and forth between the vehicle approaching too slowly and the building that lay just ahead, the initial reaction was to wait for the support from the vehicles.

The men they were chasing had disappeared around the building and there was no trace of them. The building had one set of double doors, made of steel. They had an old coat of paint on them, yellow and peeling in parts, the rust replacing the paint. There was a small concrete step in front of them, running the length of the door. Covered with the fine dust that covered everything, there were many sets of footprints breaking up the otherwise homogeneous coating.

"We gotta go in." Wallace was looking at his partner, his face worried but calm.

"Are you crazy? Let's wait for the trucks. You know, big guns, backup, more guys to help. You know . . . the smart things they taught us."

"Dude, I know. But those guys could be setting up for us. They *know* we're gonna come in. We're just giving them time. They got bad shit in there."

"Man, I don't know." Reeves's words were useless as he watched Wallace running away from him, toward the doors. The son of a bitch, he thought, he *knows* I won't let him go in alone. With that, Reeves sprinted as best he could, trying to catch up with Wallace.

Reeves turned to the left as he closed in on the doors. Wallace had already positioned himself on the right side and was crouched along the wall beside it. Reeves saw that the door opened to the left, that Wallace planned for Reeves to pull the door open to his left side and Wallace would storm through it first from the right. The first man through the door is sure to get shot if things went wrong.

Reeves planted his feet solidly so he'd have a quick start when he followed Wallace through the door. He reached across and grabbed the rusty handle firmly, flexing every muscle in his upper body as he prepared to pull that door with everything he had. He looked across at Wallace, red-faced from the heat, wide-eyed from the adrenaline, and filthy as hell.

"One, two, three," came Reeves's stage whisper, and then, "GO!" as he pulled the door open with his whole body. Wallace slid around the right side and disappeared inside. Reeves followed him, his brain trying to take in the whole picture as the inside of the room became visible. He could see three people inside, and none of them was Wallace. "Where is he?" he thought as he waited for the gunfire that was supposed to be happening.

"Get down! Get down! Now!" It was Wallace, off to the right screaming at one of the men over the muzzle of the rifle that was at the "high ready," up to his eye, finger on the trigger, safety off, locked and loaded and ready to rock and roll. Reeves was screwing up; he was allowing himself to be mesmerized by the scene with Wallace and the Hajji to his right while he had multiple Hajjis to his left—Hajjis who were doing God-knows-what. He felt like he was an outside observer watching all of this unfold in slow motion. He snapped himself out of it and started moving, deciding to figure it out as he went along. Whatever he was supposed to be doing, he was absolutely not supposed to be standing still out in the open.

Aware that he'd taken his eyes off the left side for too long, he dropped down to one knee as he swung around to take charge there. The first job was to identify any weapons pointed at him. He quickly took in two Hajjis, one of the ones they had been chasing and another one he hadn't seen until now. His most immediate danger came from the new one. He was ten feet away and struggling with an AK-47.

It's strange what the human mind will do in hyper-stressful situations. The first impression that Reeves processed about the enemy before him was his looks. He was strikingly handsome, the strong bones of the Arabian skull working their way through the fresh flesh of the young face. The man had a perfectly groomed head of jet black hair and piercing green eyes. Reeves read no fear, no hatred, and no emotion at all in the face.

He was wearing a perfectly tailored man-dress, the soldier's name for the traditional Arabian garb. It was slate grey with black trim and buttons. Heavy leather sandals peaked from beneath it. The man was showing his profile, his left side toward Reeves. His body only partially blocked the AK-47 under his right arm. The man was frozen in the process of inserting the magazine in his left hand into the rifle in his right. So, he and Reeves faced off like this. They both knew that Reeves had the advantage, his rifle locked and loaded and at the ready. With the sound of Wallace over his shoulder, screaming orders at the other man, Reeves and his Hajji provided a study in contrast, silent and completely motionless.

He just stared at the Hajji staring at him, both men absolutely frozen. Reeves decided that they both knew exactly what Reeves wanted. He wanted the Hajji to drop the weapon, and he'd simply wait for him to do it. If the man moved that magazine one inch closer to the AK-47's well where it had been headed, then Reeves would shoot him. If he put it down, Reeves would not shoot him.

To drive home the point that Reeves had control of this situation, he glanced to his left to make sure the third man was frozen too. And frozen he was, transfixed on the scene before him—Reeves and the Hajji. Reeves quickly moved the rifle to the other man, then back to his Hollywood-looking Hajji. He moved it back and forth another time or two, each change taking less than a second. He could easily kill both men if he had to, and the best guarantee against having to do that was to keep reminding them that he could.

And then the Hajji moved. Slowly, with contempt and disgust in his face, he moved the magazine hand away from his body and the weapon. He moved his arm up and away until it was extended away from his body. Then he let it hang there a minute before letting it drop. He remained frozen until the sound of the magazine hitting the ground announced his surrender; neither man's eyes followed it to the ground as their stares persevered unbroken.

The Hajji's body relaxed at the sound. Reeves did not. He waited with his rifle at the ready. He wanted the Hajji to dispose of the rifle as definitively as he'd dispossessed himself of the magazine. Reeves confidently looked to his left again to check on man number three and then his eyes were back on the Hajji in the grey man-dress. Hajji ducked his head under the sling as he moved it off his shoulder. When the AK-47 was unslung, he bent towards the ground to drop it off to his right. He never took his eyes off Reeves as he dropped it and stood erect with the same deliberate quiet strength. Finally, he turned his body fully around to face Reeves and he stood there, arms at his side.

Reeves motioned for him to back up. He walked toward him as he did so, and when the Hajji reached the wall, he motioned for him to turn around. Coming up behind him, he tapped his elbows with the muzzle of his rifle, "Up, up on the wall. Put your hands on the wall." The Hajji did so, slowly, as Reeves leaned his upper body back and moved his right foot in between both of Hajji's feet. "Spread them. Open." When the Hajji didn't move them far enough apart, Reeves moved his foot first to the left, then to the right, tapping the inside of the prisoner's calves until he moved his feet farther apart.

When Reeves was satisfied that the Hajji was sufficiently impotent, he moved his rifle to his left side and tucked it under his arm. It was now only marginally pointed at Hajji as he smoothed his hand over the man's arms, up and down his back and flanks. Reeves took his time frisking this, his first prisoner of the war. He finished the way he was taught, by pushing his whole body up against the Hajji's back and pushing him into the wall while his feel were still spread and his arms still extended.

From there, he reached his right arm around the man and moved his hand over his torso and then down the front of his legs. He opted out of the recommended step of feeling inside his legs and genitals. That was one experience he was determined to avoid unless it was absolutely necessary. Here, he thought he had methodically covered the man's body, close enough to the skipped area from each direction, that he determined there couldn't be anything there. If there was, Hajji'd have to pull his dress up to get at it. Not easily done.

He turned the Hajji around and told him to pull the dress up some. Reeves only wanted him to pull it to his knees and Hajji's flush of anger disappeared when he realized this. Reeves needed to look at his ankles. More than one regular soldier had been caught by his telltale ankles. The ankles of the average soldier would be pale and compressed, and usually hairless. There'd be a clear line about six inches above the ankle where his usually worn combat boots would have ended. This particular Hajji didn't bear this evidence. He had instead, a perfectly pedicured pair of feet. There was no discernible break in the appearance of his ankles. He was not a regular soldier in anyone's army.

Reeves had him turn around again and he pushed him up against the wall. He pulled a zip-tie restraint from his cargo pocket and put it on the man's wrist. The Army equipped the soldiers with plastic, zip-tie handcuffs, convenient and disposable. At this, Reeves saw the first sign of fear as his Hajji became vulnerable.

Reeves then pulled the other arm around to the man's back and secured this hand to the other hand with the zip tie. He was about to put him on his knees so that he could deal with the third Hajji, still frozen off to his left, when the sounds of the Humvees pulling up outside and the soldiers dismounting stopped him. With the rest of the squad arriving on the scene, it was best for everyone to freeze, lest the adrenaline-pumped new guys come in shooting at anything that moved. This didn't happen, but the building became chaos once again as half a dozen soldiers came pouring through the door.

"What do we got?"

"You guys okay?"

"Whew, look at this!" It was Dexter's voice from the back corner. He'd come upon the contraband that Reeves and Wallace hadn't seen yet. Two other soldiers, noticing the lonely third Hajji still at large, were on top of him immediately. Rougher and tougher than either Wallace or Reeves had been with their catches, the new soldiers were dragging the third man outside. They had him on his knees and blindfolded in a few seconds, his hands cuffed behind him. The man didn't resist at all, but his passivity did not serve to assuage the manhandling at all. He was forced to his knees with a thud, then blindfolded and handcuffed so tightly that his face and hands were disfigured. Two soldiers were screaming obscenities at him.

Reeves and Wallace led their men outside and placed them on the ground next to the blindfolded man. The contrast in treatment usefully calmed the whole situation down. Reeves and Wallace helped their prisoners to their knees rather than throwing them to the ground. The men were not blindfolded but placed to face the wall, so that they wouldn't see the equipment, weapons, or unit insignia of their captors, the purpose of the original blindfold. Reeves called for two of the younger privates to come and guard them as they moved to collect the third Hajji, who needed a bit of rescuing.

Apparently Bennet had offered the man some water and other soldiers took exception to this.

"Don't give that mothafucka any water! What the fuck are you doing?" Martinez was screaming into Bennet's face. Martinez was a kid from Brooklyn. Smart and dedicated, he'd been tempered on some mean streets and this vicious side of him had remained hidden until now.

"I'm giving the man some water. What's wrong with that?" Bennet was a maker of friends. Some modern psychologists might call him a people pleaser. His first reaction on meeting someone new was to determine if there was something he could give him. Likely there wasn't a man in the platoon who hadn't been a beneficiary of Bennet's outgoing generosity at one time or another. The Hajji would be no exception. The classic Bennet simply saw a man who might be thirsty and offered him some water. Martinez had charged him and—placing himself between Bennet and the kneeling man—had knocked the bottle from Bennet's hand to the ground. Then the screaming started.

"Don't give shit to this muthafucka! He kills soldiers!" Martinez had turned around and had the man by the upper arm and was shaking him, using the prisoner's body to add emphasis to his words. Each accented syllable would jerk the man violently over and the next syllable would find him being yanked back up to his stationary position.

"I'm just giving him some water. He's handcuffed."

Growling now and even louder, "No! Goddamn it! No!"

The Platoon Sergeant arrived on the scene and as always, he knew what to do. Kramer put his hand on Martinez's shoulder and turned him so that they'd be facing each other. "Jose, could you check everybody? Smitty and Ski look like they could be heat casualties, maybe some of the others, too."

The anger and fear left Martinez's face as Kramer's words served to remind him of who he was. The anger that had caused him to hate the Hajji came from his love of the soldiers, his desire to see all his comrades get home in one piece. The anger and hate were replaced by the dedication and work ethic the men were used to seeing from Velez.

"Yes, Sergeant! I'll get right on it." Martinez adopted Army–manual, perfect military courtesy when he felt "his calling." Martinez's role as an Army medic *was* a vocation. He began to hurry from one man to the other, looking in each man's eyes, feeling the back of each man's neck, asking a half dozen questions of each one.

"How do you feel? Did you pee since we left? How much water have you drunk since we stopped at the IED? Don't know? I told you to keep track. Get in the shade and sit down. You too, soldier." The medic, who was outranked by most of the soldiers on the detail, was entitled to take command and issue orders to those who outranked him when medical situations demanded it. This was one of those situations as he ordered three of the men to the shade.

He tended to them within minutes. Each man had an IV in his arm in no time. "The needle" was in common use in the desert. Any question at all as to the man's state of hydration and he was ordered to sit in any patch of shade that could be found and was administered a liter of saline solution—chock full of electrolytes—intravenously. Martinez had three men on the needle and he barked to the rest that they'd soon be joining them if they each didn't drink another liter of water immediately.

Having recovered his sense of perspective, he looked over at the Hajji he had been manhandling and was pleased to find that someone had removed his blindfold and moved him to the shade at the wall, alongside the other two prisoners. Martinez had surprised himself with his reaction on coming face to face with his first enemy combatant, and he was disturbed about his own behavior. He didn't exactly feel guilty, so he wasn't going to be making amends to the Iraqi. In fact, he thought the Iraqi deserved the worst treatment imaginable. He just wanted to be able to think of himself as being better, above the evil of the place, a man whose character and intellect provided the means by which he controlled his emotions. He tucked this away, resolved to think about it and straighten himself out later on, when this mission was done.

True to Martinez's character, he never lost control again. He never let anger get in the way of his professionalism and he never had to be counseled on it. He got there himself, bootstrap character development.

Meanwhile, inside the building, Dexter and his two soldiers were inventorying the spoils. They recovered six AK-47s, hundreds of rounds of ammunition, and dozens of magazines. There was a pile of boxes of electronic parts. Hajji was an industrious little shit. He'd be able to make weapons out of anything with a wire or a chip in it. The soldiers had seen IEDs wired from washing machine and oven timers. They'd seen IEDs detonated with pagers and cell phones. And here today, there was over a hundred pounds of the most eclectic assortment of electronic junk imaginable, the stuff that Hajji bombs are made from.

There was a cooler loaded with food. To the American sensibilities, it was garbage. The meat, vegetables, and bread were all lying in piles unwrapped. Flies walked on top of this mess, unmolested. The cooler was warm and there was visible dirt on the walls of it, as well as on the top of the food.

"Jeez, no wonder these guys don't mind dying. Life sucks for them."

"No way they eat this shit," said one soldier, immediately realizing how wrong he was when he looked up to see the Hajji outside looking in at him, anxiously worried about what the soldiers might be doing with his dinner.

By the food was a sleeping mat and blanket, neatly rolled up to the wall. When they moved it aside, they found the pamphlets they'd been trained to look for. Written in Arabic, the words were indecipherable, but the pictures sure as hell weren't. The pamphlets had instructions on how to use common electronic devices to wire bombs. Most of the illustrations were of a technical type, but some had grotesque caricatures of American and British soldiers being bested by valiant Jihadists. Some had drawings of Mullahs on them. All in all, this particular part of the find would seal the fate of the Hajjis. There'd be no doubt as to who they were or what their intentions were.

SFC Kramer was on the radio with the brass in the BDOC. There was some debate as to whether the soldiers were to bring the prisoners in or to stay put until the MPs came out to pick them up. At issue were the availability of MPs and the necessity of the soldiers carrying on this mission of clearing the road for the convoy that waited to go. As is the norm, this highly predictable situation—that of U.S. soldiers capturing enemy combatants while out on a patrol whose mission it was to find enemy combatants—had not been planned for. Holy shit, what do we do now?

Finally, the order came for the men to stay put. This good news meant they would be able to avoid the tedious round trip all the way back to the BDOC and then out to the road again. Also, they'd get to rest for an hour or so until the MPs got there. Two men and a sergeant were assigned to guard the prisoners and the trucks were placed in the familiar 360-degree-security posture. In this heat, the gunners would not be required to man the turrets for the entire period. Each man of each crew was cross-trained in each job, so each man would spend fifteen or twenty minutes on the gun and would then be relieved by another crewman. There was no need to set up a schedule or give any orders. These guys cared for each other and took their turns without having to be ordered, before being asked. Silent, unsupervised teamwork became the MO in Iraq.

So, they stayed this way for much of the afternoon, the MPs taking a bit longer to get out to them than they'd anticipated. The MPs arrived with the EOD guys. They had coordinated with each other and made the trip together. This explained why there was such a wait; two different commands from two different services having to coordinate a task could be weighty at the top. In the field, at the squad and platoon level, coordination of effort and teamwork came naturally. Marines and soldiers worked well together in Iraq. The Marine EOD team worked on the IED while the Army MPs retrieved the prisoners.

The transfer of prisoners took twenty minutes, which was nineteen minutes longer than it should have taken. The cops re-frisked and re-cuffed the Hajjis, as though regular old grunts couldn't do that sort of thing properly. They called the Hajjis *sir*, in the manner that a street cop in the States might call everyone *sir*, and they made Sergeant Kramer sign paperwork that he was turning over the prisoners. The entire process struck the soldiers who cared to watch it as absurd, the professionalism of a stateside police department juxtaposed to the chaos of a guerrilla war in the desert.

In that little time, the Marine bomb guys wired the IED and blew it in place. They didn't even bother to clear the explosion with the soldiers at the prisoner site, having gauged the distance and deemed it far enough away to eliminate any safety concerns. They were correct as far as that goes, but they didn't give much thought to the effect the surprise explosion would have on the soldiers. Not realizing at first what or where the explosion was, the soldiers all hit the dirt and frantically looked around.

"Incoming!"

"No. No, it's the IED."

"On purpose, I hope."

"Well anybody see tiny bits of Marine falling around here?"

"Jeez! You think the jarheads would have let us know!"

The MPs got on the radio. They were already set to the frequency of the Marine EOD team that they'd just traveled there with. They confirmed a successful detonation in place and notified the rest of the soldiers that it was safe to head towards the road.

The men crossed the few hundred yards out to MSR Bronze and resumed their mission. They were clearing MSR Bronze, and would patrol the rest of the 35 kilometers to MSR Uranium where they'd turn around and come home. Another unit was assigned to clear MSR Uranium from where they would turn toward home. The rest of the route would have to be cleared because there was no rule that said there could be only one IED on a route, or that if there was an IED found, there could be no ambush further on either. Rather, having found the IED, each man's senses were heightened and that much more aware of the reality of the danger.

When they crossed through the dust to the road, each man stared at the hole where the IED used to be.

Half the road was gone as well as a considerable section of the shoulder. The road was still passable though, in an all-terrain vehicle. Since the IED had been laying on the surface of the road, it only damaged the surface. When they are buried they make big craters. The craters of the buried ones go deeper and make neat cones. The ones on the surface make more irregular damage, across a much wider area.

The men drove for another six hours, traveling at about twenty kilometers an hour and stopping frequently at intersections, gullies, and bridges. At these places, they'd set up a three-sixty—a 360-degree-security posture—and the dismounts would get out and walk the area. They'd walk slowly, almost leisurely in sweeping arcs extending outward from the vehicles, or they'd walk in ever-increasing concentric circles. They'd be staring at the ground while the gunners in the turrets stared at the hazy horizon. This was one of those times that the gunners were particularly diligent. Their comrades were on foot, away from the armored vehicles, exposed and vulnerable. Depending on the nature of the terrain, a reconnaissance stop like this could take from a few minutes up to an hour.

The return trip was made completely in the dark. In this sort of environment, there were no discretionary ground reconnaissance stops. The trucks stayed close to the road, the gunner's job aided by high-intensity search lights. There's no rule that says Hajji can't place an IED on the road behind you, in anticipation of your return trip. The soldiers assumed, or rather the soldiers knew, that they were always being watched, that Hajji was always adapting his procedures to the American procedures. The soldiers knew that Hajji knew how they did things.

It was 3:00 AM when they arrived at the welcome sight of the gate at the Flea outpost. They were inside the wire and heading to the BDOC within a few minutes. At the BDOC, the gunners dismantled and stowed the guns, the drivers stored the rest of the equipment, and the crew chiefs went inside to brief the bosses on the events of the evening.

SFC Kramer and the rest of the NCOs were surprised to see the Hajjis from the afternoon's mission sitting on the ground outside the BDOC. They had expected they'd be transported to the higher headquarters where the civilian police and the officers from military intelligence would detain and interrogate them. Instead, they were sitting on the ground beside the entranceway to the concrete bunker that housed the BDOC. They were still handcuffed, but they were now cuffed in the front where there could be some use of their hands. The blindfolds were off, and each had a bottle of water in front of him. There were two soldiers posted to guard them, and they were instructed to stop the Hajjis from talking to each other.

"You guys get back to the men. Get them to chow and back to the cans. It's late. Just one of you hang back when they are all done and get over here with the truck to give me a ride back. This shouldn't take too long." Kramer was primarily concerned that his tired and hungry troops get rest and food, but he also wanted as few soldiers at the BDOC as possible. He had a suspicion that things might not be quite right regarding the Hajjis, and he wanted to find out what was happening while attracting as little attention as possible.

The NCOs turned away and headed to their crews as Sergeant Kramer disappeared inside the BDOC. He made his way down the two short familiar hallways, more like tunnels, until he came to the briefing room. There were half a dozen officers there, all paying close attention to First Lieutenant Bradley, Kramer's platoon leader. The Lieutenant was briefing the operations officer, the executive officer, the intelligence officer, and two Marine lieutenant colonels on the operation that netted the three insurgents.

The Lieutenant stood before a long table on which were stacked the contraband that the soldiers had captured that afternoon. The now familiar Al Qaeda propaganda was being passed around the room, each officer eagerly receiving each piece passed to him, then carefully studying each page and taking in the remarkable diagrams and caricatures.

Bradley was on. He had the men's attention as he described the afternoon's operation. He was relaying each detail as though he were there. Kramer noted that he didn't get a single material detail wrong. Kramer's thoughts returned to the previous afternoon's activities as the Lieutenant brought it back for him as well as for the officers, "My platoon then set up security around the IED and sent a detail after the men on foot." Etc.

Something wasn't quite right, thought Kramer. The Lieutenant had been in the BDOC when SFC Kramer was on the radio with them. The Lieutenant had taken in every detail and had called in these officers from intelligence to brief them. He didn't exactly claim to have been there, but it was clear to Kramer that the L-T was making the impression that he was.

Seeing Kramer, the L-T wrapped it up. He thanked the officers for coming and offered his services should they have any further questions. Then, scooping up his paperwork, he bid them goodnight. "Gentlemen, please get in touch with me if I can be of any service at all. If there are no further questions at this time, I'd like to get back to my men."

"Please do, Lieutenant. And by the way, great job to-night."

"Yes, Lieutenant. Your platoon did tremendous work."

"Glad we put the right men on this tough job, Lieu-tenant."

"Congratulations. Keep up the good work." The Lieu-tenant Colonel who was the executive officer beamed as he shook the Lieutenant's hand, slapped him on the back and sent him on his way.

Bradley's eyes met Kramer's as he approached the Ser-geant standing in the doorway. He ushered his Platoon Sergeant outside and, once out of earshot of the brass, absolutely gushed praise. "Tremendous job tonight, Ser-geant! Are the men taken care of?"

"Yes, Sir. The crew chiefs are putting the gear away and they'll secure for the night. I was just coming in to do the debriefing paperwork."

"No problem. I took care of it for you."

"*You* took care of it?"

"Sure, I figured you'd be exhausted. You can head

back and get some rest. You sure deserve it."

"I will, Sir, but first I wanted to visit with a few guys inside."

"Okay, well don't stay too long. Big day tomorrow. I told the Colonel you guys would be hitting the road again tomorrow."

"Tomorrow? Sir, tomorrow is the one day we had scheduled for these guys to be off. Tomorrow is their first day off in two weeks."

"Uh, I know, Sergeant. But today's capture was the first big break we've had this quarter. The brass wants their top soldiers to get out there and make it happen some more. This is the price we pay for being good at what we do."

("*We?* This sonofabitch has been outside the wire *once!*") "Sir, the men need the day off."

"Sergeant, I don't think I need to remind you there's a war on. We are in a *war*. Good night!"

"I dunno . . . ." Kramer's voice disappeared into the darkness behind the Lieutenant who was disappearing faster.

Kramer headed back into the BDOC and walked to the operations department and, stopping at Gunnery Sergeant Tanksley's desk, picked the Lieutenant's report from the top of the Gunny's pile. The Gunny, Kramer's Marine counterpart and the gatekeeper for the operations department, leaned back in his chair and stared at Kramer, waiting for the reaction he knew was sure to come.

"The sonofabitch!"

". . . and worse."

"You'd think the bastard was there! He can't get away with this."

"Yes he can. I read that piece of shit. His report never claims he was there. He talks about his platoon and his men. You'd *think* he was there."

"Uh, yeah, you would!"

"But he never directly says he was there."

Kramer's face was red hot and his eyes bloodshot within seconds. His clenched fist dropped the papers on the Gunny's stack. "I am going to beat the shit out of that sonofabitch. He's been making like body beautiful at the gym since we deployed. I am doing double missions because he doesn't do shit. I think he's been outside the wire once. I am going to kill him right now."

"No you're not." Tanksley was almost as intense as Kramer as the Marine stood to get on the same level with the soldier. "You and I are NCOs. We have men to take care of. Your soldiers need you. You go to the brig and there is nothing between them and Bradley."

"I don't give a shit. He's not going to get away with this."

"Officers have been getting away with this shit forever. You *do* give a shit and you will put the welfare of your men before your personal feelings." This was not a command but rather a statement reminding Kramer of the truth the two NCOs knew. The Gunny knew Kramer had heard him—though he'd disappeared down the tunnel.

Kramer's top crew chief was outside in the Humvee. Kramer opened the door and got in as the crew chief started the engine. These men knew each other and the junior sergeant knew Kramer was angry.

"What's up? How'd it go?"

"Fine." Kramer growled.

"Anything wrong?"

"No. I'm just bushed. Let's get home."

Both men knew he was lying, and both men knew that was the way it was going to stay. Kramer, like so many NCOs in the middle, just sucked it up and soldiered on, keeping the incompetence or dishonesty of their commanders from the attention of the men. They did this because it was in their soldiers' best interests to instill and maintain their confidence in their superiors.

Kramer, however, wouldn't sleep a wink.

The
Sergeant Major

The day the battalion was "federalized"—that is, trans-
formed from National Guardsmen of the Commonwealth
of Pennsylvania into soldiers of the United States Army—
was the happiest day of Tom Poloski's life. In front of the
thousand men in his battalion, Sergeant Major Poloski
had the chevrons of his new rank pinned on his collar
points, set gloriously in place by a retired general who'd
come to see the boys off. And when those boys stood at
attention, each and every one of them, they had a look of
respect drawn across their faces for the new top dog.

On that cold day in January, in the middle of the
biggest blizzard of the year, each man in that battalion
was experiencing extreme emotion. For most, it was sadness. These citizen soldiers were leaving their families
and homes and heading for war. First there would be a
five-month train-up in Mississippi and then they'd be
dropped into the middle of the war in Iraq to spend another year away. They were worried.

They worried about how their families would get
along for so long without them. They worried about
missing all the important moments that mark the lives of
families—from first steps to graduations. They worried

about whether their jobs would be there when they got back. They worried about an infinite number of things but most of all they worried about not coming back at all. If the planes that were to take them away managed to negotiate their way through the blizzard, they would be on their way to a long period of uncertainty, anxiety, and suffering. In that situation, who wouldn't worry?

But Sergeant Major Tom Poloski didn't worry. He was the senior enlisted man in this battalion. He'd achieved the highest grade to which a soldier could aspire. And now, in that capacity, he'd go off to war for the first time. He was the Colonel's right hand. He was the man on whose desk the buck would stop. But more important to him, he outranked every enlisted man in the battalion. After twenty-five years of eating shit, he'd finally be able to spoon it out to others.

The Sergeant Major hadn't come by his rank easily. Throughout the twenty-five years he had served with the National Guard, he'd taken every dirty job that had come along (or at least that's how he saw it). He thought he'd been made to work too hard and pay too much for the reward he received. But now those times were over. Now, it was time to set things straight. Now, all those college-educated officers would have to deal with him. Now, all those other Sergeants who had competed so hard for the rank he now wore would learn why he, Tom Poloski, had been chosen. Now, Sergeant Major Tom Poloski would show them what it meant to be the top soldier.

A handful of other senior NCOs had been promoted that day and Tom hadn't cared enough to notice or to extend congratulations. So many Sergeant Majors acted like they were politicians, constantly talking with the other sergeants, offering phony praise, shaking hands. It seemed that every Sergeant Major he'd ever known was one of these guys who was always around, poking his nose into everything. Sergeant Major Poloski wasn't going to turn being a Sergeant Major into a glad-handing job. He wouldn't reduce the dignity of his office by associating with many of the junior men at all. He'd deal with them through the company first sergeants and through their platoon sergeants. "Chain of command, that's the ticket," he thought silently. It is about time that the chain of command was observed. And he would be the one to educate his men.

When they had received notice that the planes wouldn't be taking off for a few hours, that the runways had to be cleared and the wings de-iced, he had retreated to the peace of his office. It had been necessary to figure out how almost a thousand men would be housed and fed for another evening but that's what the junior sergeant's for. Poloski had spent too many years coddling the countless kids who were in his charge. It would now be somebody else's job to wet-nurse the lads.

There, in his office, he found the bottle of Jack Daniels he'd been saving for this very day. He poured an inch into his empty coffee cup and sipped the caramel-colored peace. However, there had been strict rules promulgated about drinking. The drinking lamp was out. The men were not to touch a drop of alcohol after they arrived at the armory. Both were good orders, ones that Sergeant Major Poloski agreed with. He believed it was important to ensure good order and discipline that the men observe the rules. Considering the emotions of the day (as well as the importance of the tasks that lay before them), it was best they be sober. But certainly he'd be able to handle a nip or two. After all, he had become the Sergeant Major, and rank has its privileges.

When the warmth of his cup had made its way from his gullet to his head, he grabbed a cot from the warehouse and set it up in his office. The entire battalion would all be scrambling for the few cots that were in storage tonight and those that didn't get a cot would sleep on the armory floor. But this was of no concern to the Sergeant Major. The men were young and could certainly handle a night on the hardwood floor. After all, they were soldiers heading off to war.

The blizzard cleared the next day and Tom was the last to get on the plane, arriving only after the sergeants had ensured all the gear was aboard and that all the men were accounted for. Having polished off half the bottle of Jack Daniels by the end of his one-man celebration the night before, Tom was nursing a small hangover. The nap on the way to Mississippi took care of that. After a day of waiting in lines, and shuffling between planes and buses, he grabbed his duffle bag and darted towards the barracks area as soon as the bus pulled to a stop in Mississippi. He'd arranged for a special barracks for the senior enlisted men and he was concerned he'd not be able to find it before one of the rank-and-files made the mistake of commandeering Sergeant Major Poloski's room for himself.

The training at Camp Shelby, Mississippi was conducted by various units of the Army Reserve. The logistics were all managed by the resident command and his time at Mississippi was spent providing administrative oversight to ensure that the work of others was properly documented in good order. When the five-month train-up was done, he didn't bother to take the ten-day block of leave that all soldiers were entitled to. He'd found a rhythm and routine in the camp life at Shelby. His days were spent lazily taking care of one odd task or another and his nights were spent at the NCO club. During these nightly visits he got to sit and exchange experiences while enjoying beer after beer with the other top soldiers. Here, he was among men like himself, for only sergeant majors and first sergeants had both the liberty and the time to enjoy the privileges the club had to offer. No, Tom Poloski, Sergeant Major, saw no need to get home any time soon.

At home, he was the resident handyman. And to his kids, he was an ATM. He was a machine whose sole purpose was to dispense cash on demand and then be dismissed at the completion of the transaction. But now, they'd all just have to get along without him for awhile. His wife had been writing him over the past few months, whining about the chores that had gone undone in his absence. Many times while at Camp Shelby he realized how small a frame of reference this woman had. Could she not understand that here at Shelby, he was Sergeant Major Poloski, head soldier of an entire battalion? Surely she could not, for if she did, she would not trouble him with such mundane details of home.

He was assigned the job of leading an advance party

to the base in Iraq where they'd be staying for the next year. He was already on his way there before the troops returned from their ten-day leave. The trip, which was conducted on high priority orders, had him flying along with the other wartime VIPs (generals, diplomats, and business executives) in commercial aircraft. Sergeant Major Poloski went off to war in style, sipping cocktails and enjoying in-flight movies almost the entire trip. That is, everything except the last leg. The final flight, the last segment of his first journey into war, was flown in a C-130 cargo plane traveling from Kuwait to Al Anbar.

When he (along with the half dozen other NCOs he took along) arrived on the base, he immediately set about inspecting the living quarters. The refurbished shipping containers—or "cans" as the troops called them—were more than adequate for their needs. A quick count indicated that they might not have enough for the NCOs and the troops, so he was sure to grab a dozen cans at the end of the compound where he and the others would be closest to the latrines, showers and company tent. This ensured that he, the first sergeants, and the Colonel's staff would have their cans right away. They needed the good ones, the ones closest to the amenities. They needed to be close to one another as well as to the center of the action. The Colonel would be pleased.

Within a few days of the battalion's arrival in Iraq, they had all been assigned their missions. Most of the men were acclimated to the environment by manning watchtowers and gates. Some were assigned to command posts where they watched screens, monitored radios, and marked wall maps. The officers and top sergeants were given rotating shifts as Officer of the Day. Schedules were drawn up and offices—really, plywood cubicles—were assigned.

The Sergeant Major spent his days in Iraq shuttling between his plywood office and his steel home. He had some mandatory paperwork to fill out and he was in charge of the battalion finances. As such, he was assigned, as were all sergeant majors, the custody of and accounting for the special services money. Special services money was a Defense Department line item in the budget. It amounted to just over a dime a day for each man in the hostile fire zone. These dimes added up and there'd be thousands of dollars in the till in no time. The taxpayers had allocated these funds for the morale, welfare, and health of the soldiers. Most units would assign a committee of men from all the disciplines and ranks to oversee the spending of the money. Poloski would have none of that.

The last thing he expected to deal with was some nineteen-year-old PFC telling him what to do with the money. He was the Sergeant Major and he'd know best. The other battalions wasted the funds on sports equipment, soda, and snacks. Some had built barbeques. Some bought computers, TVs, and other electronic equipment. Tom Poloski knew that that was no way to spend the taxpayer's money. There was enough food in the chow hall. There was a PX for the extra things. Most soldiers could order sports equipment online and they were all paid plenty of money. There was nothing Poloski could buy for the soldiers that the soldiers couldn't buy themselves. Besides, he knew that if he saved the money, there'd be one hell of a party when they all got back. That's what he planned on doing. He'd rent some big campground, hire a country band, and buy all the beer in Northeast Pennsylvania. They'd get drunk for a week and the soldiers would thank him for it.

A few months into the deployment, some of the soldiers got the nerve to ask the Sergeant Major about the special services money. The neighboring battalions had some useful computer centers set up and they had all used their special services money to build them, to buy the equipment, and to contract satellite services. Those Internet cafes were a godsend in that each man could traverse the 8,000 miles that separated him from those he loved. Each man could contact his wife and children, or his parents, or his sweetheart. Specialist Long was elected to represent the soldiers. He walked the two miles to the Sergeant Major's office on a day off and asked to see him. Ignoring the obvious annoyance he had caused to the Sergeant Major, he entered his office and asked, "Sir, the men and I were wondering if we could get some help with the Internet."

"What Internet?'

"We need a satellite and a contract with a supplier. The other battalions have this and they told us they used special services money."

"What are you all using now?"

"We sneak into the computer shacks in the other battalions. It is getting harder as they know who we are."

"Well, I'll look into it."

"OK, Sir, but . . ."

"I *said* I'd look into it. Now find something to do before I find something for you to do."

"But . . ."

"For the last time, I SAID I will look into it. Now get out of my office before I kick you out!"

Long left the office pissed. Later on that night, he slashed the tires on the Sergeant Major's ATV. Poloski had been driving around in a new four-wheeler he had had shipped in from the States. Each man was convinced, but had no way of proving, that this extravagance was purchased with their special-services money. Not only was it a galling luxury for the fattest man in Iraq to be driving past combat troops who had to walk miles to get a meal or a haircut, but it just looked ridiculous. Poloski was getting fatter by the day and the juxtaposition of the fat and the ATV was an assault on the psyches of the soldiers.

Long slashed the tires at about midnight and anyone who had the good fortune to be asleep at 8:00 the next morning when Poloski waddled out to his four-wheeler was rudely awakened. The man yelled about nothing else for two days, straight. He cursed the air and threatened the cloudless sky. He ranted. He raved. He railed at anyone he could get to stop and listen for a minute. He vowed someone would pay. Between his fireworks and the lovely sight of that ATV sitting in the middle of the compound on four flat tires for two weeks while it waited for new ones, the men had the best time in months. The smiles and spontaneous laughter in the compound was infectious.

After a few days of this, the Sergeant Major took the propane tanks. The men had two propane grills in the common area. The propane tanks were regularly filled by the magnanimous Sergeant Major, or rather by his clerk. The Sergeant Major unhooked them and dragged them to his can. He told anyone with the balls to ask that he could no longer afford to keep them filled as he needed the money to buy new tires.

The men had a bus, a civilian passenger bus that they took turns driving. During meal hours, it would shuttle men back and forth across the sweltering two miles to the chow hall. The Sergeant Major confiscated the bus. He drove everywhere with it and he drove it alone. He never missed a meal, and when he drove along the road on the way to the chow hall, he'd honk as he passed his men dragging their too-old-too-soon bodies to the same place. The Sergeant Major was not to be trifled with.

It was on one of those days, one of those 125-degree days when so many men chose not to eat rather than cross the two miles on foot, that Specialist Long had his next bright idea. He never got over being treated so shabbily by Poloski. He was sitting on the ground outside his can, eating a bag of beef jerky and drinking warm water when he saw the Sergeant Major walk on by coming from the parking lot to his can. Long sat and stewed awhile and when the anger wouldn't leave, he got up and walked to the parking lot outside the compound.

He looked the lot up and down and then he looked again. He meant to ensure that he would be unobserved. When he was certain he was alone, he quickly walked to the bus and in one fluid motion, he was on his back underneath the engine. He lay there a full ten minutes, enjoying the relative cool as well as the excitement of the moment. He reached up and pulled the brake line down. He cut it, using the Gerber Multi-tool all the soldiers carried. He wiped both line halves with his bandanna, even though he knew this was an unnecessary precaution. There was no competent police lab or detective agency out here in a combat zone.

Sliding down out of the way of the leaking hydraulic fluid, he lay under the other end of the bus for a few minutes. Then, he rolled out, and was on his feet heading back to the cans. It was his luck that the trash collectors were emptying the dumpster outside the compound, and as he passed them, he tossed the dirty bandanna into the garbage—which was burned every night.

Opening the door of his own quarters, he looked down the long line of cans and could see the Sergeant Major sitting in the shade just in front of his own. Long felt a swell of pride and a touch of resolve as he took a long satisfying look at the huge belly of the useless man.

Tower Talk

Towers and gates. Duty on towers and gates had gotten tedious. This hated work, supposedly easier because it was deemed less dangerous than patrolling outside the wire, was so boring it was painful. The Guardsmen had been in Iraq for just over a month and had spent all of that time on towers and gates. If assigned to a major base, as these men were, soldiers spend the first month manning the gates and towers that ring the perimeter. This is the typical schedule for National Guardsmen whose full tour of duty is one year.

Tower duty can be grueling, twelve-hour shifts spent standing atop metal towers. The towers are usually covered by sheet metal and surrounded by sandbags. The soldier wears his full body armor and Kevlar helmet, carries his personal weapons and enough food, ammunition, and water for the tour. He's driven to the tower by the Sergeant of the Guard and is posted there, along with another soldier.

The trip from the ground to the tower is a chore in itself. If he's in full battle rattle in the heat, lugging a case of water, another case of food, and a couple of cans of ammunition up the ladder is a cardio workout in itself.

There's normally a crew-served weapon in the tower, either a machine gun or an AT-4 anti-tank weapon, and these weapons have turnover procedures that take a few minutes. The soldiers coming off the tower hand over the weapon and ammo; the soldiers coming on count the rounds, check the gun, and sign the log making themselves responsible for the stuff. In all cases, there is a briefing provided by the soldiers coming off duty. In this, they inform the new guys of the happenings on their shift—enemy contact, civilian activity, radio traffic. This is all noted in the log book they sign and turn over to the new guys.

The turnover is conducted within earshot and under the watchful eye of the Sergeant of the Guard and is complete when the SOG invites the outgoing soldiers into his vehicle and fires up the engine. Within moments, the group of soldiers disappears ahead of a choking cloud of dust and the two soldiers remaining are left choking, too, gasping against the deadly heat and contemplating spending the next twelve hours in each other's company.

On this day, PFC Bennet and Specialist Short were paired. They'd known each other since they first enlisted in the Guard after high school graduation two years before. Bennet came in for the college money and Short signed up out of boredom. Bennet hadn't gotten much education yet, and Short just got more boredom. Neither man had lived the adventure so far. Bennet was overdue for promotion to specialist and wasn't particularly motivated to press the issue. It was all the same to him. In the combat zone, it's easy enough for routine promotions like that to fall between the cracks.

Short liked the rank structure and took it seriously. He saw himself as being in command of this two-man army and he intended to exercise leadership when he had the opportunity. Working this shift with Bennet provided that opportunity. The area inside the walls of the tower was four feet by four feet and much of this was taken up by the ring of sandbags inside the metal frame. The space was designed to be as small as possible so that it would be a small target and also to discourage soldiers from taking extraneous gear with them or from getting too comfortable. Comfortable soldiers are not vigilant soldiers, or so the thinking goes.

When the men were both atop their perch, Bennet immediately made himself busy by moving some sandbags from the top row to the deck below. He arranged them into a small nest, kicking out the lumps as he went along. Annoyed, Short waited till Bennet was entirely satisfied with his creation and had settled down onto his seat.

"What the fuck you think you're doing?"

"Baking in this shithole of an oven—same as you."

"Yeah well bake standing up. You know we are supposed to remain standing, facing thataway," he said, gesturing out towards the desert.

"Give me a break, tough guy. I can see just fine whether I'm sitting or standing." As he said this, Bennet looked out toward the desert and had to crane his neck to peer over the ledge.

"Yeah, looks like you can see perfectly. Now, get on your feet and replace those sandbags."

"You're kidding!"

"Nope."

Bennet stared at Short just long enough to make sure his contempt registered and that Short knew his actions were a decision born of resignation rather than fear, then slowly stood and started picking up the sandbags. Getting no reaction from his lethargic compliance, he sped up and slammed the last two in place, getting some satisfaction from the obnoxious noise that came from the bags hitting the sheet metal. As he straightened up, both men turned to face their ugly desert. Neither spoke. They stayed this way, shoulder to shoulder and less than a foot apart for some time. Neither would speak until the silence was comfortable.

Bennet took the binoculars hanging from a hook directly over his head and began to scan the horizon with them. Once he had the boiling desert in focus, he started the methodical scanning procedure that soldiers are taught, first sweep a large area to get a context for your field of vision, then break it down into sectors and diligently stare at each—one after the other. He quickly forgot his resentment towards Short and surrendered to his instincts, scanning to ensure that if anything was out there, he'd see it before it came within lethal range. He let himself relax a bit when he gained a certain sense of comfort that, at least for now, there'd be no interruption. The desert was empty. He'd have to create his own entertainment.

"A weekend a month and two weeks a year, my ass!"

"And nothing but buckets of money for college and high times from there." Short surprised him by taking the bait.

"I haven't finished a semester of college since I joined the Guard."

"How many did you start?"

"One, last fall."

"How come you didn't finish that?"

"Got the deployment orders in November, then the SRP in December. I had to drop the course."

"One course? Your *semester* was one course?"

"Yeah, they didn't have anything else I wanted to take."

"Nothing but excuses. And you know how that goes. Excuses are like . . . "

"Shut up, Short! Just shut the fuck up!"

"No, I mean it. You only sign up for one course and then drop it. Plenty of guys finished the fall semester. Jones and Tsongas were both at the same school you were. They managed to finish. They made some kind of deal with their professors so that they could make the SRP and get their work in too."

"Well I couldn't do that." Bennet said this with a lot less vigor than his previous comments. He knew Short was right and he didn't feel like allowing him to press the point. He let a bit of time pass and then probed for soft spots.

"Say, how come you don't go to college?"

"Got no use for it; got a wife, got a job. Besides, I had enough school. Don't much like it."

Ah, the wife. Short was extremely vulnerable when it came to the subject of his wife. Bennet thrilled at the mention of this target-rich environment, but he knew he'd have to proceed carefully if he was to get a rise out of Short and avoid becoming himself the target of Short's anxiety.

Looking for an opening, Bennet found it in the graffiti that adorned every spare inch of wood and steel in the tower. On the crossbar that supported the roof, just above eye level, someone had scribbled, "When home on leave, call Annie for a good time. She's at Tink's every night."

Tink's was the name of the local pick-up bar in Scranton where the platoon drilled. Annie was the name of Short's wife and nothing, absolutely nothing, could shake his confidence in his marriage more than her going to Tink's. She'd occasionally stop there after work with her friends and when Short found out, he'd get damn-near crazy. Many a soldier, knowing how possessive of his wife Short was, found ways to counter Short's occasional high-speed arrogance by taking a shot at his wife. It always worked and it never got old.

The only other soldiers who used this tower were the rest of the guys in their platoon. It was almost a certainty that the comment about Annie was written for Short's benefit by one of the many soldiers who had been corrected by Short, or punished by Short, or reported by Short. Bennet proceeded slowly and feigned sad resignation as he muttered, "I wonder who the blue falcon is."

"What blue falcon?" replied Short, using the stage term for *BF* or "buddy-fucker." Interested and unaware, Short had taken the bait.

"The asshole who wrote *that* about Annie." Bennet gestured toward the graffiti, the comment that Short hadn't seen until now.

Short read the comment and his eyes widened as his

jaw clenched. "The bastards! The muthafuckin' bastards!" Bennet had him. The rest of the shift would be a blast.

"Who do you think might have done it?" asked Bennet, turning his head away from Short in order to hide his smirk.

"I bet it was Ski. That asshole! Wait till I get a hold of him!"

"Oh, he just did it to get a rise out of you." Bennet could play the pal. He could be the voice of reason and try to talk Short down all night, but it wouldn't work. Short was just that crazy when it came to his new bride, the girl he married when he was home for leave just before flying to Iraq.

"Bullshit! He's been trying to get my wife for years. He knew her before I did."

Of course Bennet knew this. Short would get so irrational when it came to his wife that he'd forget he told everyone everything a dozen times before. In this particular story, Ski had indeed met Mrs. Bennet before Bennet had. They had both frequented Tink's in the years after high school. Ski had never dated her, though he'd certainly tried. They were never friends and certainly they were never lovers, but they were acquaintances and the association of Ski and Short in the deployed platoon made that acquaintance somewhat more important. Ski, for whom being an instigator of conflict and pain had become a vocation, used every opportunity he could to get under Short's skin. When he had no other creative ideas, he'd play the Annie card. It never failed.

Short smoldered, drank water, fidgeted with the binoculars, and grunted and growled for an hour. Other than that, he said nothing. It became clear that Bennet had truly outdone himself when Short got on the radio to the BDOC to ask for the Sergeant of the Guard.

The Sergeant of the Guard was almost always found at the BDOC when he wasn't out checking on the sentries, so he came to the radio right away.

"Tower Twelve. S-O-G. Send it."

"Request short relief for one."

"Somebody sick?"

"No, family emergency."

"Who?"

"Me."

Sergeant Lansbury knew this could mean only one thing. Short needed to call his wife. It was not possible for a family emergency to develop in the few hours since Short had been posted, and if there were, there was no way that Short could have been notified of it.

Short was a psychotic control freak when it came to his wife. He called her at least once a day and was in contact with her using AOL's Instant Messaging whenever he was near a computer. He'd claim he was deeply in love and that he couldn't stand to be out of contact with her, but everyone knew that his "love" was a futile and pathetic need to control her movements. From a desert, eight thousand miles away from her, he'd make sure she was at home, sitting on the couch with her mother.

"What's the emergency?"

"I have to call my wife."

"No you don't. Stay right there."

"No, really. She might be in trouble. I think she might

be in a car accident."

"That's a negative, Specialist. Call her when you get off shift. That's final." Lansbury slammed the radio handset into the receiver. Disgusted, he announced to the room, "Short is such a tool." With that, he stormed over to his desk.

On Short's end, he stood with his hand clenching the handset and said to no one in particular, "Lansbury hates me."

"No, Lansbury doesn't hate you." Bennet paused. "Ski hates you though."

"Yeah, fucking Ski. Wait till I get a hold of him."

Bennet stood with his back turned to Short. He silently scanned the horizon and tried not to think about all of this. If he couldn't drive it from his mind, he'd start laughing, absolutely gleeful at his victory over the uptight Short. Then, God only knows what would happen in the tower. Short was truly crazy when it came to Annie. In any case, Bennet was no longer bored. Mission accomplished as far as that went, but he'd have to warn Ski when they got back to the rear tonight, before Short got to him.

Yes, Short was truly crazy when it came to Annie— crazy enough to talk to Bennet about it. Dropping his guard, he let Bennet see the pain on his face and he asked, "You don't think she'd cheat on me, do you?"

"I don't know. What I *do* know is that you can't do jack shit about it." Bennet was going to play this for all it was worth, but he would have to wade very slowly into this—seeing how far he could press Short and stopping just short of the meltdown he knew Short was capable of.

Grappling
Hook

Seeing he was still safe, "You should really let go of this. Leave her alone."

"But, but I *love* her!"

"Love?" Bennet had paid some attention in his college psychology course. "This isn't love. It's control. You are trying to control her. What can you possibly talk about for *hours—every* day?"

Short jumped up and charged Bennet. In little more than a step he was on him, leaning over him and into him, screaming, "I tell her just how much I love her! And I keep telling her! I never get tired of telling her! And she loves to hear it!"

Bennet cooed, "Sure, I know you do and I am sure she loves you, too." It was time to give this fish a little line. "I just hate to see you make yourself so crazy. Ski was just trying to make you crazy." Bennet got off the skyline and put the absent Ski there.

"Yeah, right. Fucking Ski. Asshole."

"Yeah, he can be such an asshole sometimes."

Short was so anxious, he couldn't stand still. There was no place to pace in the tiny tower so he smoked and drank water, then smoked some more. He'd scan the horizon with the binoculars and, finding nothing, he'd slam the binoculars down on the sandbags, guzzle some more water, and light another cigarette. After a half hour, he surrendered to temptation and took a notebook from his pack. He sat on the sandbags and began to write his wife a letter.

Bennet was beginning to regret starting all of this.

It was so much fun to start Short up but he had no way
of shutting him down. Short was getting crazier cooped
up in the tower and he'd abandoned his own devotion to
the rules and was writing yet another love letter. Bennet
wasn't tempted to read the letter that was being written
right in front of him. He was sure it would disgust him.

Short wrote for an hour. He wrote page after page,
and Bennet was beginning to develop a bit of curiosity
about what he could possibly be saying in the letter. Of
course, he expected the usual declarations of undying love
and the copious superlatives used to describe his beloved
Annie. But by now Short had over five pages covered on
both sides.

Bennet knew that Short was minimally literate. This
was another reason for the tension between these two
men. Bennet thought Short was just plain ignorant. It
wasn't just a matter of Short's being uneducated, but of
his close-minded, limited world view. So Bennet felt that
Short deserved every ounce of pain that he, Bennet, could
dish out.

Short seemed to have gotten the peace he was looking
for, and his face was somewhat relaxed as he folded the
five pieces of paper and stuffed them in a different pocket
of his pack. He stood up, picked up the binoculars, and
caught up on his horizon scanning. Bennet wasn't going
to let the opportunity to take a break slide and he settled
down on the sandbags to rest awhile. Short started to
rear up to confront this violation—simultaneously realizing that he had just finished breaking this rule himself.
The whole breakdown about Annie had made him forget
his discipline, and Bennet was going to take advantage of

it. Rather than open himself up to some philosophical discussion about hypocrisy that he suspected he'd lose anyway, Short said nothing about Bennet dogging it.

It took some time for him to realize what he was seeing as he scanned the horizon. About five miles out in the distance, just off to the right, the scenery was slowly changing. There was a cloud of dust slowly growing bigger and getting closer. The dust itself camouflaged its own source and the soldier in Short came alive again. All six senses kicked into ultra-sensitive mode. Without taking his eyes off the desert, he tapped Bennet's leg with his foot.

"We got something out there. Get on the radio."

"Whadayagot?" mumbled Bennet as he reached for the radio and looked out into no-man's land. Short was a good soldier when he wasn't insane about his wife. So was Bennet, and he was talking into the radio handset just as his eyes adjusted and could see the growing dust cloud at the end of the boiling desert.

Into the radio, "S-O-G, Tower Twelve. S-O-G."

"Tower Twelve, S-O-G. Send it."

"Be advised we have unidentified activity right out in front of us, about five miles."

"What do you see?"

"Just a dust cloud, a few livestock or a few vehicles. Can't tell."

"Wait one. We have eyes in the sky. Hang tight."

The two Marine Cobra gunships came from the same base, just behind Bennet and Short. They shot past the tower and sped out toward the threat, each ship darting and weaving as they turned into tiny dots in the sky. Bennet loaded the ammo belt into the machine gun and slammed the cover down. Until he found out the exact nature of the threat, he knew it was prudent to be prepared in the event it was some bad guys. Of course, with two Marine Cobras between the dust and themselves, there was very little likelihood that any threat would reach them alive. Those jarheads in the Cobras don't miss, ever.

The silence was broken by the obnoxious sound from the radio.

"Tower Twelve, S-O-G. Tower Twelve."

"S-O-G, Tower Twelve. Send it."

"The eyes in the sky identify friendlies. There are two Humvees, Army. Pilot says he flew low and slow, identified U.S. soldiers in each. Unable to establish radio contact. Reason uncertain."

"Roger that. Will identify when they arrive. Choppers are hovering overhead, leading them in."

At twenty kilometers per hour, about as fast as a Humvee can manage crossing the treacherous open desert, the two vehicles would arrive in ten minutes. The time passed slowly as Short and Bennet each trained their eyes on the activity slowly getting closer. When the Humvees were within a thousand meters, the Cobras darted ahead of them, passed over the tower again and took up hovering positions to the rear. From there, they would sit and watch.

The Humvees blinked their headlights on and off as they settled outside the gate. The passenger of the front vehicle got out and ran toward the tower. As he got closer, the soldiers could see he was a staff sergeant, probably the unit's leader. He looked dirty, hang-dogged, and old.

"We've got a wounded man here. We need a medic. We lost our radios and couldn't call Medevac."

Short cupped both hands to his mouth, "You got some soldiers to open the gate?"

The Staff Sergeant didn't bother to answer as he turned to his vehicles and waved for some help. Immediately, there were two younger soldiers running from the vehicles, past the Staff Sergeant and to the gate. The gate was a long pole on a hinge. It was covered with coils of barbed wire. It wasn't particularly heavy but it was unwieldy, and the soldiers had to be careful not to get tangled in the mess.

They moved the gate, jumped back into their vehicles and rode through the opening, stopping just under the tower. The driver was closest to the tower so he leaned out and yelled to Short and Bennet, "We're going straight to the infirmary. Call and tell them we're on our way."

With that, they moved out onto the hard road and headed for the infirmary. Short had no direct frequency to the hospital, so he called in the situation to the BDOC. There was immediate confusion, first in identifying the soldiers, then in trying to figure out who was wounded and how bad. Regardless of what the answers to those questions were, the one question that would have a lot of important people concerned was one of leadership.

Why hadn't they called Medevac? Why didn't their radios work? Why weren't there at least *two* means of communication? (Other choices were GPS, Blue Force Tracker, or walkie-talkies, among others.) Soldiers are never supposed to be out of contact, and they are certainly never supposed to be without medical care.

Short turned it all over to the voices at the BDOC while Bennet climbed down from the tower, re-secured the gate, and climbed back up. The excitement was over as quickly as it had started, and the two soldiers were left with only the dust in their hair, teeth, eyes, and ears that any fast movements in this country would cause.

Later on in the shift, when the setting sun caused the thermometer to head down toward double digits, the BDOC called to update the sentries on the status of the wounded man. It turns out the Humvee was hit by an IED. It was a near miss in that the explosion happened after the Humvee passed, later than was intended. The vehicle behind the target took shrapnel through the windshield, hitting the radio and the shoulder of the driver. The driver was recovering; he'd be fine.

The troop leader however was not so fine. He was relieved of his position and was awaiting disciplinary action. His failure to have enough communication options nearly resulted in the very thing the double-means policy was supposed to prevent. The first contact destroyed the radio and wounded a man. He was unable to call for assistance or Medevac. He was unable to call for air support or artillery. Were these only hypotheses, the brass might have been able to overlook it as a learning experience, but a real soldier had a real wound. The Sergeant would answer for it.

"I'd hate to be that sergeant," mumbled Bennet.

"Court-martial."

"Too bad."

"Not 'too bad.' He was not following the rules. He wasn't looking out for his soldiers. And by the way, I wouldn't worry about your being a sergeant. No one is nutty enough to make you a sergeant. "

"Yeah, I guess," Bennet mused.

"No guess about it! An NCO needs to look out for his soldiers."

"Like *you?* An NCO like *you?*"

Short let that go. He knew Bennet was going to take the opportunity to chastise him for writing the letter when he should have been scanning. When Bennet saw this, he smelled blood and pursued.

"Yeah, you're a big deal when you get to tell others what to do. It's a different story when *you* don't like a rule. You're a real individual, you are, a regular free-thinker."

"Shut up, Bennet. Scan the horizon. We still got a war on out there."

"Yeah, we got a war on. And here we sit, on top of it but not in it."

"Once again, for the douche-bags in the cheap seats . . . Shut up, Bennet."

They passed the rest of the shift in silence, both of them thrilled to see the SOG's Humvee coming down the road toward the tower. It ground to a halt below them, and the predictable cloud of dust predictably choked them all. The SOG was the new SOG for the new shift. The sentries were the same two men *they* had relieved twelve hours before. They all knew the procedures by heart and barely spoke as they sleepwalked through them.

Bennet and Short turned over the gun. The new guys checked it out and counted the rounds. They turned over the log and the new guys asked about unusual events. Bennet told them about the wounded man in the wounded Humvee. "Probably get a court-martial," he stated authoritatively as he climbed down the ladder.

"Court-martial? Ya' think? No shit, Genius."

Bennet and Short were strangers once they found themselves in the company of others. They rode back to the living area in silence, and they and their gear were poured out in front of their adjoining hooches. Bennet opened his door and carried his rifle and armor inside. He put a pot of coffee on and went back outside to pick up his pack.

He got out there just in time to see Short heading down the road, walking as fast as he could. It was too hot to run, so, like many soldiers, he adopted the power walk. Short made it look particularly silly, like an old mall walker with a new hip. He was wearing PT gear, carrying a water bottle and a phone card. The phone center was in a large trailer a mile down the desert road.

Walking alone anywhere in the Iraqi theater was strictly forbidden, but Short needed to talk to his wife and *that* was *that*. He'd make sure she was right where she was supposed to be, and then he'd get back and start working on the correspondence courses he needed in order to get that promotion to sergeant.

The Irisher

The American Army has had a distinctly Irish flavor from the start. General Washington loved his Irish troops and they loved him as well, making him an honorary member of the Friendly Sons of Saint Patrick. That's as far as they allowed the General to go however, his membership in the Ancient Order of Hibernians was out of the question, what with him being the most conspicuous Mason in America and them being the most strident Papists. To the Irish, though, anyone who was shooting redcoats was a true friend of Erin.

The Irish formed the bulk of the Grand Army of the Republic, with legendary places at Fredericksburg and Chancellorsville—and at Gettysburg, where the Irish Brigade won the day and presided over the high-water mark of the Confederacy. It has been said that while Lee and Grant were in the parlor at Appomattox working out the details of the South's surrender, a soldier of the Confederacy, unable to endure the smugness of his counterparts in the Union ranks any longer, changed the atmosphere with a charge both sides could live with. "The only reason you licked us is because you had all the Irishers." The Irish in the Union ranks cheered the compliment and befriended the rebels, offering the starving farm boys their rations as well as their hands.

The Irishers filled the ranks of the Army during the Indian Wars so much that the Irish ballad "Gary Owen" became the unofficial anthem of the U.S. Cavalry. It was the preferred song of the simple cavalryman, most often an Irisher. It was being played by the men of Custer's Seventh Cavalry as they cantered to the Little Big Horn. Their tragic massacre at the hands of overwhelming numbers of Sioux warriors was not the first time that the Irish showed more mettle than brains.

The Irish were the largest single group in the American Expeditionary Force when it shipped "over there" to make the world safe for democracy. The names found on the rolls of that WWI army are repeated again and again on the rolls of troops who headed out again in World War II, Korea, and Viet Nam. The story of the American Army is a story of the Irish and that story was still being told in the twenty-first century as commercial jets were landing in Kuwait to debark the soldiers of Operation Enduring Freedom.

Peter Kelly was an old Irish story himself. He immigrated to New York in 2000, when he was 21. He was looking for American gold and thought he had found it along with the thousands of other Irishmen employed in New York City's lucrative construction trades. His uncle, who'd been in America for twenty years, invited him to stay at his home on Long Island while Peter politicked his way toward a coveted union card. The work was good, the money great, and the New York City life was pure Eden for a young man, especially a young man with humor and charm.

Like his ancestors, he found no conflict when his patriotism for America matched his love of Ireland. The Irish heart has room enough for the two biggest countries on the planet. It was a natural combination after all, to be Irish and American too. After the events of 9-11, he was one of the thousands who raced to lower Manhattan to offer assistance. The uniformed police and firemen, themselves predominantly Irish, tried to stop them, concerned about the safety and chaos of so much humanity in the midst of so much confusion. This army, armed with the compassion of the American soul, was an overwhelming force as well. Peter found some work handing out bottled water to the rescue workers and kept at that for the better part of three days. During that time, in-between the explosions of grief and the grinding labor, he came to love America even more, but more than that, he became invested in her. The bottomless well of Yankee optimism, the unassailable spirit of hope, the unqualified charity that marked the actions of these New Yorkers became his inspiration for further action.

Handing out bottled water wouldn't be enough. The cops and firemen had long processes to join their ranks, so the impatience of the youth quickly rejected those avenues. By the end of September, Peter Kelly had joined the long line at the recruiting station in Times Square. Giving each service a cursory look, he quickly decided that the Army would provide his quickest path to martial glory.

So, after a background investigation, a written exam, and a physical, he was cleared for enlistment in the Army. One didn't need to be a citizen to enlist. The road to citizenship had become a grail-like quest for Peter and his enlisting would put the process he'd already begun on hold until his return. A successful hitch in the Army, however, would move him to the front of the line for the rare and coveted spots. The recruiter told him that, in fact, his citizenship would be all but guaranteed on his honorable discharge, maybe even earlier.

He was just as excited at the thought of his attaining American citizenship as he was by his enlisting. He made the short subway trip to McCann's Bar at Trinity Place in lower Manhattan, to find his friends. He did this often enough at the end of the day, but today he was headed there for a celebration, not to wind down as he had done at the close of the long hard days before. There, within sight of 9-11's ground zero, and with the Wolfe Tones playing on the bar's jukebox, he stood the entire establishment to a round of Guinness.

McCann's at Trinity Place was much like the dozen other bars in the city that were also named McCann's. The name and the Irish decor attracted the Irish—those newly arrived and those whose families had been here for generations. The call to return home that lives in the hearts of all the children of the Gaelic Diaspora can sometimes be appeased, though never satisfied by a visit to a place like McCann's, a bit of the old sod right there on their way home from work.

The patrons who tasted Ireland from a McCann's pint as Peter's guests were instructed that tribute would be required. Peter announced that each one was expected to greet him as an American, to shake his hand and call him a Yank. And this they did, some with shouts from their booths and stools. Other drinkers formed a line that ended at Peter's barstool. Each well-wisher tried to outdo the ones who had gone before him—in enthusiasm, volume, or creativity.

"Welcome to America, General!" said a stockbroker, offering a deep bow.

"Good evening, Mr. American!" barked the construction worker while coming to attention and saluting.

"Halo there, Yank!" came from another immigrant, here twenty-five years in the construction trades and at McCann's most every night during those years.

"Congratulations and Godspeed, Son," said the aging window washer. He whispered this like a prayer rather than shouting a cheer. He was a cautious and quiet man who had come to this city to make his way in the world when he was about Peter's age. Grateful every day for America and the life it had given him, he often thought that he would never want to go back in time and do it again. America could fatten your belly, but it could also break your back. It had been so damned hard. Peter was choosing a path that could be even harder, that of achieving citizenship through a hitch in the Army.

Peter accepted the greetings and the best wishes, the smiles, kisses, and hugs. He also accepted every drink bought for him. He never put his hand in his pocket again after that first round and it was a good thing he had called his own uncle to tell him the good news about his enlistment and to invite him to the celebration at McCann's. When his uncle arrived, he found Peter well into his cups, holding court before a dozen subjects. His back was turned to the bar, and behind him was a crowd of full glasses waiting for his attention. He split his attention between these two groups until his uncle had to help him to his car for the ride out to Long Island.

Peter was on his way to Fort Sill for his ten weeks of basic training within a few days. He took easily to the soldier's life, liked the uniforms and drill, the military courtesies and martial music. And of course, he got along with everyone. Then he was off to Fort Sam Houston, outside San Antonio, Texas for his specialty school. He had chosen to become an Army medic and the rigorous sixteen-week school was commonly called "ninety-one whiskey" school, after its designation code *91W*.

He had not chosen this specialty; it had chosen him. During his three days at ground zero, he had come to admire all the rescue workers, but he was particularly impressed with the EMTs and other medical personnel. He was awestruck at their courage and compassion. Further, he thrilled when they were able to save a life or resuscitate the dying. For them, this was just part of the job. From Peter's perspective, these men and women were agents of God, working His miracles.

He thought it would be a privilege to be so graced as to have a hand in saving another's life. When the Army recruiter told him that his test scores were high enough to qualify for 91W School and that there was a great need for medics, all other options disappeared. Peter would be an Army medic. He graduated from this competitive school near the top of his class and was therefore allowed to choose his reporting unit. He chose an infantry company because he wanted to be close to the action and the company he chose was headed for Operation Enduring Freedom in Iraq.

He was attached to an infantry platoon and threw himself into his work. As the platoon medic, he was not required to take part in the infantry training. He was to be at the training to render medical aid if necessary. No one would have complained if he simply sat in his ambulance, monitoring the radio or reading a magazine as so many medics did. Peter chose instead to train with the men he would be supporting. When they ran, he ran. When they fired their weapons, he drew a weapon and fired with them. He wanted to know them, wanted to know what it was like for them. And of course, this behavior got the attention and approval of all the men. Peter was part of the team and he became an integral part of the social life of the team as well. He was not far from the center of any party and he had a natural ability to attract people to him. He liked a good laugh and he liked a good story.

And he could *tell* a good story anytime, anywhere. Peter could be counted on to have just the right anecdote or quip to compliment any situation. He could start a fight or end one with a word. Like the Gaelic storytellers from centuries before, from whom he was descended, he took storytelling seriously. An Irish storyteller is an entertainer yes, but he is also a centerpiece of Hibernian heritage.

The storyteller was often the only link to the past that the Irish had in the days when learning, publishing, and even large gatherings were all prohibited by the English crown. The storyteller was a wanderer who kept the Irish culture alive by passing it out in bits and pieces all over the island. Stories were decidedly not testimony; facts would not get in the way if proper embellishment and exaggeration made the story more fun, made the point more acutely, or told the truth more fully. A story was a story—nothing and everything all at once.

The men learned that it didn't take much to get Peter going, and they invited him with them whenever they headed for the bars of Hattiesville, the "town" outside the gates of Camp Shelby, Mississippi. Not that it had to be an official party, per se. A group of soldiers relaxing around a small campfire, smoking and drinking the tasteless Army coffee provided in the field, formed an adequate forum for him as well. Peter Kelly could entertain, his cheerful stories and pithy quips filling in the spaces normally filled by DVDs, video games, MP3 players, and the other odd assorted electronic toys from the endless inventory of passive entertainment that this generation of Americans had become accustomed to.

It was at one of these campfires, towards the end of the train-up, that the men received the final word about the coming trip to Iraq. They were sitting in the dirt, smoking and joking, when the Lieutenant approached them, with an excitement and energy unusual for the last night of a field exercise.

"Hey, guys. The Captain just gave me the word. We are done here in two weeks. Then it's ten days home, then back here for five days to pack for the trip. We leave about the first of the month. We won't know the exact day till it's here. OpSec."

OpSec, or *Operation Security* meant secrecy. Troop movements of any kind fell under this veil. Troops were never told the details of a journey until the day arrived for it. That way they couldn't tell anyone else; it wouldn't find its way to the papers, etc. Terrorists can read papers too, and the certain news that a planeful of troops was taking off at an exact time from a specific location would be pure gold to a Jihadist with a bomb.

"That means we passed the training, L-T? Did they like us?" In the beginning, there was a regular threat of the soldiers not passing training. This threat became a toothless joke however, when the logical consequence of their not passing was their not deploying to the combat zone. After a few short weeks of Army insanity and absence from loved ones, the threat of being sent home a "failure" wasn't much of a threat. Some of the soldiers were patriots and eager volunteers like Peter, but many of the Guardsmen were yanked from schools and jobs and homes. They were doing a necessary duty, not pursuing an adventure.

"Of course we passed. And of course they didn't like us. We could've done half as well and they still would have passed us and we could've performed twice as well and they'd still call us 'Weekend Warriors' with that shit-eating sneer they get."

"Don't you just love it? When some fat piece of shit, armed with a keyboard, looks down on us 'cause we ain't *regular* Army?"

"Yeah, well stay away from them. All you guys. They're nothing but trouble to you and we are out of here and away from them in two weeks. I have had my fill of digging you guys out of trouble for one clash or another with these regular Army guys. Just leave them alone and they won't leave their desks to come looking for you. Their asses just wouldn't look natural without a desk chair at-

tached to them. Now *please* stay out of trouble till we're
out of here. It's *only* two more weeks."

They offered their Platoon Leader some of their coffee and he politely declined and walked away, back toward his peers. The other platoon leaders were gathered,
along with their company commander, around a fire of
their own, at another corner of the camp. This offer of
coffee was another ritual. They always offered; he rarely
accepted. The offer was expected—as was the rejection.
It was the way things were. They offered fraternity, but
he couldn't fraternize. The offer, as well as its not being
accepted, were both signs of respect and approval. In this
world, this made sense.

The platoon headed home for ten days leave, and each
man tried to fill each moment with high-energy activity.
The coveted time in familiar places with loved ones was
so valuable, but it wasn't enough to cover the quiet dread
of the coming sadness that a year's leaving would bring.
The soldiers and their families counted each minute as
they lived them to the fullest, trying not to think about
the inevitable suffering to come. For the second time in
six months, the soldiers had their tearful goodbyes at air-
ports and lifted off into danger. They were back together
and it seemed as though they'd never been apart.

The trip to Kuwait took two days. They landed on
an airstrip in the middle of the desert and waited there
for the buses. They'd be bussed to Camp Buehring in
Idairi, Kuwait as soon as the buses arrived, the time
uncertain. Alongside the airstrip were boxes of bottled
water, MREs and portable toilets. The toilets were filled
to the brim and simply unusable. The men walked into

the desert dust cloud for fifty feet or so and just urinated there, anywhere.

There would be a short stay in Kuwait for the purpose of getting the equipment issued and acclimating the troops to the incredible heat of the desert. The soldiers couldn't help but get acclimated. After all, what choice did they have? Much of the time in Kuwait was downtime though; the anticipated equipment issue proved to be more rumor than fact. The troops would go to combat with the equipment they trained with at Shelby, light armor, cannibalized engines, and outdated technology.

They touched down in Kuwait at about midnight and were herded into a huge tent, desert tan with plywood floors. At the entrance of the tent were boxes of MREs and bottles of water. The soldiers were told to take an MRE and two bottles of water and find a seat. The water and food tables bottle-necked at their ends and there, just before opening up into the general seating area, was a time clock of sorts.

The soldiers were instructed to punch their ID cards into the time clock—to mark the moment they entered the combat zone. The Finance Officer posted there was a pleasant looking middle-aged woman who greeted each man with a smile as she ensured his proper punching in, "Welcome to the War, Soldier."

"Thank you, Ma'am."

"You're welcome, Soldier."

"Doesn't seem like much of a war so far, Ma'am."

"That'll change. Be safe, Sergeant."

"Nice place you got here, Ma'am."

"Well thank you, we do our best."

"Is there room service, Ma'am? I don't much care for MREs."

"There's a chow hall open twenty-four hours. You'll get that information at the briefing."

"Will I get my own camel, Ma'am?"

"Sure, but you have to catch one yourself."

"Are you married, Ma'am?"

"Yes, to a Colonel. Want to meet him?"

"No, thank you, Ma'am."

They were dirty and tired but high-strung as well. The Major was entirely tolerant of the wise guys and enjoyed the energy and humor. She'd heard each of these original funny lines a dozen times before and was inclined to let each soldier have his joke, joining him when it wasn't too bad, drawing limits when it was. She understood that the humor was the soldiers' way of masking their fear and insecurity.

She was, no doubt about it, a mom. Somewhere in America there was a home in which she also belonged and in that home lived teenagers who belonged there as well. In another time, she'd be telling them to wipe their feet at the door and wash their hands for dinner with the same easy authority with which she ensured that each of these boys punched the clock and got his water and food. Sometimes, a mom is just what a soldier needs and, in this war, America was managing to provide that, too.

Peter found a seat along the dust-covered benches, with the troopers he'd be assigned to, the 2nd Section of the Cavalry Scouts. He joined them in tearing into the MREs and guzzling the bottled water while they waited for the rest of the company to find seats. Twenty minutes or so passed by before the Major, the woman from Finance, walked between the rows and stood at the plywood podium at the front of the tent. Her rank and presence marked the importance of the moment and the soldiers quickly grew quiet and gave her their attention. No more ceremony was required than her simply walking to the front of the room.

"Good evening, Soldiers."

"GOOD EVENING, MA'AM!"

"Welcome to Kuwait. I know you're exhausted from your trip and anxious to get settled in. We keep you only as long as is necessary. Has everybody punched in?" She scanned the room methodically to make sure she was heard and that there were no soldiers who hadn't checked in.

"By punching that clock, you have entered the hostile fire zone. This starts the clock on your one-year combat tour and, just as importantly, begins your combat pay and ends your federal income tax paying. When you get your first paycheck, please make sure these changes have taken effect. The very least you deserve is accurate pay."

"You will be here in Kuwait for about ten days. This isn't Club Med, but we've tried to provide some recreational things for you to do here. Each of you will be given a packet containing a map of the base, along with a list of all the facilities and the times they are available."

"Water! Proper hydration is critical. It is a fact that we have more heat casualties than we have soldiers wounded from enemy action. The heat here, as well as up north, can kill you. Get used to constantly drinking water. The good news is that we provide it for you, everywhere. Outside of your tents, there is a pallet of boxed bottled water. It is *always* there. In addition to this, there are pallets of bottled water scattered everywhere around this base. We put pallets of water everyplace we can think of. There is no excuse for your not having a bottle of water in your hand at all times. *Please drink water.*"

"And, by the way, thank you for serving. We take great pride in our mission of providing you with all that we can because we take great pride in you. Please stay safe." With that, she scanned the room to meet as many sets of eyes as she could. Major Mom loved these guys and they acknowledged that as best they could, by rising as she left the room—walking between them on her way out the back flap, through the dozens of *Thank you, Ma'ams* and *Good night, Ma'ams.*

"Three-sixty-four and a wake-up!" she yelled over her shoulder on the way through the tent flap, getting the clock started on the daily countdown till the end of their war. For the next year, each soldier would always know how many "days and a wake-up" were left till he went home.

On her way out, she was passed by the next speaker, striding to the front. He was a British sergeant, and he was tasked with teaching the troops the basics, the things they needed to know immediately. He covered friendly fire (how to avoid it) and coalition troops (how to recognize and get along with them). Most of the troops thought the Brit was hysterical; Peter didn't; he'd had his fill of these fellows who were so full of themselves years before in Ireland.

The Brit had a heavy cockney accent and was a most

confident fellow. He'd had thirteen years in the infantry, served in Kosovo, Bosnia, Northern Ireland and this was his second tour here. He was most politically incorrect, which all but Peter found surprising, everyone else's having thought the Brits were farther down the "social progress" lane. He advised the sensitive in his audience that he would talk like a soldier because that's what he was—and that they ought to be able to handle it if they thought themselves able to be soldiers. So he was salty as hell.

"*I* speak fucking English. *You* speak fucking English. *I* don't have an accent. *You* do. *I'm* the only one here was *born* in fucking England, so I'll hear no nonsense about my fucking accent. Thank you kindly."

He had slides showing the other coalition forces they were likely to encounter and he told them various idiosyncrasies of these forces that were useful to know, like which force viewed a muzzle in the air as non-threatening (Danes) and which viewed a muzzle facing the ground as non-threatening (Americans). He showed us their uniforms and told us which were likely to be so cavalier regarding uniform that we might be inclined to mistake them for someone else. (Uniforms have a real purpose.)

He put up a picture of the Japanese soldiers standing by one of their armored vehicles. Along the side of the vehicle was draped a large white flag with the red-ball sun in the center. "The Japanese are here to give the Hajjis target practice, as you can see."

He ran down the list of all the countries of the coalition that were represented and at the end said, "Know who's *not* here?" "The fucking French, *that's* who!"

The Brit strode down the aisle and out the back flap just as the Major had done. Peter's company's First Sergeant replaced the Brit at the podium up front. He told the men their quarters were not far from the tent where they were now sitting, that they'd be walking to them, and that they needed to form up and march—as there was zero visibility outside, what with the darkness and the dust.

"So, get out and form up outside, on the double," he said, pointing towards the back flap of the tent. Within a few minutes, the entire company was assembled, each man in his familiar place. They marched through the dust, unable to see where they were going, or even to see more than the three or four men immediately around each of them. The quarter mile seemed much longer as the exhausted men endured the complicated struggle of marching to cadence and carrying a hundred pounds in the desert heat, completely blind.

They lived in *festents*, white vinyl tents about half the size of a football field. Peter's entire company, with all their gear and equipment, had to fit in one tent. They had to set up their aluminum cots immediately, the cot being the means by which each man would claim some territory. The din from two hundred men aggressively banging the aluminum poles together and flinging the completed cots in all directions was deafening. Peter managed to get his assembled and on a piece of ground near his squad in one of the four corners. Corners were prime real estate, the tent walls providing limited privacy—in two directions, at least.

The ground under the cots was retail-grade outdoor

carpet laid on top of the desert sand. It had been pounded down and compressed by the thousands of troops who'd passed through during the previous three years so that it had a certain firmness, but there was no mistaking that there was only a quarter inch of bright green carpet between the cot and the sandbox. In order to make the cots level, soldiers would bang on or press in the higher ends, often jumping up and down on the cot itself. This just punched holes in the carpet and the legs pushed on down into the sand.

The tents were white, in order to reflect the sun's rays, but this did nothing to assuage the body heat from the two hundred men sweating inside. The word was quickly passed that the uniform of the day was PT gear and everyone was out of the heavy utilities and boots and into the nylon shorts, cotton T-shirts, and running shoes that was the Army PT uniform. Gone were the badges of rank and specialty as the mass of individuals became truly uniform. From the newest private to the Colonel, each man was identified only by the five-inch-high letters across his chest, ARMY. Thank God that those who chose the uniform had made that clear, as if there were any way to forget who they were, where they were and who owned them. Thanks.

By the time all the cots were laid out, they took up the entire tent, six rows of cots, laid side by side, from one end of the tent to the other. There was only room for a few feet between each cot and each row was separated by two or three yards. The soldiers had to stack most of their gear under their cots and there'd still be a need to stack a duffel bag or footlocker at the end of most cots.

These crowded the aisles in between so that the two or three yards shrunk to two or three feet.

Peter and his fellow medics had additional gear—footlockers and crates of medical equipment. Not knowing exactly what they would need, the medics grabbed all they could requisition or steal while at Shelby. The result was tons of boxes, bags, and crates. There were boxes of patches, pumps, and pills. There were bags of bottles, bandages, and band-aids. Many of the soldiers were already gone from the tent before the medics were done unloading their gear, so they'd find on their return less room than they'd had when they left. The medics had to compress most of the rows of cots as they made room for their gear.

When Peter and his fellow medics were done, they went off to do their own exploring. The word had been passed that the time spent here at Kuwait would include a lot of downtime and that there were recreational facilities for their enjoyment. The Army had more urgent things to do than to turn the Kuwaiti desert into a resort, so the recreational facilities were a bit sparse.

At the center of the tent city that was Camp Buehring could be found the common area. There were a number of outdoor facilities, and using them at this time of year was anything but recreational. The wind, dust, and heat made using the volleyball and basketball courts most unpleasant, so they stood dormant. The wind kept knocking the volleyball net down, and the basketball backboards shook and waved in the constant wind. Both courts were covered in the fine grit brought by the wind.

There was an outside pavilion of sorts—a steel frame and plywood roof with a dozen picnic tables underneath. Peter and his friends weaved their way through the tables and headed for the PX, a trailer located at the end of the square. The trailer had doors on both ends, one for going in and one for going out. There were two aisles between two double rows of goods, and these aisles were full of soldiers, sailors, airmen, and marines, each one wearing the PT gear of his service. The plywood shelves on either side were stocked with the basics. There were cigarettes, cigars, and chew. There was candy, gum, chips, and pretzels. There were plenty of bags of beef jerky and boxes of Slim Jims.

There was a section for gear that was most in demand but not issued. There were things like bandannas and goggles. There were pens that would write in the dirt and watches that wouldn't allow the dust in the works. There was a healthy section for socks and underwear as these things normally wore out faster than the Army could supply them. There were magazines and books. Nothing intellectual and nothing pornographic, just the great grey mass of mind muddle in between. The kind of stuff a soldier could buy in the PX was normally not the kind of thing he'd consider bothering himself with in any other time or place.

After a few weeks of boredom with life in a war zone, Peter would find himself flipping through the periodicals about video games, sports, and popular culture, but at this point, with the real world fresh on his mind, he couldn't generate any real interest in them. The same was true for the paperbacks. Nothing on the bestseller list was in this PX, but the shelves were stocked with war books (of all things) and fantasy adventure novels, mostly written at a junior-high-school level. Peter made a mental note to have his friends back home, who'd volunteered to send anything and everything he might want, to mail their Time Magazines and National Geographics.

There were some CDs and DVDs. Peter and his team would discover that most soldiers had laptops. They stored and listened to thousands of songs. They watched movies; any movie at all would find a home, a soldier who was willing to sit through it. They followed most popular TV series from home, though usually a season later. They followed "The Sopranos," "CSI," and "24" and they shared everything. There was always plenty to watch in the living areas, but a soldier needed to own a laptop.

The soldiers lived in their laptops. Laptops were not only entertainment centers but were their links to the real world, the place where they could communicate with their loved ones and learn about the goings-on back in the world—that is, providing they were in a Wi-Fi Internet zone. Kuwait was tuned in; Iraq was only starting to get there.

There were stacks of soft-drink cases by the register. No beer, no booze, no ice—so the hot soft drinks served as the only liquid refreshments to be found, and the piles moved fast enough. At the end of the aisles, Peter found a souvenir section. Like everything else in the PX, these items were covered in dust, but the dust was particularly unattractive on these items—items meant to be attractive rather than useful. There weren't many takers for the "I was in Kuwait" T-shirts and the Camp Buehring shot glasses.

Peter bought a twelve-can sleeve of Coke, a box of Oreos, and some handkerchiefs, just to make the trip make sense. He headed out the door into the hot dirty wind and moved to the next trailer down the line. He entered the trailer where the door had been replaced by a heavy drape—blood red with gold trim. Inside this trailer was what was supposed to look like a sheik's tent. There was an Arab sitting at a desk at the other end, indifferent to the presence of his guests. Along the left side were two mannequins. One was wearing a white headdress and white man-dress. The other was female, dressed in a black burka—this one so form-fitting it was supposed to make the mannequin look sexy.

Along the right side was a glass counter filled with useless crap. There were tinny scimitars, plastic camels, cheap lighters, and key chains. Everything in the store was covered in the khaki-colored dust, and Peter's intent was to exit the trailer as soon as was polite. He didn't want to offend the man sitting at the end—the owner, employee, slave, whatever. Peter needn't have been concerned, however, as the man continued to read his yellowed newspaper, the grey smoke curling up from his nicotine-stained fingers. He was indifferent to Peter's presence.

The next trailer was the coffee shop, with the now familiar long line in one door, assembly line chaos within, and the men drifting out the far end, singly and in small groups, coffee in hand. Peter waited ten minutes in this line, small-talking with the other soldiers in line until he got inside and to the counter. Behind the counter were three young Arab men making and serving coffee. They were surly, indifferent, and slow. "It looks like the DMV at home," Peter thought. And the product was just as disappointing. He paid $2.75 for a tepid latte in a paper cup and didn't even receive acknowledgment that he'd spoken at all when he thanked the attendant. He ended up tossing it in the large garbage can outside the next trailer, just below the *No Food or Drinks* sign.

The next trailer was an embroidery shop. There were three men busily working sewing machines, embroidering all manner of clothing with all types of personalizing. They sewed in soldiers' names, hometowns, and units. They added pictures of characters from American cartoons and movies. Some had Arabic writing and pictures too—camels and palm trees and the like. They tried to bring a little American culture to the mix, too, but were decades behind. They'd embroidered Scooby-Doo, Dudley Do-Right, and Dennis the Menace on a few things.

Peter had nothing to turn in for embroidering and there was nothing sold there for that purpose, but Peter made a note to return. He had a mind to get a desert hat in the PX and have it embroidered with his name in Arabic underneath the crossed American and Irish flags. He'd save it for sunny summer days at New York construction sites when he returned. It would be a unique conversation piece.

New York. Home. There was a dramatic shift of thinking in each soldier's mind that happened the minute he touched down in Kuwait. For months and months, these soldiers had thought of nothing else but the coming deployment in the Middle East. That was the entire future, each man's part in his war. At the very moment that deployment began, the focus shifted to the return home. Thinking of the here and now was always avoided. The future, spent in happy homes and successful lives, was idealized and fantasized from the start. "Three-sixty-four and a wake-up" was what the Major had said.

The next trailer was the barber shop. There were six chairs down the center. Peter saw one wall covered with mirrors and the other wall lined with servicemen, seated in folding chairs. The six barbers couldn't speak a dozen words of English between them. From what Peter could gather, they were Indian. India, like so many nations in the developing world, provided thousands of workers in Iraq and Kuwait for the American Department of Defense. Many spoke English but some, the ones recruited from the lowest rungs on the Indian social ladder, did not. Iraq service attracted many of these.

This was unheard of in American history, the need to import civilian workers. Whenever Americans had secured a country in the past, the task of ensuring the peace and returning the country to the people it belonged to had always begun immediately. One important part, maybe the most important part of the plan, was the providing of thousands of civilian jobs to the local population. The dignity of work would be restored; the people would be usefully occupied. The economy would get a big infusion of cash and the infrastructure would begin to emerge anew. This wouldn't happen in Iraq or Kuwait.

Kuwaitis, long rich in oil money, had stopped working years ago. Children were schooled well enough and there was, of course, the sort of work that people did at home in their gardens and kitchens. There was a professional class and most of the management jobs were done by Kuwaitis—though they trimmed hours and effort in the process. The great mass of laborers would come from the less developed countries. At Camp Buehring, Peter ran into men from Hong Kong, Sri Lanka, India, Pakistan, and West Africa. He was told to expect the same thing up north in Iraq, though the struggling Iraqis couldn't use the excuse that they were wealthy to eschew the work ethic. The British soldier from the first night there had made frequent references to the lazy, angry Iraqi men when he tried to explain the real-world problem of raising and training an Iraqi military.

Peter stood in the doorway and watched the barbers for a few minutes. There were no empty chairs anyway, so the standing itself was not conspicuous. Each barber gave only one kind of haircut. He used a clipper with no guide from the hairline all the way up to the crown of the head and then used a number-two guide for the top. He made no effort to blend the shaved side with the quarter-inch of hair on top. Whether they were soldiers, sailors, airmen, or marines didn't matter here. They all looked like jarheads when these barbers were done with them.

A young, handsome major stepped up when a chair became empty and, towering over the smiling brown man, explained his own tonsorial expectations. He was pointing to the side of his head, saying, "No shave! No skin!" Then he grabbed the tuft of hair on the top of his head and, shaking and jerking it for the man to see, said, "Leave here! Leave here!"

The smiling man nodded knowingly as he opened the barber's apron for the Major to put on. Moving like the expert he was, the barber carefully draped the apron around the officer's neck and reached for the seldom-used comb in his pocket. He inspected the hair on the Major's head as he carefully combed it and put it in place. The Major's face began to relax as he, comfortable that the man understood his needs, pulled a magazine from under the apron and began to flip through it.

That split second was just enough time for the barber to run that clipper right up the side of the Major's head. Looking at the two-inch-wide strip of pasty white flesh where the Major's curls used to be, Peter turned on the balls of his feet and headed for the door. His resolve not to get caught laughing died on hearing the Major finally finding some words. "What the . . . ? You stupid bastard!" was the last thing Peter heard as he closed the door behind him and broke out in a good belly laugh.

There was only one haircut in this combat zone, shaved sides with some fuzz on top. For some ungodly reason, the Army as well as the Marines thought that a shaved head was attractive, military, and professional. The remotest hint of a shadow on the face was cause for disciplinary action, but it was considered a damned fine appearance to have a head covered in stubble. Then again, it only cost two dollars and there was no one to care what you looked like either.

Peter's next stop was the Burger King trailer. The comforting and familiar logo and colors draped the trailer and two little brown men worked the window. This was a take-out Burger King only. Peter ordered a Whopper, fries, and a Coke, just like he'd do if he were in Manhattan and paid the same five dollars too. He was given a number, and took a seat on the picnic bench out in front. It was ten minutes till his number was called and he was handed a familiar Burger King bag. Inside was a Whopper and fries, sort of. He'd find out later, the tasteless mushy mess was made in the States, quick frozen, shipped to Kuwait, and then micro-waved in that trailer. The Coke was in a ten-ounce can. The label informed Peter that it was "bottled" in Kuwait. At least it tasted like a Coke. The Coke was the only thing that he finished as the bulk of the Burger King meal joined his latte in the trash can.

The soldiers he'd come to the town square with started to appear. They'd all gone their separate ways when they hit the square and were now coming together again. Most had bought some supplies at the PX, tried the Burger King or coffee (and gave them the same lukewarm reviews), and checked out the souvenir trailers. Like Peter, they'd found nothing worth buying.

Randy, the chubby kid from Pennsylvania, and Dave, his born-again buddy, had both availed themselves of the barbering facilities. Each had what would become the signature cut of the Iraqi campaign. With their shaved sides and a short mop on top, they looked ridiculous. Adding to the humor of the image was that Dave was tall, thin, and pale while Randy was short, fat, and dark. They were immediately dubbed Bert and Ernie, after the

Sesame Street characters. They took it good-naturedly, aware that resisting the perfect nicknames was useless. They'd be *Bert* and *Ernie* for life, or at least the part of their lives they'd share with these soldiers.

Peter saw they were all covered with the fine, tan dust that was blowing all around them. Wondering if he had been taking on the same khaki hue, he ran his fingers through his hair, over his face and down his arms. He felt grit in his ears, around his eyes, and in his hair, and he became aware that, having not had anything to drink since the Coke, five minutes before, he had grit and dust in his mouth and between his teeth.

Having experienced all that the Kuwaiti town square had to offer, the men decided to head back to the tent. On the way, they stopped into the three tents that served as a gym, a recreation center, and a library. These facilities had the older, probably Viet-Nam-era tents that were manufactured before there was such an acute need to keep dust out. They didn't have the double flaps, sealed seams, and curved bottoms of the new tents. In each of these tents, everything was covered with dust.

The soldiers didn't stay long in each tent and had an increasingly difficult time getting their bearings each time they left a tent. The dust storm was constantly shifting and changing the landscape and vista. They found their living quarters by stumbling onto them by accident and they quickly ducked inside, each man heading for his AO, his area of operation, defined by his cot. For the most part, the soldiers' time in Kuwait would be spent in their tents, on their cots, listening to Ipods, reading, playing cards, and waiting. The recreational facilities were unappealing and once they'd been to the town square, a return trip was pretty much unnecessary.

The one thing that was remotely impressive was the chow hall. Peter headed there for dinner and experienced one of the most pleasant disconnects of this war. Soldiers in the War on Terror were often treated to dining facilities that their veteran grandfathers and fathers couldn't have imagined. Run by Halliburton, they were fabulous. There were hundreds of menu items, many made from high-quality fresh fruits and vegetables. There was ice cream, cold soft drinks, fresh-baked pies and cakes. There was an attentive and busy staff of civilian servers, cooks, and busboys. While the combat soldiers and marines would always find ways to burn off the calories from these irresistible cornucopias, the servicemen and women who worked on the bases would often find themselves getting fat.

New to the experience, Peter managed to find the dining facility through blowing sand and had to wait outside in line for about five minutes. The long line moved quickly as the facility's staff worked at breakneck speed to keep the serving lines full and the tables cleared and clean. Peter had steak, fries, and a salad. He went back in line for some fried chicken and made a third trip to the dessert bar where he found a gooey piece of chocolate cake. He topped it off with two scoops of vanilla ice cream and grabbed a cup of hot coffee with real cream. He never finished all of this but delighted in the first real meal he'd had since returning from leave.

The next week found the soldiers filling their time independently. There were occasional formations and classes, all geared toward making the soldiers familiar with the world they'd live in for the next year. But most of the time they were off, instructed only to stay out of trouble and travel in pairs. The officers and staff NCOs were planning and arranging for the movement north. The unit's gear and equipment would move in a truck convoy along the four hundred miles of highway to Ar Ramadi in the Al Anbar province where they would be stationed. Most of the troops would fly out the same day but a small number were asked to volunteer to escort the convoy through the desert frontier. This convoy would leave a few days ahead of the flights.

The troops who were chosen to volunteer were the scouts from Peter's company. It made sense that the Lieutenant volunteered his men for this. Scouts are specifically trained in convoy escort and the platoon-sized unit provided just the right number of soldiers that the command had asked for. The medics scrambled to get included, everyone eager to experience the adventure they'd signed up and trained for. Besides, dangerous and dirty as a four-hundred-mile convoy through the Iraqi desert might be, it couldn't possibly be worse than another flight crammed on cargo nets inside a dark and dirty C-130, almost certainly what the "movement by air" would be like.

Peter and two other medics got the assignment to accompany the scouts. The medics would be strategically placed. One would be toward the front of the convoy, one would be in a lightly armored Humvee somewhere in the center of the line and Peter would be in the last vehicle.

He had been warned of the dire consequences of his not reporting on time so that he was terrified to sleep the night before the convoy was to leave. He hauled his gear out to the truck in the twilight of the night before and crawled up into the cab to sleep. He was awakened by the noise of the first troops, the truck drivers, opening the doors to the trucks at 3:00 AM. The next three hours were spent checking and re-checking lists, taking roll calls, and looking for the inevitable two or three idiots who did manage to miss the start time.

The solemn-looking officers took turns having intensely important radio conversations with various important people at sundry critical headquarters. The chaplain arrived to see them off and offered a quick non-denominational prayer service. The Catholic chaplain surprised Peter by explaining the Catholic practice of confession and offering a general absolution to all those who wanted it, Catholic or not.

"Well, what do you make of that?" Peter said to no one in particular.

"Make of what?" asked a strange soldier to his left.

"I spend my whole life having to follow this rule and that regulation and just anybody at all comes along and gets absolution without so much as a genuflection."

"What's a genuflection?"

"Ah, forget it."

The Chaplain relayed divine forgiveness for the lifetimes of sins for the dozens of soldiers present, offered the sign of the cross, along with his best wishes and a promise to see them all at Ar Ramadi in a few days. And with that, they turned to their trucks to take their places and head out. It would still be more than an hour before Peter's truck would move, as each truck before him was placed carefully and methodically in its position and the leaders were satisfied that the convoy was ready to roll. By the time they moved out, the sun had taken its place halfway up the sky, but it wasn't visible to Peter for the tons of dust the hundred trucks before his had raised.

It was noon before the convoy reached the border into Iraq. Peter had spent the morning riding shotgun in a combat-modified six-by-six U.S. Army truck. The only passengers were Peter, the driver, and the gunner, who stood on the divider between Peter and the driver. The gunner's bottom half was in the cab and he was outside from the torso on up. He had a .50-caliber machine gun mounted on a ring that rotated on the gunner's power. It was perfectly counterbalanced so that the gunner could move it with little effort. He was strapped to the ring and could rotate it using only the movement of his body. This would work as long as the truck was level, as this trip was likely to be.

At the Iraq border, the convoy had to pass through a security gate cut through the center of a berm built eight feet high and more than ten feet deep. On top of the berm were steel spikes connected with rusty barbed wire. The troops at the gate were Iraqi regulars, and as Peter's truck halted at the checkpoint between the berms, he rolled down the window to speak to the soldier standing on his side. Peter smiled and, waving, said hello. The Iraqi stared for a bit, turned towards the rear of the truck and walked to the back. The rude treatment made Peter un-comfortable, but he couldn't decide if the rotten attitude was the individual soldier's alone or was a normal state of affairs in the relationship between the two armies.

The trucks moved all afternoon through the Iraqi desert on a two-lane road, arriving at the destination for the night's lodgings while the sun was still high in the sky. The convoy rolled through the stockade-style fort built for this purpose and found its place in the tent city allot-ted to it. At the stockade's gate, the soldiers who took in these lodgers daily had long since developed efficient sys-tems to eliminate the confusion that had marked these movements early in the war. The officer at the gate spoke with the convoy commander and gave him a packet and a map. The commander was given clear instructions as to where to park the trucks, where to sleep, and where to find the chow hall. These were the only things to be found at these overnight truck stops—parking, fuel, food, and sleep tents.

Peter showered in a field trailer modified for that pur-pose, and found a decent enough bunk. Like the other soldiers, he was in a deep sleep within minutes, as the next day's 4:00 AM jumping-off time would come early. The night passed almost unnoticed as the soldiers began rising at 3:00. Most viewed the chance for a good break-fast and a filled coffee thermos as being worth the little sleep they'd give up. They weren't disappointed. The food was good, the coffee hot, and the men were excited. To-day, they were to be on the main highway north. They were promised a modern, eight-lane highway with things to see, towns, rest stops, people.

Midmorning found Peter rumbling along the highway. On macadam, with fifty meters between each truck, there was no dust to contend with. There was the occasional roadside stand, and rest stops were small patios with two or three tables made of poured concrete, steel umbrellas providing some protection from the merciless sun. The charcoal grey of the road surface and the whitish grey of the concrete provided the only relief from the light-khaki world that is Iraq.

Peter's peace was disrupted by the gunner rolling the gun mount left to right, back and forth, quickly. He was up on the balls of his feet and Peter looked skyward to see he was frantically waving his arms and trying to get the attention of something behind the truck.

"Stop! Stop!" he yelled as he waved. As quickly as he had started this, he stopped. He leaned down and retrieved the flare from the ammo box at his feet and instantly straightened up. Peter found the source of the gunner's alarm by looking in his rear-view mirror. He could see a small white Volvo bearing down on the truck, seeming to speed up rather than slow down at the gunner's warning.

The gunner struck the base of the flare on the top of the cab and Peter was startled at the "WHOOSH" as the blast of warm air hit him in the face. The flare would alert the rest of the convoy of the threat as well as warn the driver to back off.

Peter saw the car was still bearing down on the truck and he couldn't quite accept what he was seeing. He thought there must be some reason for this aggressive behavior other than evil intent. His mind raced in search of another explanation beyond the obvious. Peter could see that the car was manned by a single male—a danger sign in itself, the British Sergeant had advised. And he was traveling fast, trying to overtake the convoy. "That's his second mistake," he thought just as he heard the gunner fire his warning shots. The gunner was discharging his M-16 in the air, hoping this would ward off the threat. All of these things, the waving, the flares, the warning shots were required actions in this theater.

Rules of Engagement or ROE, were pounded into the soldiers' heads. They were more important than any military objective this war might be trying to achieve. They were more important than defending America or freeing the Iraqis or fighting Islamo-fascism. Following the ROE, designed by the lawyers and managers who steered the corporation called the U.S. Army, would keep the soldiers out of a court-martial and off CNN. The gunner, scrupulously following the procedures outlined in the ROE, had to wave and yell first. He then had to fire a flare. He then had to shoot his M-16. While doing all these things, he had to take his hands off his machine gun. And as this was all happening, the old Volvo with the new tires was getting closer. While he waved and shouted and shot off flares and warning shots, the old Volvo with the unresponsive, determined, solo male driver was gaining ground.

And when the gunner had exhausted all the preparatory procedures for firing his weapon and eliminating this obvious threat, he returned to his mounted machine gun. He was in a cold sweat and his hands shook. He knew for sure that this car was the enemy, probably a car bomb. He knew he was the only one in the world who could stop the car and he'd never felt lonelier, thinking that no one else even knew about it. He was furious that he, of all people and now, in this of all places, had this ridiculous responsibility. He was terrified, lonely, and angry all at the same time.

He lined up the car just before it was to disappear from view behind the long high truck. He pulled a trigger at an enemy in combat for the first time in his life. Rather than experiencing the power of a dozen rounds of .50-cal ammunition pounding out the muzzle, he felt the bolt slam home and stop without discharging a round. Horrified, he looked and saw that the belt of ammo had slipped from the feed tray while the gun was spinning around on its own, while he was firing his M-16, or looking for flares, or waving and yelling.

Peter saw this, too, and was furiously gathering the belt that had dropped and coiled to his left, at the gunner's feet. Peter's hands were pushing the rounds up to the gunner while the gunner's hands were reaching down to get them. There were four hands on the pile of life-saving bullets when the driver of the Volvo pushed the plunger duct-taped to his steering wheel and slammed into the back of the truck.